THE PROMISE OF PEACE

CAROL UMBERGER

INTEGRITY®

P U B L I S H E R S

Nashville

DEDICATION

To the men and women, past and present,

of the US Military Services.

You know the true price of freedom and peace.

God bless you.

ACKNOWLEDGMENTS

My sincere thanks to the many readers who have written to encourage me and to ask for another story. Here it is, as promised.

A warm thank you to the Thursday night Improv group at Barnes and Noble—you know who you are. Thanks for your smiles and encouragement. May you each write to whatever level of success suits you best.

A huge thanks to Maureen Schmidgall, who bravely read the manuscript at its worst and always put smiley faces with her suggestions for improvement.

Thanks to Donnell and Beth for insights into teenage rebellion. Best of luck in your own writing endeavors.

A big thank you to Angel Smits, a wonderful writer who understands when I tell her the symbolism isn't working and then helps me fix it.

Thank you, Betsy Wintermute, for sharing your knowledge of horsemanship and all things medieval.

Thank you, Heather Peterson, for allowing me to ride the real Shadow, a magnificent eventing and dressage thoroughbred gelding. And to Shadow himself, who made jumping 18" seem as exciting as a sixfoot fence!

As always, a big thanks to my wonderful editor, Lisa Bergren.

And thanks and praise to the God who promises us peace beyond our understanding, if only we believe.

Author's Notes

Dear Readers,

I hope that you have enjoyed this final book in the Scottish Crown Series. Like you, I will miss these characters who have become friends. But there are more characters waiting in the wings for me to tell their stories.

Despite his many successes, Robert the Bruce's one regret was that he never fulfilled his promise to go on Crusade. On his deathbed in June 1329, he asked James Douglas to take his heart to the Holy Land. After Bruce's death, Douglas had the king's heart embalmed in a small silver casket that Douglas then wore on a chain around his neck. On March 25, 1330, Douglas rode into battle at Zebas de Ardales and was killed in the ensuing fighting. The casket was removed from Douglas's body and returned to Scotland, where it was buried at the Abbey of Melrose.

Scotland's peace with England was short-lived. By 1331, Thomas Randolph was also dead, leaving young King David to reign without the help of his father's most trusted advisor. Two years later, Edward III disavowed the treaty he'd sealed with the marriage of his sister to David Bruce, on the grounds that Edward was under-age when he signed it.

Warfare between England and Scotland broke out again and continued on and off for the next four hundred years. Never again did a king or general with Bruce's gifts arise in Scotland. But Bruce had forged a sense of nationality that has not deserted the Scottish people to this day.

I have tried to capture some of the history and customs of fourteenth-century Scotland, and I beg forgiveness where I felt it necessary to take liberties for the sake of clarity. If you would like to learn more about this time period, I highly recommend *Robert the Bruce, King of Scots* by Ronald McNair Scott.

For news about my upcoming releases or to contact me, please visit my website at www.carolumberger.com, or you may write in care of Integrity Publishers.

God Bless.

PROLOGUE

Scotland, June 1306

FRESH FROM A DECISIVE VICTORY over Robert the Bruce, Ian Macnab and his older brother followed the Prince of Wales and his retinue of knights. In pursuit of Bruce and what remained of the Scottish army, the English knights and a handful of Scottish loyalists were anxious to blood their swords again.

But Bruce had melted into the highlands. Seeking an enemy, any enemy, the prince ordered an attack on the small, unarmed village of Midvale. The English were destroying the village for no other reason than that it lay in their path. As anxious as his comrades for more of victory's promise, this was too much for Ian. What madness had swept over these men? He watched as the thatch on a cottage caught fire and its occupants raced for the cover of the nearby woods. The smell of smoke and screams of women and children filled the air. Village men armed with pitchforks tried in vain to turn back the attack. Ian longed to come to their rescue, but even with Angus's help, there was little they could do to affect the outcome.

In the confusion of the charge, Ian spurred his horse next to his brother's. "This is wrong, Angus. We must not attack innocent people. Come, let's be gone!"

Angus hesitated.

"Stay then. I'm riding out." He turned his horse and rode to the top of the hill overlooking the village. There Ian watched in shock, shaking his head as if doing so would make the carnage before him disappear. He clutched his sword as anger, fear, and finally revulsion raced through him.

Angus soon joined him on the hilltop.

It might be futile, but he couldn't just sit here and watch. "We must find a way to stop them!" Ian took up his reins to ride to the rescue of the innocents being slaughtered before them.

Angus Macnab grabbed at Ian's reins. "Nay, don't be foolish. Ye were right not to be party to this but ye'll not stop the prince when the bloodlust is on him."

"We must try. What if this were Innishewan?" Their home and village were safe well across the country in Argyll. But that didn't make it any easier to see this unfamiliar hamlet senselessly destroyed. Angus shook his head as Ian's bay pulled and shied from Angus's grasp. "If we attempt to stop the prince, he will have us cut down, and then we will be no help to anyone."

Ian had no doubt what Angus said about Prince Edward was true. The prince's capricious emotions and mighty temper were as feared as his father's.

Angus Macnab let go of the reins and pointed to the west of them. "There, brother. There ye may do some good."

Ian looked to where Angus pointed and saw a tree-lined creek and, yes, movement and color within the woods. Some of the unfortunates had managed to escape from their homes to seek refuge where it could be found.

"Those will need help and I'm for it," Angus said. "But them in the village are beyond our help."

Though everything in him cried out to rescue those still in the village, Ian knew his brother was right. No sense in seeking a needless death. They were going to be in enough trouble for refusing to attack in the first place. Reluctantly he nodded.

Angus said, "We'll help as we can and then slip into the hills for a time." They raced their horses to the creek, where they found women and children, many of them wounded. Innocents, every one. *The Prince of Wales.* Ian spit on the ground.

He and Angus were joined by a cousin, Duncan, who had also declined to join the prince's butchery. Though none of them were experienced healers, all of them had tended to battlefield wounds before, and they set to work with little conversation.

Ian bound a gash on the arm of a woman not much older than his daughter, Morrigan. A warrior in her own right, Morrigan had ridden with them earlier today. She had suffered a nasty cut in battle and he had sent her home for his wife, Eveleen, to tend.

Then he turned to face a young woman who was wailing over a dead infant in her arms, his tiny leg slashed to the bone. The child had bled to death. With agonizing motions, Ian caressed the young mother's face and gently pried the boy from her arms.

"Please, let me hold him . . . just a wee bit longer." She bit her lip, nodding as tears streamed down her red face. She sank to the ground, weeping, face in hands.

Ian turned to face his brother, raising the child to make sure Angus could see. "I'm glad Morrigan did not witness this." He drew a breath, determined that Angus should understand how he felt, staring down at a lad who would never have the chance to wage his own battle, never have the chance to look out for his own family, his own country. "I'll not follow the prince in battle again, Angus. He disgraced the title of knight today, he and the men with him."

Angus said nothing, probably hoping Ian would get his emotions under control and see reason. Angus's reason. 'Tis how it had been all their lives. Except once.

Ian turned and helped the woman to her feet, then returned the

3

child to her arms, whispering assurances that he would help bury the child; that while all seemed lost, God had not abandoned her. He looked down the hill to the smoking village. The English were gone now, and the people were returning to what was left of their homes. They looked as dazed and disoriented as Ian felt. But he was rapidly regaining his bearings.

Scotland's king had been treated with treachery, with no hint of honor. The Earl of Pembroke had declined to fight when Bruce challenged him, saying the day was too far gone. The two generals had made a gentleman's agreement to commence the battle the next day at first light—a customary agreement. Bruce and his army had made camp and bedded down for the night.

However, despite his assurances to Bruce, Pembroke had waited until the Scots were sufficiently off guard—with tents pitched and supper cooking—and then he'd attacked, routing the Scots and nearly capturing Bruce in the chaos. "Where was the law of chivalry yesterday, Angus? Pembroke did not keep the faith, and neither did the prince. Mayhap Gordie had the right of it, giving his loyalty to Bruce."

This war with England had divided the loyalty of many highland clans. Ian had sided with his brother Angus—laird of clan Macnab—and against his son, Gordon. Gordie had died fighting with Bruce at Dalry Pass against one of their own clansmen, John of Lorne.

Angus looked around—the three Scotsmen were alone now. He said, "I'll not speak poorly about the dead. Gordie did what he felt he had to. I accept that, though I disagreed with him. 'Tis bad enough yer son defied his laird. Ye and I can't change sides now without incurring the prince's wrath, and through him, King Edward himself."

"Which king shall we serve? An honorable Scot or a butcher and his son?"

"King Edward had nothing to do with the prince's behavior

today. Clan Macnab will fight for Edward so long as I'm laird. And that's the end of it."

Ian looked at his brother, at the deep reddish hair and blue eyes they shared. Barely a year separated them, and they'd often been asked if they were twins. But they were not alike in any other way, which meant they were oft at odds. "I'll not fight for England again after what I saw today."

"War is evil, and sometimes the innocent pay a price, Ian." Angus stood and faced him, then gazed about at the last of the wounded. "We've done all we can here. Let's be gone."

Duncan moved to stand beside Ian.

But Ian didn't move. "I said nothing, fought beside ye this day despite Pembroke's lack of chivalry against Bruce's army. Treachery and war against armed men was one thing. But this savagery against women and children—that I won't abide. Not for any cause."

Angus shoved his shoulder, trying to provoke him. "Get on home with ye, then. Ye aren't fit to be a warrior."

Duncan wisely moved across the rock-strewn ground to stand with the fidgeting horses.

Ian stood firm and Angus shoved him, harder this time. Ian stepped back. "I don't want to fight ye, Angus."

"Then don't disobey yer laird."

"I'll not join Bruce. That much I promise. And I'll help ye however I can. But I'll not take up arms for the king of England again." Ian turned to leave.

Angus grabbed his sleeve, pulling him around to face him. He let go of the cloth and poked Ian's chest with his beefy finger. "Will ye fight me, then? Because that's the only way I'm going to let ye have yer way in this."

Ian held his hands at his sides, even though he wanted mightily to hit his brother. But he would not dishonor himself by striking his laird in anger, brother or not. "Aye, ye've wanted an excuse to fight me ever since the last time. Ye won that fight, Angus. I still have the crooked nose to prove it."

"I didn't win and ye know it. Ye may have got a broken nose but ye still got Eveleen."

Mustering patience, Ian said, "She didn't necessarily pick the best man, Angus. She picked the man she loved."

Ian turned again to walk away but Angus grabbed him once more, spun him around, and struck Ian's cheek. His eyes watered from the sting of the blow, but he refused to strike back. He waited for Angus to hit him again.

"Stop it, both of ye!" Duncan yelled, coming toward them as if to calm them down.

But Ian waved Duncan off. Long-simmering animosities and buried hurts often welled up between the brothers. Trying to avoid further confrontation, Ian wiped his sleeve over his eyes to dry them. "We finished this years ago, Angus. I'll not fight ye again over Eveleen." He stood there, daring his brother to strike him again. When the other man stood still, Ian turned and walked toward Duncan and the waiting horses.

With a roar Angus crashed into Ian from behind. Ian had no time to react and fell headlong to the ground, striking his head before Angus's body came to rest on top of him. Ian heard bones crack, then all went silent. One thought filled his head and heart before the world went dark.

Eveleen.

ANGUS SCRAMBLED OFF HIS BROTHER and knelt beside him. "Ian. Ian, man. Wake up!"

Duncan ran to him. "He hit his head."

Then Angus noticed the unnatural angle of his brother's neck and, at the same time, watched as Ian's breathing stopped. "Ian?" Angus felt for the pulse. "Ian! Oh, God, please no. I didn't mean it, none of it." Angus clutched his brother's body to his chest and sobbed. He was laird; he was in fact his brother's keeper, the keeper and protector of the Macnabs. He and Ian had survived so much together, and it came to this? A freak accident, and now Angus had his brother's blood on his head.

Why had he allowed anger to overrule love? And how would he ever explain to Eveleen? Would she believe it was an accident?

When he could delay no longer, Angus motioned for Duncan to help him. With few words between them, they hoisted Ian's body over his horse, tied it fast, and made the long ride back to Innishewan.

As they neared the keep Duncan said, "I don't think yer sister-in-law can take another heartache. Would ye like for me to break the news?"

Angus, his voice choked, said, "'Tis my duty to tell her. I have caused her nothing but pain, all my life. May God forgive me."

When they approached the castle, a cry went out from the sentry. Angus, leading Ian's horse, rode into the bailey. Shock and dismay covered the faces of those who came to greet him. They must have assumed Ian died in battle, for no one asked what happened, sparing Angus from having to confess.

Weary and dreading what lay ahead, Angus halted his horse and dismounted. "Duncan, see to Ian while I go to Eveleen."

She wouldn't be in the castle but at the small cottage inside the walls that she and Ian called home. Angus left his tired horse and walked the short distance, dreading his task with every footstep.

She stood there just outside the cottage, her beautiful dark hair streaked with gray. Wiping her hands on her apron, she said, "What is it, Angus? Ye look as if ye've seen a . . ." She clutched the apron. "It's Ian, isn't it?"

"Aye." He wanted to make everything right between them. Turn back the clock twenty years and start over. Would anything ever be right again?

Not if he told her the truth.

And so when he stood before the woman who'd taken his heart years ago, he couldn't bear to tell her that he'd killed her husband. "He fell from his horse, Eveleen."

She said not a word, just stared in disbelief before she crumbled. He stepped forward and caught his brother's wife in his arms. He carried her into the small cottage she had shared with Ian and their children but couldn't think what to do. He stood there, Eveleen's weight in his arms, as his niece, Morrigan, rushed through the door.

"What have you done to my mother?" she demanded.

Her accusation stung. "She fainted." He walked to the bed, laid Eveleen on it, and then straightened to face Morrigan. Working one-handed because of the wound on her arm, she stalked to a bucket of water and dipped a cloth into it, squeezed it out, and returned to sit beside her mother.

Laying the cloth on Eveleen's forehead, Morrigan said, "Why did she faint, Uncle Angus?"

He didn't answer. Didn't know what to say. He'd already lied to Eveleen. "Where's Keifer?"

Morrigan made a dismissive wave with her hand. "He's at the castle playing with Owyn. What happened to my mother?"

"Your da is dead."

"Dead? How can he be dead?" Morrigan stared at him. "He was fine this morning. I don't believe you!"

Angus wiped his hand across his face, felt the sweat on his brow, felt the pain of his own denial.

He would have to talk to Duncan, convince him to back up Angus's story. No good would come of everyone knowing. It had been an accident—whether he fell from his horse or tripped on a rock, what difference did it make? Ian was dead.

"I'm sorry, Morrigan. 'Tis true."

Morrigan had faced death in battle, had fought beside him and Ian more than once. She was stronger than any woman Angus had ever known. To see the tear that traced her cheek nearly undid him.

"What happened, Uncle? I came home and told Mother that Da would be along shortly, and then you bring him to us dead?" Her shoulders sagged. "Gordon is barely cold in his grave. How are we to bear this?"

Angus repeated the lie, hating himself but knowing he couldn't suffer Eveleen knowing the truth.

Eveleen's eyes opened, and she reached for her daughter's hand. Morrigan's tears dropped onto their clasped hands. Eveleen sat up, and the two women held each other. Angus knelt and offered his arms for comfort, but neither woman accepted his solace.

Seeing that they wanted nothing to do with him, Angus pulled back, still on his knees. "I'm as sorry as I can be, Eveleen. Morrigan. What ever ye need, I'll see to it. Ye won't suffer for lack, I promise."

"Aye. All I'll lack is my husband," Eveleen whispered. "Go away, Angus. Go home to your wife. I cannot look at you."

Stung, heartbroken not only in the loss of his brother but also the loss of the esteem of the only woman he'd ever really loved, Angus rose and left the cottage.

Though he would not dishonor his wife by breaking his marriage vows, he could still love Eveleen and see to her welfare. 'Twas the least he could do.

Aye, Eveleen would come around once her grief diminished.

STORM-TOSSED LEAVES covered the ground around the Macnab graveyard at Innishewan. Damp dripped from the trees, but Morrigan's eyes remained dry. She had no more tears left to cry. How she wished her older brother was here to tell her what to do! But Gordon lay nearby in a grave covered by new spring grass.

Two men with shovels dropped rain soaked ground onto the casket, the mud splattering as it hit the wood. Morrigan held her little brother's hand as the grave was filled, shovel by shovel. A few feet away stood her mother, leaning on Morrigan's younger sister. Opposite them stood Angus Macnab with his mousy wife and son, the only one of the couple's children to survive infancy. He was small and wiry but healthy.

The boy, the same age as Keifer, would one day be laird of clan Macnab.

Morrigan knew the story well of how Angus and Ian Macnab had both courted Eveleen MacTaggert. In the end she had not chosen the laird but his younger brother. Morrigan wasn't sure if Angus had ever forgiven Eveleen or Ian. But Angus's grief at his brother's death seemed real, palpable even.

Angus came over to Eveleen and once again assured her he would take care of her and Ian's children.

"I'm sure ye would do well by us, Angus. But the children and I are moving to Inverlochy to be near my family."

"But ye belong here. Ye are a Macnab now."

She looked at him for a long moment. "I belonged here while Ian lived. Now I want to go home."

Morrigan hated to leave the relative safety of Innishewan, but her mother didn't want to stay. Morrigan didn't have the heart to argue. Too many bad memories here. And Uncle Angus—well, Morrigan had never trusted him. Best to leave as Eveleen wished.

"Morrigan, can ye not reason with her?" Angus beseeched.

"I will do as my mother wishes, Uncle."

Shaking his head, the man walked back to his family.

Morrigan would grieve the loss of her father. How much worse must it be for a boy to grow to manhood without his father to guide him? As she stood by her father's graveside, she vowed to see that Keifer received the training Ian could no longer give. And when the time was right, she would join Bruce's army and fight against her uncle and his English king.

Morrigan looked down at her two-year-old brother. He must have sensed her glance, because he looked up. So forlorn, his expression! She held her hands in invitation, and he darted into them. She picked him up and he put his arms around her neck, clinging so tight she had to loosen his hold so she could breathe.

Still, the small wooden horse in his hand—a toy that Da had whittled for him—dug into her back. A trickle of wetness rolled down her neck and under her tunic. She felt the boy's shuddering breath.

"Hush now, wee one. Hush." She patted his back, offering solace. The priest had finished speaking and the mourners were beginning to leave.

Her father's cousin, Duncan, came over to pay his respects. When he saw Keifer's tears, he said, "You take care of yer mother, Keifer. Ye're the man of the house now." He stared at Morrigan and seemed about to say something more when he glanced up at Uncle Angus. Duncan didn't make eye contact with Morrigan as he said, "God bless ye, Morrigan." Then he spun about and left them.

Her da would have made a better laird, Morrigan thought, unable to control her bitterness. Angus inspired fear where Ian had gotten people to see things his way with persuasion and charm.

Morrigan gathered her family and they returned to the cottage to finish packing their belongings. Keifer, silent all this long day, sat by the fireplace playing with his wooden horse figurine.

Morrigan looked at her mother, who picked up the only book

they owned—a beautifully copied collection of the Psalms. Eveleen's eyes shone, and she looked almost happy.

"What is it, Momma?" Morrigan asked.

"I will see your father again, Morrigan. The thought relieves my grief—'tis the only way I can get through this."

Keifer stopped his play. "Papa coming home?"

Distracted, her eyes staring off in the distance, Eveleen replied, "Aye child. We'll see him again."

"Gordon?"

"Aye. Gordon too."

Keifer said, "Good."

He was too little to understand what his mother meant. And what could it hurt if the child hoped for a reunion with his father, no matter where it would take place?

ONE

Dunstruan, Spring 1315

From behind a high spot on the parapets, Keifer Macnab watched the activity below in Dunstruan's bailey. Today he was to leave here to foster with the Mackintosh laird. The horses were nearly ready, but Keifer was not. Angrily he forced back the tears that threatened.

He was so tired of holding everything inside. So tired of waiting for his father to return. The years at Inverlochy had been good ones. His mother's father had been there to teach him to fish and how to use a knife and to overcome his fear of horses.

Then Grandfather had died two winters past and they'd moved to Dunstruan. Here he'd been tutored by the warrior monk, Ceallach. And just when Keifer had come to feel attached to the people of Dunstruan, especially Ceallach, once again he was forced to leave behind all that was familiar.

It isn't fair.

He raced to the stairs and then down them, turning at the bottom—not into the bailey where Ceallach, his sister, and the others expected him.

No.

Instead Keifer ran through the kitchen, careful that Cook didn't see him. Running as fast as he could, he headed into the oak forest behind the castle.

Following the well-worn path of Dunstruan's flock of sheep, he ran until he came to the overlook, stopping briefly to stare at the blue loch below. Then he ran toward the water, and now the tears couldn't be held back. Anger and frustration welled up and flowed down his cheeks.

He ran until his lungs hurt, until he nearly choked on the tears and his fury. Finally he reached the water's edge and momentarily considered running straight into the water and swimming as far as he could. Swim until his arms gave out and he sank beneath the surface. There would be an end to his problems. His pain.

The boy skidded to a halt in the mud and drew in rapid breaths. He hung his head. He knew such thoughts were evil—they solved nothing, just as running away would do no good. 'Twas no use—they would find him and he would have to leave.

But until then he would sit right here and wish he'd never been born.

MORRIGAN MACNAB FOUND HER BROTHER sitting on a log by the edge of the loch. The future laird of the Macnab clan drew back his arm and threw a rock into the water with a fury that alarmed her and made her glad she, and not her mother, had come to find him. The woman would have taken one look at her son and changed her mind about allowing him to be fostered so far from her.

Fostering was usually done with a nearby family, but Morrigan knew this move was in Keifer's best interest, to keep him safe. The boy had become quite attached to Dunstruan's laird over the months they'd lived here. She understood Keifer's reluctance to leave what had become familiar and dear. Hadn't he suffered enough losses in his short life?

But something in the angry set of the boy's shoulders told her more was at work here. She walked closer, deliberately scraping her foot. Keifer's head jerked up at the noise and he faced Morrigan. His face was streaked with tears, and Morrigan's heart stumbled. She hadn't seen the boy cry since their father's funeral. She'd known Keifer didn't want to leave Dunstruan, but perhaps she'd misjudged how deep his feelings ran.

He didn't speak to her, just turned and heaved another rock into the lake. A gentle breeze ruffled his curly red hair.

Morrigan wished she could spare Keifer this upheaval. He would learn a hard lesson today, but learn it he must. Ceallach had returned from the war in Ireland to keep his promise to escort Keifer to Moy. "It's time to leave, Keifer. Ceallach is waiting."

Another rock splashed into the lake. "I'm not going."

Morrigan didn't argue, seeking instead words that would comfort while letting him know that he must eventually give in. "I know you don't want to leave, but you must learn to be laird. One day you will take over the clan. You are Da's only living son—the duty is yours."

"I don't want to be laird. I want to be a soldier, a knight like Ceallach." This was not a new argument. Ever since their earliest days at Inverlochy, Keifer had made his wishes known. However, King Robert the Bruce had disinherited their Uncle Angus and his son—first casting them out of Scottish-held territory and then imprisoning Angus when he came back fighting. The Scottish king made Morrigan head of the Macnab clan until Keifer came of age. But Keifer remained adamant that he wanted to be a knight, not a laird.

Morrigan said, "Adam Mackintosh is a knight, Keifer. 'Tis an honor to be fostered by the laird of the largest federation of clans in the highlands."

"But he doesn't know how to joust or, or . . . he can't teach me to use the claymore."

Keifer was right about that—Adam Mackintosh had been gravely wounded years back. Though still an admirable adversary with a broadsword, Adam's fighting abilities were limited. "Aye, that's true. But his warlord, Seamus, can teach you to use any weapon. He will teach you the ways of the highlands, and Adam will teach you to be a laird."

Morrigan put her hand on the boy's shoulder. "And you will be safe at Moy, should Uncle Angus be released from prison."

With a shrug of his shoulders, Keifer went back to throwing rocks.

Plink. Plop.

Morrigan sat down on the log and looked out over the peaceful loch. Would Keifer tell her what else weighed so heavily on his young shoulders? Was it only the prospect of being sent away or something more?

She said, "You look like you lost your favorite toy."

Panicked, he reached into the folds of his plaid and pulled out the leather-bound ball Ceallach had made, looked at it, and carefully put it back. "No." He threw another rock, with less force this time, then sat down next to her, resting his chin in his hands. "Why can't I stay here?"

She wanted to put her arms around him, shelter him, keep him close, just like her mother did with him. But he would not appreciate the gesture. And he could not stay. For his own good, he must go to Moy. She feared Keifer would be a virtual prisoner here. At Moy, he could have a more normal life. "I've told you. I cannot protect you here—too many men loyal to Uncle Angus remain nearby. Adam and his warlord can train you to be a laird."

"Fergus could train me."

"Much as I admire Fergus, Keifer, 'tis a fact he grew up as a servant at Homelea. He's an able steward but doesn't have the training to lead a clan."

"Ceallach then."

Morrigan drew upon her patience. "He is a wonderful soldier and he is learning to be a laird—"

"But I want to be a soldier like him."

"War has already exacted a heavy price from our family. No more. You need to learn to lead the clan. And I need you to be safe. You could learn much from any of these men. But I want you somewhere that Uncle Angus won't think to look, should he be released from prison."

"Uncle Angus wants the ring, doesn't he?"

"Aye. He wants the laird's ring back so he can pass it to his son."

"He can have it."

"No, he can't. King Robert has punished Uncle Angus by taking away the clan leadership and giving it to us. To you, once you are grown."

"You can keep it, pass it to your son."

"It is *your* birthright, Keifer."

"Wouldn't you like your son to lead the clan?"

"No!" She gentled her voice. "No, Keifer, for that would mean you'd forfeited your right or that you were dead. I want you safe and healthy and grown to be a man. I promised Da in his grave I would see to it, see that you would be trained to take your place one day."

He stayed very quiet and still. Morrigan sensed that whatever deeper issue plagued Keifer might soon be revealed.

"Da will never find me at Moy."

Morrigan jerked as if punched. "What are you talking about?"

"Da is getting out of prison. He's coming for me, for us. How will he find me?"

"Don't be ridiculous, Keifer. Da is dead. Coming on nine years now." Morrigan and her mother rarely spoke about Ian Macnab, but how could Keifer have come to such a conclusion? Had Keifer harbored such a hope all these years? "You know what it means when someone dies, don't you, Keifer?"

He nodded. "But when Da died, Mother said it gave her peace to know she would see him again. I don't remember much about him, but I know he wouldn't go away and not come back."

"We'll see him in heaven, Keifer. Not here on earth."

"Why doesn't Mother ever talk about him? Is she angry with him for leaving?"

"Perhaps she still grieves, Keifer."

Morrigan found it hard to believe that the child had clung all these years to the fantasy that his father was in prison and would return when the war ended. That he remembered anything at all about their da, so young was he. Now the boy must deal with the reality that his father would not be coming back, and she regretted to see some of the light go out of the child's eyes.

He sighed. "I guess he must be dead or he'd have come back by now. Gordon is dead, too. I don't remember him at all."

"Then when you get to Moy, you must ask Adam to tell you about Gordon—he and Gordon were good friends."

Keifer turned to her. "Don't you remember him either?"

Pain stabbed Morrigan. "Oh, aye. I remember him well. He had your hair and slanted eyes, just like Da. Both of you." She smiled. "Gordon used to tease me something awful. Once he chased me with a rotten apple on a stick, threatening to smear it on my new tunic. I tripped and fell and sprained my elbow." She laughed and saw that Keifer smiled. "He caught it good from Da for that one."

"Why did he do such things?"

"Well, now I realize it was his way of showing that he liked me."

"Oh." The smile left Keifer's face. He looked so serious, too serious for such a young boy. "Everyone leaves me or sends me away."

This time she reached out and pulled the child into her embrace. "'Tis not because there is some deficiency in you, lad."

Keifer hugged her back, and they sat together for a good while. Eventually he pulled away, and she saw resignation in his expression. But the hurt still lingered in his eyes, and she wondered what it would take to heal his sense of abandonment. She would pray every day for him to find comfort and peace.

They stood and walked back to the keep and the future that awaited Keifer in the highlands.

TEN DAYS LATER, Keifer and Ceallach arrived at Moy. They stopped on a hillside overlooking a loch with a castle sitting on an island in the middle of it. Cattle and sheep grazed nearby, and despite his intention not to like the place, Keifer could feel himself drawn to the enchanting, midday view.

As they rode over the causeway, the watchman shouted a welcome. They rode into the bailey and were greeted by the castle folk. A tall blond man and an auburn-haired woman came out of the keep. The woman held a boy child of about two, and a somewhat older lad clung to her skirts.

Ceallach dismounted, but Keifer held back as a wave of shyness overcame him. And just a little resentment. Despite the danger from his uncle, he didn't see why he must be relegated to the far reaches of the highlands. Granted, Castle Moy looked able to withstand any siege, but there were other castles that could have protected him. Castles closer to his mother and Ceallach.

A small girl a few years younger than him raced into the courtyard and careened to a halt in front of the man and woman. The girl's spiraling red hair had escaped its braid and hung in complete disarray. Her forehead displayed a fresh-looking bruise. A daub of dirt on the end of her pert nose crowned the urchin's face, and Keifer grinned in spite of his melancholy.

Ceallach said, "Come down from the horse, boy."

Keifer did as he was told, and the girl marched up to him, arms crossed. "I'm Nola. I already have two brothers. What I need is a sister, not another boy."

"Nola! That's quite enough," her father said. "Apologize."

Arms still crossed, she said, "I'm sorry." Then she turned and stalked up the stairs and through the castle door.

Well, there was at least one person as unhappy about the situation as Keifer.

Ceallach said, "Adam and Gwenyth Mackintosh, this is Keifer Macnab."

Keifer mumbled a hello.

The woman shifted the child in her arms from one hip to the other. "When you men have seen to the horses, come inside for food and drink."

Keifer decided right then that he liked Lady Gwenyth. She had included him with the men. He led his horse, following behind Sir Adam. Keifer and Ceallach tied their horses outside the barn and Keifer unfastened the girth. He lifted the saddle off, struggling a bit with the weight of it. As he swung away from the horse, the heavy saddle collided with the girl.

"Watch out, clumsy ox!" she cried as his load smacked into her.

He dropped the saddle from one hand and scrambled to pick it back up out of the dirt. Once he had a firm grasp on it, he said, "Please excuse me, my lady." Then he looked at her in her disheveled state.

She giggled. "I'm not a lady."

Keifer struggled but managed to keep his features stern. "And I'm not a clumsy ox." He reined in his temper—mustn't lose it and embarrass himself or his sister so soon after arriving.

He brushed the horse and cleaned its feet while the girl, Nola, chattered about her father, her brothers, the new calf, and a cat about to have kittens. She didn't seem to require answers for her questions, which suited him fine.

"Nola, leave the boy be," Adam said, halting the flow of words. "Come, Keifer, I'll show you where to put your horse."

Keifer led the horse, Nola at his side.

She said, "You don't talk much."

"You don't give a body a chance."

At her crestfallen face, he quickly made amends. "I'm sorry."

With a shrug that seemed to offer forgiveness, she said, "Do you have brothers and sisters?"

He put the horse in the stall Adam indicated and made sure it had hay and water.

"Aye."

"I'm the oldest," she said. She leaned down and picked up a gray kitten, petting its head.

"I'm the youngest."

"Oh. Do you have a best friend?"

Keifer thought about it for only a second. "James is my best friend." A stab of homesickness hit him as he remembered his friend so far away at Dunstruan. If this Nola was the oldest, then her brothers were going to make poor friends for a boy as old as he. Some of his sadness must have shown on his face.

"I'll be your friend. If you like."

She looked so hopeful, he couldn't be mean. "All right."

She beamed at him and handed him the kitten.

He gave the cat a friendly pat and set it down. Though glad to have pleased her and just a little grateful for her offer of friendship, Keifer reminded himself not to become too fond of her.

Ceallach and Adam walked toward them, and Keifer fought to tamp down his resentment. He'd allowed himself to care about the big knight, and yet soon Ceallach would abandon him. This place, these people, would be no more permanent in his life than his father, brother, or Ceallach.

Keifer would not make the same mistake with Adam Mackintosh or anyone else at Moy.

TWO

Sᴏ ᴀᴅᴀᴍ ʟᴇᴅ ᴛʜᴇᴍ ɪɴᴛᴏ ᴛʜᴇ ᴋᴇᴇᴘ where they sat down for the midday meal. Keifer sat quietly, listening to his host and hostess and taking their measure.

"We are pleased to have you here, Keifer," Sir Adam said. "The children have been allowed to sit at the table rather than being banished to the nursery so that they may welcome their new foster brother."

Keifer couldn't think what to say.

Lady Gwenyth came to his rescue. "I remember leaving my parents to foster—it seemed cruel at the time. But I became fond of my new family."

One of the younger boys spilled his cup of milk, and the lady calmly wiped the spill while Sir Adam gently admonished the child to be more careful.

Keifer had expected to be afraid of the man, but he dealt easily with his children and spoke with respect to his wife. Maybe he wouldn't be so bad after all.

Keifer kept a close watch on Nola, who sat across from him. She squirmed in her seat throughout the meal, and at the earliest possible moment, asked her father to be excused.

"Wait until Keifer is finished. Then you may show him the castle grounds."

She fidgeted, sending meaningful stares his way. Keifer didn't want to be escorted by a six-year-old child, especially a girl. However, he had no more swallowed his last bite of bread than Nola shot up from her seat, knocking the trestle top and shaking its contents. She raced around the table and grabbed his arm. "Come on, Keifer."

He looked to Adam for a possible reprieve, but the man just raised his eyebrows and nodded.

Keifer slowly stood, was granted permission to leave, and was nearly dragged off his feet when he didn't move fast enough. He had to jog to keep up with the red-headed sprite attached to his arm. They breezed through the kitchen and the chapel before heading outdoors, Nola chatting all the while.

Determined not to succumb to her exuberance, he scuffed his boots in the dirt, raising dust. She let go of his arm and skipped ahead. Looking back over her shoulder, she shouted, "Come on!"

As Keifer followed her at his own pace, he took notice of the well-maintained buildings and the high, stone curtain wall. Morrigan had chosen well; it would be nigh on impossible to breach these walls. Trying not to feel as if he'd been sentenced to a prison term, he looked for his companion, who had disappeared.

Her head popped out from the doorway of a wooden building and she gave an impatient wave of her hand until Keifer followed. He stepped inside, and though it took a moment for his eyes to adjust to the dim light, he knew from the smell they were in the sheep shed.

He thought of the sheep at Dunstruan and of the weaving hut where he and Ceallach and Lady Orelia had worked together on the very plaid he was wearing. He fingered the cloth, remembering the English noblewoman who'd been a prisoner at Dunstruan. Lady Orelia had taught Keifer how to weave. Then she, too, had left him. He knew she had to go back to England and why, but it didn't make the parting any easier.

Aye, he'd allowed himself to care and what good had it done? *Stupid sheep.* Fiercely he shoved the memories aside as he and Nola stood outside one of the pens. Nola asked, "Did you have sheep at Dunstruan?"

"Aye." He bent down and picked up a clean piece of sweet-smelling hay. Sticking the end into his mouth, he picked his teeth and tried to ignore the girl.

"Did you help with them?"

He nodded. She was difficult to ignore.

Nola put her hands on her hips. "Did you have a favorite?"

"No." He threw down the makeshift toothpick. "You ask too many questions."

She stopped talking, and he feared he'd hurt her feelings. But apparently she wasn't easily hurt. She turned from him and switched her attention to the sheep inside the enclosure. "Oh, dear."

"What's wrong?" He didn't care. Wouldn't care. He only asked because he was pretty sure Nola would tell him whether he wanted to know or not.

An ewe stood at one end of the pen, feet planted in defiance. Opening the gate, Nola entered and Keifer followed. Nola ignored the ewe and walked to her lamb, curled up in some straw at the opposite end of the enclosure. Keifer feared the mother would charge them to protect her lamb, but she lowered her head to the hay lying on the ground and began to eat.

Curious at the ewe's odd behavior, Keifer knelt next to Nola and the tiny animal. "What's wrong?"

"The mother has abandoned her wee babe."

Keifer looked closer. "Why? What is wrong with it?"

"I don't know. It seems to be all right but 'tis cold and hungry. If it doesn't eat, the poor thing will soon die. Will you carry it for me?" she asked.

Keifer shrugged. "Sure." He picked up the mewling lamb and carried it out of the pen. To his surprise, they headed for the castle. "What are you going to do?" he asked, walking fast to keep pace with Nola.

"We're going to try to save it." When they entered the kitchen, Nola scampered off and returned with a willow basket lined with tanned sheepskin. Keifer placed the lamb inside.

"I'll be back—keep her warm."

Keifer sat beside the lamb, wondering what hare-brained idea Nola had come up with. The tiny creature looked so forlorn, he picked it back up and held it. Keifer knew only too well how it felt to be abandoned. He tucked the lamb inside his plaid for added warmth. He breathed in the smell of the creature's fleece and felt its tiny breaths.

Nola soon returned with a bowl of milk and a piece of cloth, as well as a spoon. Keifer placed the creature back into the basket and they took turns spooning milk down the lamb's throat, one of them holding its mouth open, the other emptying the spoon. Their sleeves and the lamb were soon damp with milk.

Exhausted from its efforts, the lamb fell asleep. Lady Gwenyth made up a pallet for each of them near the fire.

As they moved the sleeping lamb closer to their pallets, Sir Adam came to see how they were doing. "So, you are learning your first lesson about being a laird—to be a good steward of what God gives you."

"Will the lamb live?"

Sir Adam smiled. "Nola hasn't lost one yet."

Keifer and Nola took turns feeding the lamb through the night. By morning the lamb seemed stronger. They carried her outside to relieve herself. She kicked up her heels and hopped about in pure joy. Keifer laughed at the lamb's antics.

Nola called to the lamb and it came to her, butting its head against Nola's leg.

Sir Adam joined them. "Looks like she'll make it, thanks to the two of you. We must try to find a ewe that will nurse it, or you'll be getting up every night with her." Keifer sincerely hoped Sir Adam was successful in finding a surrogate mother for the lamb. He didn't want to spend too many nights awake every few hours as he had last night. "Why did her mother abandon her?" Keifer asked.

Adam reached down and patted the lamb. "Some don't know how to mother. I don't let such ewes breed again. She'll make a better stew than a mother."

Nola seemed unconcerned that the lamb's mother would be slaughtered.

"How can you be so indifferent?" Keifer fretted.

"'Tis the way of things," Nola explained.

"Aye," Sir Adam agreed. "An ewe who can't or won't mother her lamb, well, 'tis obviously not her purpose to be a mother. 'Tis her purpose to be nourishment so that we may fulfill our purposes."

"What is our purpose, Da?"

Adam stroked the girl's hair. "Each of us must seek the answer to that question for ourselves."

"How?" Keifer asked, interested in spite of himself.

"Start with prayer. And keep praying and listening for the answer. Now. We best find that old ewe whose lamb died and convince her this one is hers."

While Adam and Nola worked with the sheep, Keifer gave thought to Adam's words.

Keifer already knew his purpose—he didn't need to pray about it. He would become a warrior, a knight of such prowess that no one could defeat him. He must become strong and skilled so that he would never be killed in a foolish accident and desert his mother and sisters like Ian Macnab had done.

That evening, as the castle inhabitants were making their way to bed, Lady Gwenyth called Keifer aside. They stood beside the huge fireplace that heated the great hall. Keifer glanced at the dying fire and the servant who banked it for the night.

When he looked back at Lady Gwenyth, she studied him. Her expression was thoughtful and kind and he relaxed.

"I appreciate you helping Nola with the lamb," she said.

"Aye, well, Nola asked me to."

The lady smiled. "My daughter can be very persistent when she wants something."

Keifer couldn't help but smile. "That she can."

"You are to let me know if she becomes tiresome, Keifer. You are not required to be her keeper."

"I didn't mind." He said it to be polite but realized it was true. He enjoyed the little girl's infectious enthusiasm. It countered his sadness at being away from his family.

"That is a kind thing to say, Keifer. Now, on another matter. I have spoken with my husband about your sleeping arrangements. We thought perhaps you might prefer to make a pallet here in the main hall with the other men rather than in the children's room."

He stared at her. At Dunstruan he had made his pallet on the floor of his mother's chamber. But now he was being treated like one of the castle guards. Except of course, the only weapon he had was his eating knife. Still. . .

"I would rather stay in the hall."

"Good. I thought so." Lady Gwenyth motioned to a serving girl who approached them carrying a bundle. "Did you bring his belongings as well?"

"Aye, my lady."

The girl and Lady Gwenyth placed the straw-filled mattress on the rushes and then handed Keifer two woolen blankets. The hall would become chilly by morning. "Thank you, my lady."

"You are welcome. Sleep well, Keifer."

The lady and the servant left Keifer to settle his belongings along side his bedding. Carefully he set down the small wooden chest that held his most treasured possessions. Keifer lay down on his pallet and pulled the blankets over him. Then he leaned on one elbow and brought the chest close to him, situating it so he had light from the fire to see by. But even in the darkest night he would have known each object by touch.

He handled each one, remembering how they'd come into his possession. And in so doing, remembering as well the people who had given each item to him. Satisfied that his treasures were safe, Keifer turned the key and set the box aside.

He lay down and tucked the blankets securely around himself, then as memories and homesickness overwhelmed him, he wept. The brief spate of tears seemed to release something inside of him, and he felt stronger, ready to embrace this new turn in his life. A comforting presence gave him to know that God had not deserted him, even here in the wilds of the highlands.

As he waited for sleep, he listened to the sounds of others readying their pallets. Keifer was certainly the youngest one to sleep in the hall, and he felt proud to be included in the company of men.

Warm and feeling more at home, he drifted into a sound sleep.

The next morning, Keifer awoke to the bustling sounds of the main hall. Everyone else seemed to be awake and dressed and ready to break his or her fast. Keifer didn't want to earn a reputation as a stay abed. With hurried movements, he folded the blankets and placed his chest in the mattress before he bundled it all together for storage.

He stacked his roll against the far wall with the other men's. Then, remembering from Nola's tour where the chapel was located, he made his way there to begin the day in prayer.

As he stood with the others in the chapel, he gave thanks for his blessings. Morning prayers didn't last above a quarter hour, and soon he left and went to the main hall to eat. When he entered the hall, Sir Adam waved to him, indicating he should join him at his trestle table.

Keifer sat down with his new master. "Good morrow, sir."

"Good morrow to you, Keifer. Did you sleep well?"

"Aye."

"Good. You'll need to be well rested." He indicated the red-haired man sitting across from them. "Seamus, meet your new pupil."

The big man nodded and mumbled a greeting around a mouthful of food. Keifer stared at what was probably a normal-sized knife but looked like a toy in the man's huge hand. Seamus said, "So, my boy. Do you know how to clean a horse's stall?"

Keifer stifled a groan, knowing that he would perform this particular chore every day until he became a knight and had a squire of his own. "Aye, sir. I do indeed."

"Good. Eat up. The day's a wasting."

"IT'S NO USE," Nola muttered. The key she'd found this morning in the main hall lay in her outstretched hand. Its silver gleam had caught her eye as it lay in sharp contrast to the rushes on the floor. No doubt she should have taken it straight to her mother, but what fun would that be?

Nola had spent most of the morning saving her mother from the trouble of finding what the key belonged to. Except it didn't seem to open any of the doors in the entire house. Where else could she find a lock in need of a key?

Perhaps she should just give up. After all, there had been no promise of treasure, no guarantee of success. Still, curiosity compelled her to keep looking until she realized that it might belong to Keifer since she had found it near his bedroll. She would go and ask him.

She had seen him leave the hall with Seamus. They would have cleaned the stable stalls first thing. Perhaps they would be ready for an idle moment by now. Even though she knew that Keifer would have chores and lessons, she hoped he would also have time to explore and play. The idea of having an older brother—even a foster brother—appealed to her.

Whistling at the prospect of time with her new friend, she skipped through the hall and headed for the stables. She held tight to the tiny key, afraid of losing it. If it didn't belong to Keifer, maybe he would help her search. One way or another she would find the secret this key protected.

As Nola neared the stable, she opened her hand to look at the key. The key slipped through her fingers and into the dirt under her feet. She came to an abrupt stop, dropped to her knees, and searched the ground, but didn't see the small silver object. Nola scrabbled in the dirt in an effort to uncover her treasure.

A shadow fell across her just as her fingers located the key. She looked up and discreetly palmed it.

"What are you doing in the dirt?" her father asked.

Nola stood and faced her father. He didn't look angry, just amused. Though she hated to lie, she didn't want to hand over the key resting safely in her hand. So she smiled. "I thought I saw something in the dirt." It wasn't really a lie—she had seen the key, after all.

Her father looked at her as if not quite sure whether to believe her. "Well, come along. Your mother has need of you."

Nola breathed a sigh of relief as she walked beside her father, resigned to solving the mystery of the key later.

KEIFER USED A BRANCH to sweep the ground and erase the signs of digging. Then he gathered loose stones and leaves and scattered them. He surveyed the site. How would he find this spot again if he disguised it too well?

A large tree limb lay nearby. He could drag it over to mark the buried box. But then suppose someone gathered up the limb for fire-wood? He should find a rock, something heavy and more permanent, and place it there. However, the nearest big rock he might possibly be capable of moving lay some distance away.

Maybe this hadn't been such a good idea. Keifer kicked at the dirt and then took up the shovel. Carefully he removed the dirt covering the area where he'd buried the small wooden box. But as he dug, the chest remained hidden from sight.

Panicked, he dropped to his hands and knees, clawing the dirt with bare hands. He almost shouted in relief when his fingers brushed the edge of the box. He retrieved it and held it up to the light.

If he hadn't lost the key, there would be no need to look for a hid-ing place. But the key had disappeared. He would have to break the clasp to get into the box. But until then he must find somewhere else to hide his treasure. If he had his own room, he would be able to pro-tect it from prying eyes and thieves. But his choices had been to sleep with the other children or bed down in the hall. Sleeping with babies was out of the question.

Which brought him back to the object in his hands. He was old enough to be given privileges and responsibilities. He feared that if anyone knew what he kept in the box his sister had given him, they would laugh at him.

Let them laugh. He didn't care what others thought. These items were all he had of home and family, and if Nola or anyone else thought less of him . . . He must not lose any of these precious objects like he had lost that blasted key.

Keifer needed to find a place where he could be alone to look at the contents when he felt the need. With that in mind, he made his way to the gallery behind the fireplace in the great hall. A narrow ledge ran across the length, hidden from the tables below by a cross work of wood strips. Perfect. Here he could see and not be seen and maybe even be safe from that pest, Nola.

NOLA COULDN'T FIND KEIFER. He hadn't been with Seamus, nor was he here in the main hall. Could he be hiding from her? As she stood still, her kitten meowed and began to crawl up her skirt.

"Shh." Nola reached down and brought the kitten up into her arms. She climbed the stairs beside the great fireplace, lost in thought. When she reached the top, the kitten launched itself from her arms and ran behind the screen in front of the gallery's narrow walkway.

Nola had spent many hours on the overhang, looking down into the main hall when her parents were entertaining. But the hall was empty today and she didn't have time to dawdle. She needed to find Keifer.

"Here, kitty." Nola walked closer, sure she heard the cat pounce on something.

Thud. The kitten screeched and Nola raced onto the narrow walk-way, grateful that the screen stood between her and a long fall to the floor below. Her kitty needed her! She stumbled over the hem of her skirt and crashed into . . . Keifer.

"What have you done to my cat?" she demanded.

He held the animal out to her. "Nothing. The daft thing attacked my leg."

Nola set the kitten on the floor. "Why are you hiding?"

He ignored her. She thought he must be unhappy at being forced to live here with her family. She couldn't understand why. Castle Moy was great fun to explore, and he could be happy if he'd just try.

He'd shunned her offer to be his friend and avoided her. That she could abide. But she wouldn't let him get away with hurting her cat.

She kicked him in the shin.

"Ouch! Why'd you do that?"

"You hurt my kitten. And you don't want to be my friend." Nola noticed the small chest in his hands. "What's that?"

Looking as if he'd lost his very last friend, Keifer shook his head. "You don't give up, do you? Just go and leave me be."

But Nola could imagine only too well how hard it would be to leave her mother and family, all that was familiar and dear. And to have her father dead! Her heart hurt just thinking what life would be like under such circumstances. This boy needed a friend, and she would be Keifer's whether he wanted her to or not.

"Why are you up here?"

His chest heaved with a huge breath. Was he trying not to cry? Nola looked away to give him time to compose himself, looked again at the small box in his hands and noticed it had a locked latch on it. A very small lock. Just the size of the key she'd found.

She put out her hand. "I found this in the rushes of the main hall this morning. Is it yours?"

She opened her fingers to expose the key laying in her palm. He nodded but didn't reach for it at first. Nola could see the relief on his face. What was in the box?

He reached for the key.

KEIFER MADE AS IF TO HIDE IT in the folds of his plaid, then thought better of it. Placing the key in the lock, he turned the key, removed the lock, and opened the lid of the chest. He stared into it for a moment, unsure whether or not to share the contents with this girl.

Then he offered the box to her.

Nola peeked inside but she did not try to touch anything, as if she respected such treasures. "Will you show them to me?" she asked.

Keifer reached in and picked up the wooden horse. "My da made this for me." He laid it in her hand, and she closed her fingers around it and lifted it in front of her face. She turned it about, examining it. "It's beautiful. It must be nice to have a father who can make such a wonderful toy."

"My da is dead." He hadn't meant to sound hurt, but his pain must have come through in his voice.

She looked at him, her expression stricken. Tears welled in her eyes. "Oh, Keifer." She handed the figure back to him. "Here, take it before something happens to it."

He took the horse from her and put it back in the box.

"Will you show me the rest?"

"There's a fish hook and some string. Do you fish?"

"Da has taken me a few times, but he's usually too busy. Maybe you could take me—you are old enough to go without an adult." She looked so hopeful, Keifer puffed his chest at her adoration.

"Perhaps." He picked up the ball. "My friend, Ceallach, made this for me."

"Who is Ceallach?"

"The man who brought me here. He's the laird of Dunstruan, where I lived before coming here."

"He was your friend? The laird?"

"Aye. He taught me to use a sword and started my training as a warrior. He was a great warrior himself."

"And do you want to be a great warrior too?"

"Aye. It is my heart's desire." Now why had he confessed such a thing to this meddlesome girl? Keifer put the ball back.

"Do you miss your family terribly?"

He didn't answer.

"They most likely miss you, too. Why did they send you so far away to foster?"

"Because my uncle wants to kill me." Keifer looked at the final item in the box.

"Kill you! Why?" Nola followed his gaze. "What's that?"

Keifer hastened to cover the ring, but he wasn't fast enough.

"Oh, it's shiny. What is it?"

He hadn't known her long, but he knew enough that there would be no placating Nola once she had made up her mind. Still covering the ring with his hand, he said, "I will show it to you, but you must not tell anyone about it."

"Why? Did you steal it? Will you get in trouble for having it? Why can't I tell?"

"I did not steal it, but yes, I could get in trouble for having it." He lifted his hand and picked up the ring, laying it in her outstretched palm.

"It's a laird's ring," she said.

"Aye. The Macnab ring. It belonged to my Uncle Angus, but King

36

Robert took it from him and put him in prison. I will wear the ring when I'm old enough to be laird of my clan."

"Why will you get in trouble? Is it yours or isn't it?"

"It's mine, but my Uncle Angus wants it back for his son—my cousin."

"That's why your uncle wants to kill you, then."

"Aye. He thinks my sister has it, but she sent it with me for safe-keeping. So you mustn't tell. Promise?"

She nodded vigorously. "I promise!"

"Good. It will be our secret."

"We must find a good place to hide the key to the box. I know," she said. Reaching behind her neck, she pulled her braid over her shoulder and unfastened a ribbon from it. Taking the ribbon, she laced it through the hole at one end of the key and tied the ribbon in a loop. "There, now you can wear the ribbon and keep the key close to you. No one will be able to get into your treasure box and steal your memories."

Keifer took the ribbon she held out to him. "Thank you, Nola." He placed the key around his neck.

Without a word Nola hugged him, and Keifer's loneliness eased.

THREE

Castle Moy, 1318

As THE MONTHS AND YEARS WENT BY, Keifer settled into the routine at Moy. He missed his mother and sister less and less and convinced himself he was better off at Moy. News came slowly to the far reaches of the highlands, but eventually they learned that Edward Bruce, the last of Robert the Bruce's brothers, had been crowned King of Ireland. Later still, they heard that he had been killed in battle.

Berwick, that unlucky border town, was retaken by the Scots as Scotland and England continued to feud. These tales of far-away conflict fueled Keifer's desire to become a warrior, perhaps to even be knighted for his bravery in battle. Every morning he attended chapel, broke his fast and headed for the lists to train with Seamus.

He was tall and strong for fourteen, a fact that gave him great pride, though it was none of his doing. Just yesterday Nola's mother had taken Keifer aside and impressed upon him that she held him responsible for the younger children's safety when they were together. Though it was a compliment to have her trust, he couldn't help resenting being in charge of them.

This morning he and Nola had met before daybreak, and now Keifer walked up the path from the stream where they had spent the morning fishing. "Hurry up, Nola. What's keeping you?"

He turned to urge her to move faster, but the path behind him was empty. "Nola, come on. We're going to be late for chapel." There was no answer.

The bushes that grew along the path prevented him from seeing what delayed Nola. "I'm going to be in trouble with your mother. Again," he shouted.

"Keifer. I need your help!"

"Of course you do. I'm not falling for that ruse again. Hurry up, we're late." *As if the girl didn't know it.*

Keifer heard a loud splash and, fearing what it might mean, he dropped his pole and the fish he'd caught and ran back to the bank of the stream.

Nola thrashed about in waist high water.

"What in the world are—" A plaintive bleat filled the air as the lamb Nola clutched shoved its head above water.

"Don't stand there yapping, help me with this *gòrach* lamb," she sputtered.

Each springtime the two of them took on the care of the orphaned lambs, and each year at least one of them followed Keifer and Nola around like a dog. Keifer felt a kinship with the abandoned animals and Nola had the patience to deal with the stubborn creatures, wooing them into her family circle just as she had him.

But as he waded toward her in the cold water, Keifer thought this year's lamb had met its match in Nola. The creature lunged and pulled Nola off her feet and into deeper water. Keifer fought the current and reached out for her hand, but her fingers swept past just out of reach as the water swept her away.

"Let go of the lamb, Nola!" Her head disappeared beneath the water. *Foolish girl.* He abandoned his sure footing and moved toward where she'd gone under. Treading water, he jabbed his hands below the surface. Nothing. For the first time, he tasted fear.

Nola's head broke the surface some distance away. The current carried her downstream faster than him, and Keifer swam after her with frightened, fast strokes.

She still clutched the panicked animal.

"Let go of the dumb sheep and grab a branch," he shouted. The cold water would have felt good on a warm summer afternoon, but so early in the day, without the sun's full warmth, it sapped Keifer's energy. Afraid Nola would weaken, he swam harder.

Nola went under again, but this time she let go of the lamb, which struggled toward the shore. Nola was a good swimmer, but with her heavy skirts weighing her down, Keifer feared she might not surface again. The current was carrying her to the deep pool where they'd caught their fish.

Keifer prayed for strength and for Nola's head to again emerge. With luck the water would carry her to more shallow water, but could Nola hold her breath that long? Would she sink too deep for the current to move her? When he reached the spot he'd last seen her, he took a breath and went under, searching for her until he grew faint from lack of air.

Lungs nearly bursting, he surfaced without Nola and panic threatened to overtake him, just as it had the wild lamb. He prayed again, teeth chattering. He'd been carried to the shallows and was able to stand now—why didn't Nola push herself up out of the water? Had she hit her head?

Desperately Keifer searched under the water, along the shore. Seconds passed like hours before Nola's head broke the surface. He moved with as much speed as the water allowed and pulled her to him.

"Nola!" he shouted. Her eyes were closed, and he dragged her to the shore. Warm tears joined the cool creek water on his face. He hugged her tight, crushing her to him.

The action must have jostled her lungs, for a gush of water came out of her mouth. She sputtered and struggled and opened her eyes. "Nola. Thank God." He helped her to sit and retch up the rest of the water. When the spasms passed, she looked at him, swiping the water from her eyes as if she'd just taken a leisurely swim. "Did you save the lamb?"

His laugh came out strangled, and she tried to push him away. But he clung to her, saying a heartfelt prayer of thanksgiving and promising himself that they would never miss chapel again.

He pointed to the bedraggled animal just upstream from them. "The lamb swam to shore and is probably laughing at us both. You could have drowned!"

"Aye, but I didn't. I knew you'd save me."

He shook his head, wondering at her faith in him. "That I did. You could thank me, you know." Keifer stood and helped Nola to her feet. "Come on. By the time we change clothes, we'll miss chapel for sure."

"I do thank you. You were very brave." She looked to the east and the rapidly rising sun. "We're going to catch it for sure unless we can convince Mama we went to chapel before we went fishing." She shrugged and proceeded to walk back to where she'd left her pole.

They gathered their belongings and walked up the path toward the castle. Nola said, "You won't tell on me, will you?"

"We'll be in enough trouble for missing chapel. Just promise me not to do anything foolish like that again."

"I promise."

Keifer doubted that she would try that particular stunt again. But he could be sure she would find some other mischief. Nola's impulsive nature made her a delightful companion. He just hoped she could learn to curb her impulses as she matured without destroying her joy for life.

GWENYTH SAT ON A WOODEN BENCH in Moy's chapel, her husband beside her and their sons between him and his mother. Gwenyth smiled as Eva removed Tom's hand from his brother Rob's hair. What would Gwenyth do without her children's grandmother to help with her active brood?

As she looked up at the beautiful stained-glass window above the altar, Gwenyth remembered the day she'd taken vows with Adam in this very place. She bowed her head for a prayer of thanks for God's many blessings since that day. Two of those blessings sat here with her. Little James was still asleep in the nursery. Her fourth and oldest child was late for chapel. As was Keifer. No doubt they were into some mischief together. Such had been the case ever since Keifer's arrival three years ago.

When Gwenyth finished praying, she lifted her head and glanced about the chapel, looking once again for Nola and Keifer. Still not here. She would have to scold them both.

Adam had also finished his prayers and stood up. While his mother took Rob's hand, Adam reached for Tom. As they walked from the chapel, Adam asked his wife, "Where are Nola and Keifer?"

"I was wondering the same thing. Neither of them asked permission to skip chapel this morning."

Eva said, "I'll take the boys inside to break their fast if you want to look for Nola and Keifer."

"Thank you, Mother," Adam said.

Eva took the children by the hands and walked into the main hall while Adam and Gwenyth remained standing outside the chapel.

"I suppose we'll have to look for them. They aren't still abed—Keifer's spot by the fireplace and Nola's bed were empty."

"I worry about them," Gwenyth said.

"Attending chapel faithfully is but one way of worship," Adam reminded her.

"Perhaps for an adult. But children must learn the discipline—and rewards—of regular prayer."

Adam nodded. "Where should we begin our search? And what will you do when you find them?"

Just then Nola's head peeked around the doorway leading into the hall. Just as quickly it disappeared.

Gwenyth strode forward. There stood Keifer and Nola, both soaking wet and each carrying a stringer of fish.

"Was it necessary to miss chapel?" she demanded.

Keifer looked at her with disdain, as if she couldn't be expected to understand. "Fish bite best early in the morning."

The boy's defiance would have to be dealt with, but Gwenyth chose to fight one battle at a time. "Surely they would wait a quarter hour until you'd been to chapel?"

Neither child had an answer to that.

Adam said, "How did you catch them—bare handed?"

"Nola fell in and I had to pull her out." Again that strain of defiance in his voice. Gwenyth would have to speak to Adam about the boy's uncooperative disposition. "I could have gotten out by myself." Nola flicked water from her clothing, and Keifer got her back by flinging his wet hair.

Drops of water sprinkled Gwenyth's face. "Enough. Go and get dry clothes."

Apparently her voice conveyed her displeasure, because the two left without further argument.

Gwenyth watched after them. "Have you noticed Keifer's bearing of late?"

"Aye. He's pushing to see how far he can go. Seamus has mentioned it, and he and I will deal with it. Let me know if Keifer becomes disrespectful. 'Tis something boys do, Gwenyth. A firm hand will guide him through it."

"They both need a firm hand. Neither he nor Nola seems to take their faith, nor us, seriously."

"Aye." As they walked toward the main hall, Adam continued, "I am surprised Keifer continues to put up with a child so much younger."

"She's closest in age to him. Why wouldn't they strike a friendship?"

"Because she's a girl, perhaps?" He stopped and turned to her. "Have you given any thought to the future should they move past friendship when they are older?"

Gwenyth halted as well. "Part of me doesn't want to worry so far ahead. But I suppose we should be prepared. Would such an alliance be acceptable?" Gwenyth asked.

Adam said, "It's acceptable, but I had thought that Nola might marry a Macpherson to strengthen those ties."

"Well, time enough to worry about it later. For now I must go see that they don't catch their deaths from their adventure."

AFTER CHANGING HIS CLOTHES and downing a bowl of porridge, Keifer hurried to the lists. He looked forward to the effort of training to ward off the chill he'd taken in the creek. Keifer enjoyed working with Seamus but sometimes his demands seemed pointless. Still, Keifer did his best to arrive on time and learn what Seamus had to teach him, harboring the hope that someday he would become a knight.

Seamus stood by an outcropping of the courtyard's stone wall. A variety of weapons lay there, including the sword that had belonged to Keifer's father. But Keifer did not have permission to fight with it yet. Another promise for the future—that when he'd earned the right, he would be allowed to carry his father's sword.

Keifer walked over to Seamus, who said, "Good day, Keifer. Are you ready to work?"

Picking up his sheathed weapon, Keifer replied, "Aye."

"You will have an opportunity to show our laird what you have learned this week." Seamus lifted his chin and pointed across the bailey.

Sir Adam strode toward them, a scowl on his usually smiling face. That did not bode well, and Keifer had his first inclination that the laird's presence had some meaning beyond simply watching.

After a curt "Good morrow," Adam stood directly in front of Keifer and said, "Let me see your sword."

Keifer's heart pounded. The sword had not been cleaned in several days. He glanced to Seamus, whose expression gave no hint of what to expect. Dreading the laird's reaction, Keifer took the weapon from its scabbard.

Hands held out, Adam demanded, "Give it to me."

Why was the laird making such a fuss? Keifer handed it to him, wondering what the point was.

Adam examined the weapon, turning it over and back. "Needs cleaning."

Keifer stared at the dirty blade.

"Well, have you nothing to say?" Sir Adam asked.

Keifer dared not lie—he'd already learned the hard way that Sir Adam's punishment for such an infraction was a whipping. And even though the stripes had stung his pride more than his bottom, he did not care for a repeat of the episode. "Aye, my laird, 'tis dirty."

Seamus said, "I told you to clean it when we were finished yesterday. Didn't I?"

Sullenly Keifer replied, "Aye."

Seamus and Adam exchanged a glance. They treated him like a babe.

Adam said, "'Tis Seamus's job to train you, Keifer. 'Tis your job to obey him as you would me. Do you understand?"

"Aye." He understood his role well, yet he couldn't seem to overcome his need to resist. He'd spoken with the priest about his willfulness, and the man had suggested that Keifer pray for strength from the Holy Ghost. Keifer prayed daily for such strength but so far found it lacking.

"Good. When you are finished with your lesson, you will clean all the weapons in the armory as well as your own."

"Aye, my laird."

"Now I will watch your lesson—I hope you are not as sloppy in your fighting as you are in preparing to fight."

Adam nodded to Seamus before standing to the side.

Angry as well as nervous, Keifer moved into position. Seamus instructed him as to what they would practice first. The lesson began. They worked on several different moves as Seamus explained yet again the advantages and disadvantages of size, quickness, and stamina. "You must learn to recognize your opponent's strengths and weaknesses as well as your own. Watch the weapon, not the body. Body movement may prove false—the weapon is the key."

After a time, Keifer's arm ached. He parried a thrust and blindly attacked, not striving for form, only wishing for the bout to end.

Seamus deflected the blow with ease and called a halt. "There, Keifer. That is the longest bout you have managed yet. Well done."

Adam walked over to them and put his hand on Keifer's shoulder. "Well done indeed, lad. I am pleased with what I see."

Keifer leaned on his sword, drawing in gulps of air. His arms felt like stones and his legs trembled, but it was worth it to receive such a compliment.

Seamus ruffled Keifer's sweaty hair. "You will make a fine warrior yet."

Adam withdrew his hand from Keifer's shoulder and walked over to the weapons, picking up a broad sword. "Come, Seamus. If young Keifer hasn't tired you, go a round with me."

Seamus grinned. "My pleasure, my laird."

The morning sun had grown warm, and both men pulled off their sarks. When Adam removed his, Keifer stared at the ragged mark on Adam's left arm. As the men engaged their swords, they explained what Adam did to compensate for the lack of strength in his shield arm. Adam's prowess was admirable, but Keifer's gaze returned over and over to the scar.

When both men were breathing heavily from their efforts, they halted and put up their weapons. The three of them walked across the bailey to the place behind the kitchen where a crock of water was kept for drinking. Filling the crock each morning was Keifer's responsibility. Only now did Keifer remember that in his hurry to go fishing he had failed to do so today. Hopefully there was water left from yesterday, or he could expect another rebuke.

Adam picked up the drinking ladle and lifted the lid.

"What's this? No water?" He turned to Keifer. "This chore is to be done before breakfast. Why was it not done?"

Keifer rolled his eyes. "I will fill it now, my laird."

Where Adam's face had earlier reflected approval, now he scowled. "Aye, you will. And you'll not roll your eyes in disrespect, either. See that this crock and the one in the kitchen are filled at the assigned time from now on."

Keifer grabbed the bucket to head to the well, mumbling, "I don't see what difference it makes."

Adam grabbed him from behind and spun Keifer to face him. "I'll tell you what difference it makes. I am thirsty, as is Seamus. And Cook needs water first thing, not when you are good and ready. Everyone must work together for the good of all, Keifer. Just because you don't see the need doesn't mean you can forgo your chores. I have reasons for my orders, and I expect you to obey. You want to be a knight? First you must learn this lesson. All true knights obey their master without thought of it twice."

Keifer hung his head.

"Do you understand?"

"Yes, my laird."

"Now fetch us some water."

Keifer took the bucket to the well and returned to fill the crock. Without being told, he checked to see if Cook needed water, but someone had already taken care of it. No doubt Keifer would get a scolding from Cook or Lady Gwenyth yet today as well.

Seamus drank his fill and handed the dipper back to Sir Adam, who said, "Keifer will be along in a few minutes to clean the weapons. And for this other transgression, see that he sweeps out the armory as well."

Nodding in approval, Seamus said, "Aye, my laird," and walked away.

Keifer drank his fill in silence. He glanced at Sir Adam, and the man stared off in the distance, as if he'd just noticed a hole in the high wall surrounding the castle. Keifer thought it best if he remained quiet.

Keifer replaced the dipper on a nail meant to hold it and looked up at his laird. He expected the man's expression to be angry, but it was not. Adam pulled on his sark, covering the scar. Keifer stifled the desire to ask how Adam had been wounded.

"Let us sit here in the shade a moment, Keifer." They sat side by side on a wooden bench.

Keifer wiped his sweaty forehead with the sleeve of his tunic. A soft breeze felt good on his face. The rest of the castle folk must have gone into the hall for the midday meal, because the bailey was deserted. Keifer's stomach rumbled, and he looked forward to eating. But he could tell that Adam had more to say to him.

"A good warrior is a disciplined warrior, Keifer. Part of that discipline is obeying orders. Part of it is self-control. A superior warrior masters both his strengths and his weaknesses."

"I understand, sir." Hoping to direct the conversation away from his own transgressions, Keifer said, "You fight well, my laird. May I ask . . . How did you receive the scar?"

A pained look crossed the man's face.

"Forgive my boldness, my laird. I should not have asked."

"No, Keifer. I'm glad you asked. When I tell you to master your weaknesses, your willingness to give in to temptation, I speak from painful experience."

Keifer nodded, anxious to hear about the great battle and Adam's heroic deeds that earned him such a magnificent scar.

"I do not consider my wound a badge of honor, Keifer, if that's what you're thinking. I gave in to temptation and nearly lost my life."

"Temptation?" Keifer was disappointed at the direction this was headed. Had Adam been hurt in a senseless brawl and not in the midst of battle?

"Aye. The lure of things that are not good for us." Adam stared across the bailey before continuing. "I served with your brother Gordon. Did you know that?"

"Aye. Morrigan told me you knew him well. I don't remember him myself. Only what I've been told."

"If I had been as good a friend to Gordon as he was to me, he might not have died at Dalry Pass."

Adam recounted the events of a hot August day, when his head had ached from too much drink. "I was so weary from my revels the night before, I was incapable of mounting a successful defense when my companions, including the king of Scotland and his family, were attacked. I barely escaped with my life, and I could not come to Gordon's rescue."

Keifer's heart pounded and his stomach clenched. He'd never known the details of how Gordon had died. "Was my brother a good fighter?"

"As good as any highlander with little or no formal training can be. But he was a very good man, Keifer. He died protecting his king, a hero's death."

Hero or not, Gordon's death had been a blow to his family, especially to Keifer. "My mother and sister never blamed you."

"No, to their credit, they did not. They proved that tenfold by entrusting you to my care."

Keifer didn't know what to say to that and remained silent.

"I can't help wondering how it might have been different if I had been sober and alert. 'Tis only by the grace of God that I am alive, Keifer. And all for the want of a bit of self-discipline. Most of the time I am able to accept God's forgiveness, though it is still hard after all these years."

It would be easy for Keifer to blame Sir Adam, to see him as less of a man after this confession. But his pain and regret were obvious, and Keifer couldn't help admiring him for being willing to expose his own shortcoming in order to teach Keifer. "Thank you for telling me this, my laird. I will keep my weapons clean, I promise."

"I'm sure you will. Learn from the mistakes of others, lad. Now go and see to your chores. When you are finished and Seamus has inspected your work, see if my wife has any duties for you to perform."

Keifer resolved to do better. If he did not, then Sir Adam might not recommend that Keifer receive further training. And Keifer wanted to be trained by the best of King Robert's knights. Gordon had died when he might have lived had he been better prepared. The same would not happen to Keifer.

FOUR

THE DAY TURNED UNSEASONABLY HOT by afternoon. Keifer put the broom away and pulled his tunic on over his head. Seamus had inspected the cleaned weapons and gone home to his wife, telling Keifer he was free to go once he finished the sweeping.

Keifer went in search of Nola and found her with her mother in the sewing room. "Lady Gwenyth, Sir Adam said I should ask what chores I might do for you today. And I'm sorry about the water this morning—I will do better."

"That's good to hear." She grinned at Nola. "If the two of you would help me wind the rest of this thread onto spools, I think it might be an excellent day for a swim. Without the sheep, this time."

Nola jumped up. "Aye! Let's go!"

Keifer, newly mindful of his responsibilities, said, "First the thread."

Working quickly, they finished in less than a quarter hour and Lady Gwenyth sent them off. Dense undergrowth provided a screen of privacy, and they took turns changing into something suitable for swimming. Keifer wore an old pair of breeches. Nola had a shirt of her father's with the sleeves cut short and a pair of Keifer's breeches he'd outgrown long ago.

Now the sound of the waterfall soothed Keifer as he and Nola floated in the pool beneath it.

With each lesson from Adam or Seamus, Keifer became more

aware of the responsibility of leading his clan. The more he learned, the more he doubted his ability to do the job. It took everything in him to care for himself! How did a man go about caring for a great many people? How did Robert the Bruce do it? Let alone Adam? The thought of such great responsibility overwhelmed him.

King Robert had recently brokered a truce with England, though Adam didn't seem to think it would hold. Still, there was hope that this truce might lead to peaceful negotiations. Keifer just hoped that he would have a chance to use his skills before the two countries settled their differences. He was eager to try his hand in battle. Lairdship could wait.

"Do you ever think about the future, Nola?"

"Well, I am worried that Mother will make me take care of my brothers tomorrow while she sews."

He splashed water at her. "No, I mean when you're grown. Where will you live, and will you know everything you need to take care of yourself and your family?"

She had ducked the spray of water and paddled off a short distance. "I worry more that I'll never get to see anything outside of the glen."

"Really? You'd like to travel?" Nola the adventuress. Somehow this didn't surprise him.

"Aye. Mother told me about France and about the great cathedrals in Paris. I asked if we can go there sometime, but it would cost a lot and my brothers are too small to travel so far."

"Maybe you can go when you are older. With an escort," he added.

She stopped swimming and stood up. "You could take me!"

"I've no desire to see France." Unless of course he was needed to guard the king of Scotland on a royal errand.

Nola resumed paddling about. "Well, if I can't see Paris, I would at least like to see Edinburgh, and maybe even Stirling Castle. You could take me there, couldn't you?"

"I could, but I have to complete my training, and that will take years. And I'm hoping that your father will recommend me to train with Sir Bryan Mackintosh."

"Can't Seamus teach you everything you need to know?"

"He's a very good teacher, and so is your father. But I want to be knighted, to gain experience in the tourney, and perhaps in a real battle."

"You don't have to be a knight to do that."

"Perhaps not. But I have a more practical reason. Innishewan is in need of money—money I could earn in tournaments, if I'm good enough."

Nola didn't give up. "I don't see why you have to become a knight. You could marry a wife with money."

He laughed. Practical Nola always had a solution. "I could. But maybe . . . maybe if I am the very best fighter, I won't die senselessly and leave my family without protection." He had never admitted that to anyone.

Nola paddled over to him. "Keifer, no amount of training can guarantee that."

"Maybe not. But I'm going to do all I can to stay alive."

"I still don't see what the great danger is, but I guess I can understand you not wanting to die and leave your family like your father did."

Nola understood too much, despite her tender age. She amazed him with her maturity. Oft times, like now, she seemed more his own age instead of years younger.

Keifer feared that he would not be there for his loved ones—that he would one day have a child who would grow up not knowing him, just like Keifer. Sometimes the aching emptiness of that loss nearly sent Keifer into despair.

"You miss having a da, don't you?"

He shrugged. "Your da is all right, when he isn't lecturing."

She laughed. "He just wants what is best for you. For all of us."

"Aye, well, he needs to take a lighter hand sometimes."

"Is that the kind of father you will be, then?"

"No. I'm not going to marry."

"Not going to marry? You have to get married."

"No, I don't. I have decided to name Morrigan's son as my heir. I will devote myself to the protection of my sisters and their families."

"Morrigan doesn't have a son."

"She will someday, God willing." He shook his head. "Enough of such serious talk." He splashed Nola and she retaliated. They continued to play until they churned up the bottom and the water began to cloud with mud.

Tired of swimming, they made their way to the bank where Nola threw herself onto the grass. Keifer sat beside her. "So, I take it you do want to marry but you want to see the world first."

She pushed her wet hair behind her ears. "Aye, but I'll settle for a trip to Edinburgh."

"You're only nine. Are you planning to marry any time soon?" he teased.

She shook her finger at him. "A girl must think of these things, Keifer. Before you know it, you're betrothed and married and having babes. I want that; I'm just not in a hurry for it."

Keifer had never considered that a woman might want anything other than a husband and babes. The idea intrigued him. "Do you ever wonder who you'll marry?"

She hesitated.

He smiled. "What?"

Again she started to shake her finger at him and he made a grab for it. She was too quick, though and he missed. She wasn't smiling when she said, "Don't laugh or I swear I'll, I'll—"

"I won't laugh, Nola. What poor fellow have you set your cap for?"

She jumped to her feet. "Don't make fun of me!" She began to pull on her dry clothes over the wet.

Keifer followed her and when he drew close, he suspected some of the water on her face was tears. He reached for her and she pulled away.

"Nola. What did I say wrong?"

When she faced him, her heart was in her eyes and it startled him. She was just a child, though he would never call her such to her face.

"If ever I change my mind about marriage, I hope I find a companion as agreeable as you, Nola." He pulled her to him. "Ah, lass, I'm sorry. A man would be honored to have you care for him."

"But not you, Keifer?"

He grinned. "I'm not a man, yet."

Innishewan

MORRIGAN COOKSON left the newly refurbished kitchen of Innishewan Castle in search of her husband, Fergus. She smiled. Marriage to Fergus had proved to be everything she had hoped for and more.

It had taken longer than anticipated to make the castle livable after her uncle left it in shambles. She hadn't seen Angus Macnab—hadn't visited him in prison—in the four years since he'd been taken to face King Robert. She shook her head. Why ever was she thinking of her uncle today?

She walked through the main hall, noting with approval that the servants had cleared and taken down the trestles. Others were spreading fresh lavender in the rushes on the floor. Morrigan found, to her surprise, that she enjoyed many aspects of running a household. A few years ago she wouldn't have believed such a thing. The thought made her smile.

Because of her training as a warrior and Fergus's as a steward, they truly complemented each other, even if their roles sometimes overlapped. In many ways theirs was a marriage of true equals, and she and Fergus worked together as a team.

She placed a hand on her barely expanded stomach. No doubt when the child was born they would need to revise their roles, but even then she knew that Fergus would not use a heavy hand to force her to his will. How she loved him!

She found him poring over the ledgers in the solar. His dark hair gleamed in the light from a small window. The scar over his eye was plainly visible, yet she thought him the most handsome of men. "Am I interrupting?"

Looking up, Fergus smiled. "Come in. I'm just reconciling some figures."

She walked to him and when she stood close, he pulled her into his lap. His blue eyes shone with concern. "How are you feeling?"

She put her arms around his neck and kissed his forehead. "Fit as can be."

"Good. Then ye won't mind this." He kissed her lips and she quite lost track of time and place. Sometime later, she heard the familiar sound of her mother clearing her throat. Morrigan reluctantly pulled away—how many times had Eveleen found them thus?

But today Eveleen didn't smile as she usually did. White-faced and edgy, she stood at the open door and wasted no time with pleasantries. "We have a visitor. Yer Uncle Angus."

Morrigan jumped to her feet, romance forgotten. "But Uncle Angus is in prison."

"He's been released."

Four years ago Uncle Angus had tried to kidnap Keifer. For that offense and for supporting the English king, Robert the Bruce had imprisoned Angus Macnab.

And now he was free? How had Angus managed that? "Where is he?"

"At the gate. I . . . I refused him entrance."

Fergus stood and walked over to Eveleen. "That was wise, good mother." He took her arm as though he realized she needed his courage to bolster her own. "Come, let's see what he wants."

"What will we tell him about Keifer?" Eveleen asked as they walked toward the keep's door.

Morrigan moved to walk at her mother's other side. "The truth. He isn't here. We are not required to tell him or anyone else where the boy is."

The three of them went into the bailey and to the gate. Morrigan only hoped the man would pay his respects and be gone without upsetting her mother. Morrigan would hear him out and send him on his way. The portal was open, but Morrigan's men held the visitor at sword point.

Angus had dismounted, and though Fergus and Eveleen stopped this side of the gate, Morrigan walked forward and halted beside her guards. She could barely restrain her dislike of her uncle.

"Uncle Angus. This is quite a surprise."

He sketched a courtesy. "King Robert released me a few days ago. Bruce has given me a small tract of land an hour north of here. I thought . . . I wanted ye to know I am close by if ye need anything."

"We have never needed anything from ye, Angus," Eveleen said with quiet dignity.

Fergus said, "Are ye for Bruce, then?"

"Aye. A few years in prison gives a man time to see the error of his ways."

Morrigan wasn't sure she believed him but kept her thoughts to herself.

Angus stepped closer. "Eveleen." He looked down at the ground. "I'll not come back here to disturb yer peace. But I must speak with ye in private this once."

Eveleen looked to Morrigan.

She nodded. "It's all right, Mother, if you wish to."

"Speak to me here, Angus. I have no desire to be private with ye."

He drew a deep breath. "All right. They say that public confession is good for the soul."

Again Morrigan worried that Angus would unnecessarily upset her mother. "Uncle Angus, confession might be good for you, but it might not be good for those who must listen to what you say." She stared at him, and with a nod he acknowledged her point.

"That may be true, niece, but still these words need saying. First of all, ye need not fear for Keifer. I will not harm the boy. 'Tis the least I can do to repay—"

"You don't owe us anything," Morrigan interrupted.

"Ah, but I do, Morrigan." He turned to Eveleen. "Ye see, I killed Ian."

Eveleen frowned. "Don't be ridiculous. He fell from his horse."

Morrigan was struck dumb by this confession. What was Angus up to?

Stepping closer to Eveleen, he said, "Aye, so I told ye. I could not face ye with the truth."

Morrigan said, "You killed my father? Why bother to confess now after all this time?"

"A man has time to think in prison, time to pray for God's forgiveness. And now I'm needin' yers."

"Ye killed yer own brother." Eveleen swayed, and Fergus steadied her. "How? Why?"

"We argued. He walked away from me and I charged him, knocked him down. He fell, hit a rock and broke his neck."

"He didn't fall from the horse?" Eveleen whispered.

He laid his hand on her arm. "Nay, he did not."

Eveleen shoved at his hand, pushing it away. "Ye lied and let me believe that lie all this time." Her voice rose in obvious anger. "Why bother to tell me now?"

Morrigan wondered the same thing, though somehow his confession didn't surprise her. She struggled not to reach for her sword and cut him down here and now.

"I am not young, Eveleen. I want to die with this made right between us. I will never have yer love, nor do I deserve it. But I would ask for yer forgiveness."

Eveleen said in a choked voice, "Angus, Angus. What have ye done?" She turned to her daughter, sobbing, and Morrigan held her close.

Fergus said, "I'll take her inside, lady wife. Finish with yer uncle."

Grateful for her husband's offer, Morrigan watched her mother and Fergus walk away. Then she faced her uncle. "I should run you through and be done with it. But then I'd be no better than you." Another thought came to her. "What of Owyn? Does he share your change of heart? Is Keifer safe from him?"

Angus swiped his hand over his face. "He will obey me in this matter."

"Then are you warning me to beware of Owyn?"

"I don't know how my son feels. I've not seen him yet. But he may very well want what should be his—leadership of the clan. If so, then Keifer is not safe."

Morrigan should feel compassion for the man. He'd done a brave thing today, confessing to Eveleen. To her. But try as she might, she couldn't soften her heart enough to invite him in for food and drink. "I thank you for the warning."

With a nod, Angus Macnab turned and mounted his horse. As he rode away, Morrigan hoped it would be the last time she laid eyes on him. She didn't trust him, couldn't trust him or Owyn. Keifer must remain at Moy.

And when the boy was older and Seamus had taught him all he could of fighting as a highlander, then she would send Keifer to train as a knight. It might be the best way to ensure his safety—ensure his training was second to none. And far superior to Owyn's.

She would discuss it with her husband.

SOLACE. ANGUS SOUGHT SOLACE as he poured himself another goblet of whiskey. What had possessed him to go crawling to Eveleen and beg her forgiveness?

He emptied the glass, and the burning of the drink matched the pain in his heart.

No! He didn't feel pain. Wouldn't feel it. She was nothing to him, never had been. She was his brother's widow. Nothing more. Except that Ian had died at Angus's hands. An accident. He'd told her the truth today and it hadn't made any difference. She'd pushed him away, just as she'd chosen Ian over him all those years ago.

He poured another drink. Forgiveness. Why had he expected it when he'd never forgiven himself?

No hope now. Might as well see it through. She wouldn't speak to him, couldn't stand the sight of him. He was already damned in her eyes and God's. What was one more death? All Angus had to do was find Keifer. He could leave tomorrow and no one would be the wiser.

He rubbed his eyes. How could he even consider such a thing? 'Twould only bring Eveleen more pain and leave no chance for her to ever forgive him. Ian had been dead for a dozen years, and the lie had stood between them all that time. Maybe now that he'd confessed he would be rewarded with a second chance with her. Yes, there was a chance. Hope. He had to keep his chin up and off the tavern's table.

Resolute, he set the spirits aside. He would bide his time. He'd waited this long for Eveleen MacTaggert. A few more years wouldn't make much difference.

FIVE

Castle Moy, 1320

ADAM LOOKED UP AT THE SOUND of the knock on the solar door. Gwenyth didn't wait for his nod but strode into the room holding a knife as if she held a distasteful rodent by the tail.

But it was not a mouse, it was a knife. And not just any knife. The handle wrappings clearly identified it as Keifer's.

Adam laid down the household ledger he'd been going over and gave his full attention to his wife. She stood in front of his desk and held the object out to him. He took it. The unsheathed metal gleamed in the light, unprotected.

Adam shook his head. "Where is the cover?"

"A good question, one I should like to ask the knife's owner. I came upon young Rob just as he plucked this weapon from the trestle. Why was it left to lay there?"

Adam came out from behind his desk to stand next to Gwenyth. "Is Rob all right?"

"A nick on his thumb. Next time we may not be so lucky."

He ran his fingers through his hair. "'Tis the second time this week he let it lay, isn't it?" Adam blew out a breath. "I'll speak with Keifer again."

"You may speak all you like. He'll be scrubbing trestles with the kitchen maids for the next week, after I've had my say."

"Aye, do that. Perhaps it will help him to remember. I'll keep the knife until such time as Keifer shows a bit more responsibility."

Gwenyth sighed. "Are we doing the right thing, fostering him? Perhaps he should have stayed with his family. Fosterage isn't right for every child. Sometimes he seems so lost."

"Aye. Perhaps so. But Keifer is safer here, especially now that his uncle has been released. We must remember that the boy has had a hard time, losing his father so young. Who knows how that might affect a boy?" Adam had been an adult when his own father died, and yet there were still times when he missed the man keenly.

He continued. "As I recall, I tested my own father on more than one occasion. All in all I think Keifer's acting like a normal fourteen-year-old boy."

"Then we have this to look forward to with our own sons?"

Adam grinned. "I'm afraid so. This and more. We can only do our best, Gwenyth. And pray for patience."

"So, you rebelled against your father's rules?"

Now Adam laughed out loud at the memories of his arguments with his father. "Oh, aye. Had my bum caned more than once. We can train Keifer in the way he should go, but in the end, he must make his own choices."

"Then we must pray that God will be with him when we aren't there to guide him."

"'Tis all any parent can do, my love."

SNOW FELL IN BIG SOFT FLAKES as Nola watched the bailey from her upstairs bedchamber. Her father had sent a messenger to let them know when he planned to return from Berwick, where he'd gone to meet with the king and other nobles. The big snowflakes had begun an hour after the midday meal, and now a thin white blanket covered the ground.

Da and Keifer had been gone for nearly a month, and Nola had missed them both. Tomorrow was Christmas Eve, and Nola prayed the weather wouldn't delay the travelers. Christmas Eve was her favorite day of the year. They would all tramp through the woods gathering greenery to decorate the hall. And Da would help them search for the perfect Yule log.

Nola closed her eyes and prayed. Every few minutes she opened them to scan the bailey. As the afternoon light began to wane, so did her hopes. But she kept praying.

A loud shout and the clatter of horses' hooves awakened her from prayer turned to a nap. Snow had piled against the wavy glass of the window, but she could make out two familiar figures dismounting below.

"Da! Keifer!" Nola banged the shutter closed and raced from her room and down the stairs. She found her mother and brothers in the hall. Mama struggled to put warm mantles on James as the excited little boy squirmed. Nola grabbed Tom and Rob and pulled them back. "It's cold; put your coats on." Nola tugged her cape over her shoulders and they all went outside.

Da strode toward them, and when they met, he knelt in the snow and embraced all four children in a warm hug. He smelled of clean air and the outdoors.

He stood up with James, the youngest, in his arms, and for a moment Nola wished she were still small enough to be lifted so. Da faced Mama and kissed her.

"Welcome home, husband. We are anxious to hear the news you bring. Come children, let your da go in where it is warm."

Searching through the snow-filled air, Nola asked, "Where's Keifer, Da?"

"He's seeing to the horses."

"I'll help." Nola raced off to the barn and found Keifer rubbing down Da's horse.

"Welcome home, Keifer!" She grabbed some straw and began to work on Keifer's gelding.

"You don't have to do that," he said.

"But if I do, we can go in where it's warm and you can tell me all about your trip. Was it wonderful? Where did you stay? Did you see the king?"

"Whoa. One question at a time."

She stopped rubbing the horse's hide and with a sigh said, "I wish I could have gone, too." She resumed working on the horse. "Tell me everything. No, hurry up with the horses and let's go in where it's warm. My fingers are frozen."

"If you'd taken time to find your gloves—"

"Don't scold. You sound like Da." That always quieted him. Keifer didn't want to be like her father, for some reason.

Keifer fetched water for the beasts while Nola sat on her hands on a bale of straw.

"Are you almost done?" she asked when he came back with a second pail.

"Let me give them hay and then we can go in."

She jumped up from her seat and followed him while he fetched the hay. "Oh, I can't wait. Tell me one thing right now. The best thing."

He placed the hay in the stall. "The best part of the trip?"

"Aye."

He stood with his fingers tapping his cheek. "Let's see now. The best thing."

Nola smacked his arm. "Stop teasing!"

"Actually, the negotiations with England are stalled again, so not much was accomplished." He closed the door to the stall and they started walking toward the keep.

"So the truce may not hold?"

"Aye. There may be war!"

He was smiling. Smiling at the prospect of more conflict.

"You needn't look so happy that we may be at war again," she said crossly. But Keifer seemed unaware of her dismay, so his news must be wonderful. "So, tell me your news."

He pretended to think.

"Keifer!"

He laughed, throwing his head back in that way he had that she loved to watch. "All right. The most wonderful thing about the trip is that Sir Bryan Mackintosh has agreed to take me on as a squire. I will become a knight as I've dreamed!"

Nola forced her smile to remain on her face. "That is wonderful. When will you leave?"

Eagerly Keifer grabbed her hand and pulled her along. "In the spring."

Nola could feel her smile fade despite her effort to be happy for him. She stopped walking.

Keifer let go of her hand and they faced each other. "What is wrong?"

She sighed. "I am happy for you, truly I am. But I will miss you."

"And you will be stuck here with no hope for an adventure, right?" He made a sympathetic face.

"Aye."

"Then I will persuade your father to bring you to my knighting ceremony. It won't be Paris, but it will be out of the glen."

"That will be wonderful, but it will be years from now." She felt her shoulders droop. "Sometimes I wish we were older."

He cocked his head to one side. "Why?"

67

She took a deep breath and plunged ahead. "Because then we could marry and I could go with you."

"Marry?"

"Well, you needn't look at me as if I've suggested cutting off your head!" She turned on her heel and stalked toward the door.

"Nola! Wait!" He caught up with her and spun her to face him. "I . . . you surprised me is all, Nola. You have another year or so until you are old enough to be betrothed, let alone married."

"I could be betrothed any time father wishes. We can promise ourselves to each other, Keifer. Then when we're older—"

"Nola. I told you long ago that I don't think I want to marry."

"I know." And she did know. She had hoped he would forget or change his mind by now. "I know you are afraid you'll die and leave your unfortunate wife bereft."

"Unfortunate?"

She looked at him. "Aye. Such a glum outlook would have her on her knees praying for you half the day and into each night."

He bent down and picked up a fist of snow. "Unfortunate, you say?"

"Keifer," she warned. "Don't you dare throw that at me."

He looked down at the ball of snow in his palm and then at her, as if trying to decide. With a dramatic sigh, he dropped it to the ground, then took her arm to escort her.

They walked in the cold air, heading toward the promise of warmth in the keep. Smoke rose from the central chimney, seasoning the air with the smell of burning wood.

"If I were to marry, you would be first on my list of prospective brides," he said, his voice solemn.

"You are such a tease." She had tried to resign herself to Keifer's decision about marriage, but it wasn't easy. She could easily imagine herself as his wife someday. Would he meet someone else who would change his mind? "I won't have anyone to go fishing with when you are gone."

Keifer grinned. "Or to pull you from the water." He sobered. "And who will tease me into a good mood when I get grouchy?"

Nola wondered, who indeed?

THE SNOW ENDED with just a few inches of powder, not enough to spoil the celebration but enough to make the countryside beautiful. Keifer loved Christmas at Moy, and he awoke the next morning in happy expectation. It felt good to be home.

After breakfast he helped Sir Adam hitch the oxen to the sled they would use to haul the Yule log. While the men loaded a saw and axes, the women prepared a basket of food and drink. With a good deal of laughter and some shoving by the little boys, Lady Gwenyth and young James were settled on the sled.

The others walked as they made their way through the forest. They searched for pine, juniper, holly, and mistletoe and brought it back to the sled. Later they would use the greens to decorate the hall.

Soon the sled was too full for anyone to ride, so Keifer gave James a ride on his back. As he trudged through the snow, listening to the shouts of Nola and her brothers when they found some greenery, he felt a pang. In spring he would leave for Homelea and his training. It would be years before he spent such a day with these people again.

He shifted James's weight and dodged an errant snowball.

Family. This is what he would miss if he did not marry. Watching Sir Adam throw snowballs at the boys reminded Keifer of all that he had missed with his own father. Despite being welcomed into this family, Keifer felt like a piece of him was missing.

Adam, for all his faults, was good to his family, and treated Keifer as one of his own. Keifer had to give him credit for that. If something were to happen to Adam . . . Keifer steeled his heart. Hadn't he promised himself he wouldn't get too close to these people? Just then James grabbed for a branch and missed. He lost his balance and snatched Keifer's hair to keep from falling.

"Mind what you grab, James!" he growled. He stopped and set the boy on the ground.

"Come here, James," Sir Adam called. "Leave your brother be."

Brother. The bonds of fosterage were lifelong. He scowled, suddenly too close to tears for comfort. He did not want to love this family, but it was too late. This time with them had shown him a father's love, taught him to be a man. At the same time he'd been safely hidden away from his uncle while he grew to manhood. Aye, Morrigan had chosen well when she sent him here.

The sled had stopped, and Sir Adam led the way to the log he had picked out earlier in the fall. Shaking off his melancholy, Keifer helped Adam hitch the oxen to it. They dragged the Yule log through the woods and back to the castle. Six men were needed to carry it inside and maneuver it into the hearth.

That evening, Christmas Eve, Keifer watched as Nola lit the fire with a piece saved from last year's Yule log. Lady Gwenyth threw a bit of holly on the flames to burn up this past year's troubles.

As she did so she said, "I pray our Savior will keep us safe in the year to come."

They all sat around the great fireplace as the Yule log smoldered, waiting for it to catch fire and burst into flames. The younger children's eyes were heavy from the warmth and a day of activity in the cold air. James had evidently forgiven Keifer for his shortness earlier, because the boy snuggled against his side and yawned.

Nola said, "My favorite is the mistletoe with its bright white berries."

"Aye. It symbolizes our prayers for goodwill and peace to all our friends who will come for the feast tomorrow," her mother said.

"Too bad we can't find some of that peace with England," Adam grumbled.

Keifer prayed for peace even though he hoped it wouldn't come until he'd had his chance to fight.

The nobles of Scotland had signed a declaration at Arbroath last April outlining their grievances with England. The decree had been sent to the pope in the hope that he would recognize Bruce as Scotland's rightful king.

"Recite the declaration to us again, Sir Adam," Keifer said. "Perhaps the coming year will bring peace."

Adam went to his desk and took a piece of parchment from it. He began to read, and as Keifer listened to his country's impassioned plea, he was determined to become a warrior who could fight for freedom.

He focused again upon Adam's voice. ". . . for so long as there shall be but one hundred of us remain alive, we will never give consent to subject ourselves to the dominion of the English. For it is not glory, it is not riches, neither is it honor, but it is freedom alone that we fight and contend for, which no honest man will lose but with his life."

"Oh my," Lady Gwenyth breathed. "I am moved each time I hear it."

Even the younger children sat up a little, as if they felt the impact of the words.

Again the lady spoke. "Those are not the words of peace."

Adam responded. "England leaves us with little choice. We've sent this declaration to the pope to gain his favor for Scotland's cause. He must recognize Bruce as our king if we are to have any hope of peace with England."

Adam looked at Keifer. "Have you told anyone of your news?"

"Only Nola." He grinned and turned to Lady Gwenyth. "I'm to train with Sir Bryan Mackintosh."

Lady Gwenyth's face broke into a sad smile and she said, "I'm glad for you, Keifer. But I will hate to see you go."

Though he, too, dreaded the good-byes that would have to be said, Keifer looked forward to training for battle. Because despite the pretty words in the declaration, he doubted the troubles with England would be over any time soon.

ON CHRISTMAS DAY many guests came to share a traditional feast. Keifer recognized William Macpherson and his wife, Suisan, and their son, Will, who was a year older than Nola. Though Will was near Keifer in age, the two had never struck up the kind of friendship that would entice them to travel the half-hour walk between their homes.

After greetings and taking the Macpherson's offering of food to the kitchen, Suisan went with Lady Gwenyth.

The men took up places around the fire, the great Yule log still burning, though other wood had been added. Keifer sat with them, but their talk of lambs and farming soon lost Keifer's interest. He wanted to hear about great battles and brave deeds, not which fields should be sown in oats next season.

Lady Gwenyth came back into the hall and, seeing Keifer, called him to her. "The ladies and I will take the smallest children with us. But I would like you to watch over Nola and the others for me. See they come to no mischief."

Suddenly the planting of oats sounded rather appealing. But the lady wasn't really asking if he wanted to watch the others for her. He tried not to let his expression convey his aversion to the task. "As you wish, my lady." Sixteen and still watching children. He couldn't wait to leave and begin his training.

His dislike of Will Macpherson increased as the afternoon wore on. Will was comely and he knew it. He insisted that Nola be his partner in the games they played. Nola didn't seem to mind, but Keifer did.

At thirteen, Will resembled his father in looks—dark coloring and a well-built form. Morrigan had told Keifer that he looked like his father, Ian. Keifer wished he could see it for himself. Wished his da had been in prison instead of Uncle Angus.

Sir Adam, Seamus, even Ceallach, had all done their best to teach Keifer what he needed to know. But Keifer needed to know things about himself that only his father could teach him. Without him, Keifer wasn't sure who he was supposed to become or how he came by his likes and dislikes. Keifer envied Will his relationship with his very much alive father.

Perhaps it was these thoughts that caused Keifer to be impatient with Will.

He watched Will pull Nola's braid and remembered Morrigan telling about their older brother's teasing. If Will teased Nola, did that mean he liked her or not? Keifer scowled. Nola was his friend, not Will's.

Was he jealous? Of Nola and Will? He pushed aside the silly notion. He and Nola were friends, nothing more. After all, Keifer didn't intend to marry. And she was still a child and he nearly a grown man. Come spring he would begin to train in earnest. He most certainly was not jealous.

Until he caught Will giving Nola a kiss.

It was but a wee one, more of a brother's kiss to her cheek, but it made her blush, and in turn, made Keifer blush in the watching of it.

They were right pretty together, those two. He ought to be happy for Nola that she had an admirer.

But he wasn't happy. He felt all churned up inside, like Cook's butter. And perhaps a bit curdled as well. It was time to move on. He was not a man who got caught up in the goings-on of children playing at romance. He was a knight in the making!

WHILE THE MEN FINISHED THEIR TALK in front of the fire, Gwenyth led Suisan Macpherson to the solar, where the other women had adjourned with the smallest children.

When Eva, Adam's mother, saw Suisan and Gwenyth enter, she raised her eyebrows then went back to her sewing. Long ago Suisan had spurned Adam's offer of marriage. Adam had been gravely wounded, nearly died. And Suisan hadn't wanted to marry a man who might be a cripple the rest of his life.

Gwenyth smiled. Adam was far from crippled, and Gwenyth was glad that Suisan had been such a shallow young woman. Though her rejection had caused Adam a good deal of anguish, it had allowed for Gwenyth and Adam to fall in love and marry.

Despite Suisan's past behavior, Gwenyth had come to enjoy her visits with the Macpherson woman. Suisan was a gifted musician and a devoted wife to William, as well as a good—if overprotective—mother to her son.

Gwenyth settled Suisan on a bench and sat down next to her mother-in-law.

Gwenyth could see that Suisan was breeding again. The poor woman seemed to be in this condition every year, and yet only her firstborn, a son, had lived beyond infancy.

Children were a blessing from God, to be welcomed no matter

what. But Suisan's poor bairns rarely lived beyond a few days or weeks, it seemed. Perhaps if she were stronger she might produce stronger babes.

Gwenyth considered how she might bring up the subject without offending her guest. "Did William go down to Berwick?"

Suisan had taken out her spindle and wool. "Nay. Said it was too far to travel in winter. But Adam went, didn't he?" Suisan fed some wool onto the spindle as it dropped and spun.

"Aye, he did." She repeated the declaration Adam had read to the family last evening.

Eva looked up from her sewing. "What other news did Adam bring home?"

Gwenyth thought for a moment to decide what news might be of interest to her guests. "They have settled the succession on King Robert's grandson and namesake."

Bruce's brother Edward had been killed in battle in Ireland, making it imperative that an heir be named. Edward Bruce had been king of Ireland for less than two years and would never wear the crown of Scotland he'd coveted. Gwenyth thought it a shame that the king had lost the last of his brothers.

"Has the king lost hope for a son with his wife?" one of the ladies asked.

Gwenyth replied, "I don't know, but Elizabeth is past thirty years old."

"Aye, and nary a bairn born to them yet," Eva said, clucking her tongue in commiseration.

"Adam says we best pray for a long life for our king. A child as king, with the nobles fighting to be regent until the boy's majority, would give England more reason to come north again."

Suisan spoke up for the first time. "William says King Robert is sometimes laid low with a terrible affliction. Perhaps that is the reason they remain childless. His limbs go numb and his skin grows sores."

"Leprosy?" Gwenyth asked.

"Aye. Leprosy of some kind, though not the kind that makes body parts drop off."

Eva said, "The ailment saps his strength. I heard years back that he once had himself strapped to his horse and led into battle in order to rally his army and strike fear into the enemy."

"I wonder if it's true or if this is just a story his men tell to bolster his reputation," Suisan said.

Gwenyth looked up from her needlework. "Let us pray for his health to improve and his life to be long!"

"Aye. And for his queen to bear a son," Eva added.

For a time the only sound to be heard came from the chatter of the toddlers playing nearby.

Eva said, "I see you are breeding again, Suisan."

Leave it to Gwneyth's mother-in-law to come right to the point. Gwenyth didn't know how Eva felt about the woman who had once spurned her son.

Suisan said, "Aye. The babe should come in late March. God willing, this one will be healthy."

Eva peered at her. "And what of yer health? Ye've dark circles under yer eyes."

"I am fine. Perhaps more tired than with the others . . ."

"I grieve for your losses, Suisan. We've only lost one child so far—I can't imagine such a loss year after year." Gwenyth changed the subject. "Did you bring your harp, Suisan?"

"Aye."

"Then would you play for us this evening? I know my daughter would love it, as would the rest of us."

Suisan smiled. "Does Nola play?"

"Aye. I've taught her all I know."

"Then perhaps she and I will play a duet."

"That would be lovely."

KEIFER FIDGETED WITH HIS NEW PLAID. He'd outgrown several, including his favorite, the one Lady Orelia had made for him.
Lady Gwenyth had woven this one from the wool of his and Nola's
orphaned lambs. Keifer smiled, remembering how Nola had insisted
on helping with the shearing, and the animal had soiled her shoes in
the process.

Nola had smelled of sheep urine for weeks but refused to throw
away perfectly good, if foul-smelling, shoes. No question he would
miss her when he left.

The hall filled with people, many whom he did not know, and
some—Will Macpherson in particular—he wished he didn't know.

Nola had made Keifer promise to sit with her at the feast. A
vaguely familiar lass walked up to him and tugged on his arm. "Come,
let's take our places. I'm famished."

Keifer looked again, wondering at the girl's boldness. He recognized her voice at the same time she turned to him. "What did you
do to your hair, Nola?"

Nary a wisp had escaped from the wimple she wore.

"Mother said I could dress up." She spun about and stopped,
squinting at him. "You didn't recognize me, did you?"

He laughed. "Not at first. You know, you will be beautiful someday, Nola."

She smacked his arm. "Of course I will. Da says so all the time.
Come on, let's take our seats."

When everyone was settled, Adam spoke. "With this meal we
celebrate the birth of our Savior. We remember how our God sent his

son to take on human form that we might at last see his face. We remember that God himself came to dwell on earth, much as he once dwelt with the nation of Israel in the desert. Praise be to Jesus Christ our Lord."

A loud "Amen" rose from those gathered, and the meal commenced.

Will Macpherson had insisted on sitting across from them, and all through the meal he captured Nola's attention. Nola seemed not to mind, but she was so easygoing she wouldn't hurt the other boy's feelings by telling him to be quiet. Keifer followed her lead. It was Christmas after all, time for goodwill toward man and boy.

But Keifer would be glad to see the Macphersons leave Moy. And he faced the fact that Will would have Nola's attention all to himself when Keifer left this spring.

He didn't like the idea one bit.

Six

March 1321

NOLA PLAYED WITH HER LITTLE BROTHER while their mother sat spinning before the fire on a chilly spring morning. As she piled wooden blocks on top of each other, she stifled the resentment she felt. Her younger brother Tom would leave in two days to foster with a family on the western edge of the glen.

Her father hoped Tom would find a wife there and strengthen ties with the clans on that border. And Keifer would leave soon as well. Would she never find a way to leave the glen, even for a short while?

"I don't see why I can't go to the school in Edinburgh. If I can't travel, at least I could learn about the places I'll never see."

"I'm sorry, Nola. We can't afford to send you to Edinburgh for such lessons."

"But Keifer is going to go away and Tom too. 'Tisn't fair."

"Even if your father could spend such money, he wouldn't let you go south while England continues to threaten invasion. No, you will have to content yourself with drawing. Or find some other pursuit."

Nola had been waiting for just such an opportunity. "Well, then, I should like to take lessons on your harp."

Her mother smiled. Nola had already learned all her mother could teach her on the instrument.

"Perhaps Suisan Macpherson would agree to teach you. She is quite good."

Nola held back a groan. She had been hoping her mother would suggest the harpist in Inverlochy. Nola desperately wanted to see some of the world outside of their glen in the highlands.

She sighed. At least the Macpherson keep lay half an hour's walk away. Maybe she would be allowed to spend the night. It wasn't much of an adventure, but it would have to do.

THAT NIGHT AS SHE BRUSHED OUT HER HAIR, Gwenyth said to Adam, "I'm afraid we may have decided wrong when we chose not to foster Nola."

Adam walked over and sat on the bench next to her. "Why do you say that?"

"She rather neatly manipulated me into asking Suisan Macpherson for harp lessons today. I fear Moy isn't big enough for Nola's adventurous nature."

"Lessons sound harmless enough."

"Far less harmful than the convent school in Edinburgh she asked for."

Adam smiled and Gwenyth laid down her brush. "You smile, but she was serious."

Adam tilted his head and looked thoughtful. "Is it too late? To foster her?"

"Perhaps not." She picked the brush up again and brushed absentmindedly.

"We kept her here because you didn't want to part with her."

"I remember how fosterage with my cousins led to my betrothal to my cousin Edward."

"Fostering is arranged with the possibility of such alliances in mind, love."

"I know. But look what a near disaster that became for me."

He grinned. "I remember." He leaned over and kissed her, and she forgot the past and the future for a few minutes. Adam pulled away and Gwenyth raised her eyebrows.

Again that devilish grin. "Perhaps later."

She swatted his arm. "I told Nola I would plead her case to you about the lessons."

"It seems to me that these lessons may afford an excuse to approach William and Suisan about fostering Nola. She would be close by where you could see her often."

"You hold no grudge against Suisan, do you?"

"I'd be a fool to do otherwise. Her refusal to marry me ensured I'd be a free man when you showed up on my doorstep. I like William. He is an honest man who has led his faction of the Macpherson clan to prosperity they didn't enjoy under Leod's leadership. And Suisan is a gentle soul, though I think she is too protective of young Will."

She considered that before speaking. "Perhaps that is natural for a hen with one chick."

"Ah. No doubt that is so."

Gwenyth stroked the brush through her hair. "Am I holding too tightly to Nola by not letting her go farther away? I'm sure Morrigan and Fergus would love to have her."

"Perhaps they would, but I'd prefer to keep her within the glen. After the upheaval when my father died, I want to create a sense of unity among the clans in the federation. I'm not going to send a child to foster if there is no benefit to the clan. Certainly not just to satisfy her wanderlust. And our connection with Morrigan and Fergus is already sealed."

She laid down her brush and faced Adam. "You would like to

foster her with William and Suisan to encourage a match between Nola and Will, wouldn't you?"

"Aye. Such a marriage would strengthen the federation."

"But what of my suspicions about her feelings for Keifer?"

"I'm not against a match between Nola and Keifer, Gwenyth. But at least spending time with the Macpherson boy might open her eyes to the fact there are other men she might like."

"Aye. No harm in that. So, when will you talk to William? Their baby should be born soon. I had thought Nola and I would visit in the next day or so to see if Suisan needs anything."

"We'll all go day after tomorrow and see this settled." He took the brush from her hand. "Your hair shines like silk, wife. Come, let me muss it up again."

She smiled and went to him. And despite the passing of years and the birth of four children, Adam mussed his wife's hair quite thoroughly.

TWO DAYS LATER Adam and Gwenyth accompanied Nola to Inversie. A haggard William Macpherson greeted them at the door of the main hall.

Fearing the worst, Gwenyth said, "William, have we come at a bad time, then?"

He brushed his dark hair back with his fingers. "No, no. Come in. Suisan had the babe early this morning."

"How are they?"

"Well enough. She has such a hard time birthing them, but all is well. Come, Gwenyth, Nola. I'm sure Suisan would be glad to show off our little lass."

Relieved to hear that Suisan and the baby were all right, Gwenyth followed William through the keep, Nola at her side. Suisan's pale face and the crying of the child greeted them when they entered her chamber. A servant came in with a tray, and Suisan handed the baby to Gwenyth to hold. To Gwenyth's relief, Suisan ate well. Gwenyth peered into the little one's face. "She's a tiny thing, but she has a strong, lusty cry." Gwenyth turned back to Suisan. "We came today to ask for harp lessons for Nola, once you have regained your strength."

"I would love to teach her. She plays well."

"Excellent. We thought perhaps Nola might pay for your time by helping with the babe." Gwenyth didn't want to bring up the issue of fosterage until Adam had a chance to discuss it with William first.

"How do you feel about that, Nola?" Suisan asked.

"I would very much like the lessons, my lady. And I could be very helpful." Gwenyth wondered if Suisan sensed Nola's lack of real enthusiasm. Nola enjoyed her little brothers but often begged off taking care of them. Perhaps if she fostered with Suisan, she could do other chores and leave the care of the babe to its mother.

Gwenyth laid the now sleeping baby in her cradle and covered her. "We'll let you rest, Suisan. I'll make arrangements with William to send for Nola when you are ready."

When she and Nola rejoined the men in the main hall, Adam gave the briefest of nods. So, they had agreed. Now all that remained was to tell Nola.

They rode home, talking about everything but what lay so heavily on Gwenyth's heart. No matter that her daughter would be less than an hour's walk away. She would miss her high spirits and willing hands with the work of running a castle.

After the evening meal, Adam rose and asked them both to join him in the solar. He gestured to the bench. Gwenyth pushed aside the tapestry-covered pillows and sat down. Nola sat next to her, on the edge of the seat.

Adam cleared his throat. Evidently he feared Nola's reaction as much as Gwenyth herself did. "Nola, your mother and I have considered that you might be happier if you were to go away to foster with another family. I know you are older than most girls who leave home, but there is still time."

"I'm not unhappy, Da."

"Aye, you're so happy that you would like to go to Edinburgh for harp lessons."

Nola grinned. "Well, I would like to see a bit of the world. Mother's tales of Paris and seeing the world sound like great fun."

Gwenyth hoped to spare her daughter some of the pain that had accompanied her own journey. "You might travel thus with a husband one day."

Nola made a face. "I don't think it likely I'll marry such a man, do you? Especially if I never leave the glen to meet him."

Adam shook his head and smiled. "I'm afraid you'll have to settle for a highlander, Nola. For better or worse."

Nola's expression dimmed.

Adam told Nola of the agreement he'd made with William Macpherson.

She leaped to her feet. "Foster with the Macphersons? But you didn't even ask me how I felt about it!"

"Parents are not required to ask their children in such matters. Your mother and I believe this is best for you. You are wanting to escape the confines of Moy—here's your chance."

Nola twisted her hands in her skirt material. "To live at Inversie! That wasn't what I had in mind in the way of an adventure."

"Well, it will have to do for now. I'll not send you out of the glen."

Hoping to soften the blow for her daughter, Gwenyth reminded Nola that Suisan truly needed her and that she was willing to provide Nola harp lessons.

"The harp lessons will be welcome. But do not make plans for me to marry a highlander if the man is Will Macpherson."

"What's wrong with Will?" Adam demanded. "Uniting our families and lands makes perfect sense."

"Maybe to you. But you won't be the one tied to Will Macpherson the rest of your life!"

"And I ask you again, what is wrong with the boy?"

Gwenyth feared that the honest answer to this question was that he wasn't Keifer.

"I suppose nothing is wrong with him if you don't mind a man who has no desire to leave the glen. He's content to stay here."

Adam shook his head. "And what is wrong with that? Being at home in the glen is an attribute, something of which a man—*or* woman—can be proud."

Nola stared at Adam as if he had an extra head. "What's wrong with wanting to travel?"

Gwenyth hid her smile behind her hand. These two would never agree on this, she feared.

"Besides, Will takes for granted that I will agree to a betrothal when we are of age. If I foster with them, he will be encouraged beyond bearing."

"Would such a betrothal be so awful?" Gwenyth asked.

"It wouldn't be if my heart didn't belong elsewhere."

"I see."

Adam huffed out his breath. "There is no need to decide on your wedding plans tonight. I can accept that you don't see Will as a potential husband, Nola. But I ask that you give him a chance."

Nola looked at her father. She straightened her spine and held her chin out in that stubborn way she'd done since the cradle. "And I will accept this fostering with grace if you will but grant me one boon."

Gwenyth felt her eyes grow larger. What would the girl demand?

"What is that?" Adam asked, his expression wary.

"Allow me to accompany you and Keifer when he leaves for training. 'Tis likely to be the only time in my life when I can leave this glen."

With an audible sigh of relief, Adam said, "Very well. You may go with us."

Nola spun on her heel and left the room.

Adam looked at Gwenyth. "That went well, don't you think?"

AFTER THE SPRING THAW Adam and Nola accompanied Keifer on the journey to Homelea. Keifer could hardly wait to get there. The horses walked too slow, Nola talked too much, and Adam insisted on resting the horses too often.

By the fifth day, Keifer had tired of even Nola's company. They rode side by side with Adam in the lead.

". . . don't you agree, Keifer?" Nola asked.

"Agree?"

"You weren't listening."

"You talk all the time. How's a man to know when you have something important to say?"

"By listening, you great dolt."

Adam turned in the saddle. "Nola, that's no way to speak to Keifer."

"He wasn't paying any attention—'tis rude—"

"Enough. Give us some peace, Nola." Adam turned around.

Nola stuck her tongue out at Keifer. Why he, a nearly grown man, must put up with a child of twelve, he didn't know.

In the absence of Nola's chatter, he heard birds singing and the whisper of the breeze through the trees. But he couldn't enjoy it when Nola was so obviously unhappy.

Nola was no more a child than he was, if he would but admit it. She'd grown two inches in the past few months, and though he tried not to stare, he could not help but notice that the bodice on her tunic needed to be let out to accommodate . . . Keifer drew a deep breath and let it out. Aye, Nola was no longer a child. By the time he saw her next, she would be a woman in every way. He grinned at the thought.

"What is so funny?" she demanded.

"You."

"You think I'm a child, a pest. Well, I'm not."

"Not a pest or not a child?"

He could see her struggling to be angry; saw her lose the battle when she smiled.

"Truce?" she said.

"Aye. But a few more minutes of quiet wouldn't do me any harm."

She laughed, and all was right with Keifer's world.

Later that day they passed the site of the great battle for Stirling Castle along the Bannockburn. Adam's accounting of his part in the battle fed Keifer's agitation.

"Soon I'll be a knight and can take part in such a battle."

"You don't have to be a knight to fight in a war," Nola reminded him.

"True, but I must become a fighter second to none in order to protect my family and my clan."

"Time, hard work, and a lot of bruises stand between you and those golden spurs you covet," Adam said.

"If a thing is worth striving for, the labor is not a burden." Of course it wouldn't be easy; Keifer never thought it would be. Why must Nola's father always look at the dark side of things? Keifer refused to allow the man's pessimism to dim the glory of his quest.

Two days later they rode southeast from Edinburgh, and Homelea became visible atop a riverside cliff. As they approached, Keifer could barely contain his excitement. His dream was about to come true. Black Bryan Mackintosh was renowned for his skill with the claymore and his ability to fight from horseback. Keifer would be among an elite few chosen to train with the man.

"Have you been here before, Da?" Nola asked.

"Aye. I accompanied Sir Bryan when he first took possession of the place. 'Twas not much more than a fortified manor home at the time. I'm anxious to see the new fortifications Bryan talked about."

They rode across open land where sheep grazed outside of Home-lea village. An abbey's spire could be seen above the trees to the east. The smell of fresh-cut hay wafted on the breeze, and small stone cottages dotted the countryside.

They passed over a causeway and entered Homelea's gate. "These walls are new," Adam said.

"They look impenetrable," Keifer said.

"Aye. No one will breach them without heavy siege engines."

They crossed an open area that led to a second set of walls, far less impressive than the first. A wooden bridge guided them into a large bailey. The taller, fortified ramparts surrounded the bailey of a forti-fied manor home.

The bailey teemed with people and livestock at midday. Chickens clucked and raced out of the path of the horses while dogs barked a cautious welcome. Someone ran to the keep, no doubt to announce the visitors.

It reminded Keifer of Dunstruan, and he smiled at the memory. His family was less than a hundred miles away. Surely he would see them before he'd completed his training.

Keifer dismounted and went to help Nola down from her horse. That at least got a smile of approval from her father.

Adam strode toward a large man in chain mail whose dark hair glistened in the sun.

"Welcome, Adam!" the man shouted. He clasped Adam about the shoulders. "'Tis good to see you, brother." The men had fostered together, as well as fought together for Bruce. Both turned to Nola. "And this is . . . this can't be your daughter? Grown already?"

Adam grinned. "Aye. Nola, this is the Earl of Homelea, Bryan Mackintosh. Nola is our oldest. And this is Keifer Macnab, your newest student."

Sir Bryan looked Keifer up and down and said, "Welcome to all of you. There is still some time before the midday meal will be ready, so allow me to show you the improvements I've made." He offered his arm to Nola, and Keifer saw her blush as she accepted. As Sir Bryan walked them around the grounds, he treated Nola as if she were visiting royalty. Keifer thought he would very much enjoy serving such a man.

Adam said, "I see little evidence of the destruction Homelea sustained."

"Well, I was very, very careful when I dismantled it."

They smiled at a secret obviously shared, and Keifer hoped to hear the whole story one day soon. They stepped inside the main hall where trestles were set up and serving girls scurried to set out food and drink.

"Please sit down and help yourself. Lady Nola, I will give you over to young Keifer's care while Adam and I talk."

Nola sat next to Keifer, and the two older men moved off to await Sir Bryan's wife.

ADAM SAT where Bryan indicated and accepted food and drink from a servant. He drank the cool water, grateful to wash the dust from his throat.

Bryan broke off a piece of bread and handed the rest to Adam. "The boy looks capable—built strong. I understand Seamus has been training him. Why not let him finish the job?"

"Seamus has done well—I think you'll be impressed with Keifer's abilities. But there is some bad blood in the family—our king took the Macnab lands away from Angus and his son for their support of England. 'Tis my understanding that Angus has come to terms with this but that Owyn Macnab considers the land and title his. Keifer may have to fight to keep it, and his sister wants him to be prepared."

"I see. Seamus can teach him to fight well enough, but Morrigan wants him to have the additional skills of a knight."

"Aye. That and the contacts he'll make—you and the king among them—will give him allies he can call upon if need be."

"I'm anxious to see him with a sword. You will stay a few days and watch him train, won't you?"

"Aye. I have no desire to climb back in the saddle for a time."

Bryan nodded. "I thought you might feel that way. Stay as long as you like. You and I can catch up on news. We were unable to attend Morrigan and Fergus's wedding. Did you go?"

"No, 'twas too long a trip from Moy. They have a son and another child on the way. From what I've heard, they are doing well."

"I'm glad to hear it. Fergus is a good man, and perfect for Morrigan." Bryan looked over at Keifer and Nola. "Your daughter will soon be of marriageable age. Hard to believe the time has gone so quickly. Seems like just last week you and I arrived here and beat down Kathryn's door."

"Aye, so it does. Nola is twelve, thirteen soon, and yes, I've started thinking about her future. I've a mind to betroth her to young Will Macpherson."

"An excellent way to strengthen that alliance. Always a wise thing to do." Bryan watched Nola and Keifer again.

Adam wondered what he saw that made him scowl.

"How long has the boy been fostering with you?"

"Six years. I think you'll find Seamus has prepared him well."

"I have no doubt." Bryan pointed his chin at the young people. "Those two have become good friends."

"Aye. As befits foster siblings, no?" Adam and Bryan had shared much over the years, and many's the time he wished they lived closer to each other.

"Nola may only be twelve, Adam, but I'd bet a fair amount of silver she doesn't think of the boy as her brother."

"What? Has he done something to warrant—"

"Calm down, the boy's behavior has nothing to do with my observation. Nola wears her heart on her sleeve."

Adam considered this. "Then 'tis for the best that they be separated so she may consider other suitors." He moved his goblet in circles on the table. "Mayhap Gwenyth was right."

"Oh?"

"She mentioned the same thing not long ago. Aye, this separation will test them both. If God means it to be, it will survive this time apart and I'll not stand in their way."

"Parenting isn't easy, is it?"

"No, it is not. How are your young ones doing?"

Lady Kathryn walked into the hall, and Bryan stood and extended his hand to her. "Here's just the person to answer your question."

All through the meal, as he listened to Kathryn and Bryan talk about their family, Adam stole glances at Nola and Keifer. The boy sat tall, a proper distance from Nola. She said something, and he leaned closer to answer her. She threw her head back and laughed, and Keifer's smile held a definite fondness. Was it more?

Nola placed her hand on Keifer's arm in earnest conversation. Keifer listened, his gaze just shy of entranced. Nola, on the other hand, did not mask her fascination. The girl had a soft heart and never did disguise her feelings well. Though Adam stopped short of calling her affection for Keifer love, anyone could see that she held the boy close to her heart.

Love? Or affection for a wounded soul? For Adam recognized the boy's empty spot—the place where memories of his father belonged. Adam only hoped that he and Gwenyth had prepared the boy as thoroughly inside—as Seamus had outside—for adulthood. That Keifer would bloom under Bryan's tutelage.

Time would tell.

SEVEN

KEIFER WAITED FOR NOLA in his horse's stall. Nola and her father would leave soon, and Keifer wanted a few minutes where their words could be private. He assured himself that he didn't need her or anyone else, that he only wanted to give her something. But he dreaded her farewell.

Any other time he would have heard her whistling or singing or chattering to the animals. But today she entered the barn so quietly he jumped when she lifted the latch on the stall door.

She hesitated, and he pulled her into the stall and closed the door. Though her eyes were mirthless, she grinned at him. Then seeing his expression, her grin faded. "Why are you sad? You are getting what you always wanted."

"Aye. And you've had your adventure."

The horse walked over to see if Nola had a dried apple for him, but for once her hands and clothes were empty of such treats.

"This trip to Moy? With my father as chaperone?" She pushed the horse's nose away and the beast moved to the other side of the stall. "This does not count as an adventure. Not for me. But being here is what you always dreamed of, isn't it?"

"Aye, but I must leave all that is familiar once again. I don't like good-byes. It seems like I am forever leaving or being left."

Her eyes filled with tears, and one spilled down her cheek. "I don't want to go. I would stay if I could."

He wiped away her tear with his thumb. "I'm sorry. I didn't mean to make you cry. Here. I have something for you."

"What?"

He reached under his tunic and grasped the ribbon that held the key to his treasure box.

She gasped when she saw it. "Why are you giving me the key? How will you open the box?"

"I left it at Moy so that you can safeguard it for me."

"You left it behind?"

"Aye." He'd agonized over whether or not to bring his treasures with him. The things it held were childish mementos except for the laird's ring. But he'd felt they would be safer in Nola's care than here among strangers.

She stared at him and burst out laughing.

"Why is that funny?" he demanded, hurt that she didn't appreciate his trust.

She reached into the pouch at her waist and pulled a knotted twist of wool from it. "I made this for you to keep in the box to remember me by."

"What is it?"

"Well, I remembered mother telling us that before a tournament or battle, ladies would give their scarf or ribbon to the knight they favored. I knew that if I gave you such a thing, the other boys would tease you." She held the knotted twine of wool out to him. "So I made this bracelet for you to put in the box where the others can't chide you over it."

He took it, touched that she would think to do such a thing. He held it out to her and a tear escaped her left eye.

"No, Nola. I'm not giving it back. Since I left the box in your care at Moy, I want you to tie this around my wrist."

She swiped away the tear. "You'll wear it?"

"Aye. I'm sure it will bring me luck, and I'm going to need plenty." He swallowed hard. "And it will remind me of my ties to my family at Moy. Of you."

Nola took the bracelet and tied it to his outstretched wrist. "Does this mean you'll wait for me?"

That made him smile. "Wait for you?"

She finished attaching the bracelet and took hold of his hand. "Aye. You said you would take me on an adventure, and I mean to hold you to it."

"I may not be able to fulfill that promise, Nola. What then?"

"In that case, I suppose I may have to create my own adventure. I know I am only twelve, Keifer, and that we both will change by the time your training is over. I can't promise my heart, nor will I ask you to. But could we at least promise not to marry anyone else until we've spoken to each other again?"

She sounded much older and wiser than her years, and as always, her heart shone in her eyes. This child would be a woman and he a man grown when next they met. He feared they would change, affections going elsewhere. But he could not tell her so now, for he could not bear to break her tender heart.

"You know of my pledge not to marry, Nola. I cannot ask you to wait for me."

"You may change your mind."

He shook his head.

"If you do, then remember this promise."

"All right. That promise I can make. I promise not to give my heart to another until I speak again with you. Are you satisfied?"

She nodded. "I better go. Da will be waiting."

"I'll walk with you, but this must be our good-bye. I don't want . . ." He drew in a breath to steady his voice. A man training to be a knight did not cry.

"I know. I absolutely do not want to cry in front of my father!"

He pulled her close and, without a second thought, pressed his lips to her upturned face. But a buss on the cheek didn't satisfy, and he moved to kiss her lips. He'd never kissed a girl before, and he delighted in the soft way her lips yielded, molded, to his mouth.

She put her arms around his neck and clung tightly. She hadn't done that the time he'd caught her kissing Will Macpherson. Aye, this kiss was not the kiss of a friend, and Keifer was honor bound to end it before they promised too much to each other.

He pulled away and looked down into her face. Her eyes seemed a bit unfocused and he grinned, amused that he'd had such an effect on her. But he reminded himself she was an untried girl who might read too much into the kiss. It was time to part. "You are a minx, Nola Mackintosh." His smile faded. "And I shall miss you terribly."

"And I you."

"Come. We've sealed our vow and said our good-bye with a proper kiss. I don't want your father to come looking for us."

They walked out of the stable and across the bailey to where her father stood with their horses. Keifer and Nola didn't dare look at each other.

"There you are, Nola. We were getting concerned." But Keifer could tell from his foster father's face that he understood and was not angry.

Adam grasped Keifer's hand. "We will expect to hear good reports about you, Son."

Keifer, not sure he could trust his voice, nodded. Adam turned to mount, leaving Keifer to assist Nola. He walked over to her and expected her to face the animal so Keifer could help her. Instead she leaped toward him, throwing herself into his arms. He pulled her close and buried his face in her untamable hair. Before he set her down, he said, "Off with you now. Don't ever change, wild one."

With a determined nod of her head so familiar and dear, she drew a deep breath. He cupped his hands together and offered them for her to place her foot in them. She did so, and with a lift from him, swung her leg over the horse. He arranged her riding skirt to cover her leg while she settled her feet into the stirrups and tugged the other side of the skirt into place.

Reluctantly he removed his hand from her calf and watched her gather the reins in her gloved hands. Amid the calling of good-byes from Sir Bryan and his family, Nola and her father set off. With a final wave, they trotted out the gate.

Keifer wondered if he would ever smile again. Abandoned over and over again—Da, Gordon, Morrigan, his mother, Ceallach. It didn't matter that he had wanted this. Heart ruled over head in this matter. And it didn't matter that Nola left unwillingly. Their forced separation seemed the cruelest blow of all.

Macpherson Castle at Inversie 1323

NOLA OPENED THE SHUTTERS on the nursery's only window and stared out at the bright, sunny day. She held Mary Macpherson in her arms, and though she loved the child dearly, Nola would have much rather been outdoors. She spent a good deal of her time in this room at Inversie, not only because Suisan asked her to, but also because Will didn't frequent the place.

Mary squirmed and Nola set her down. The little girl toddled off to her box of playthings.

The door opened and Suisan came into the room. She cast an

approving eye around the tidy room and at her happy child. "You are a godsend, Nola. I don't know what I'd have done these last two years without you to help with Mary."

"I've enjoyed it, Lady Suisan." She wrinkled her nose. "Well, most of it."

"When Mary goes down for her nap, come to the solar and we'll have your harp lesson."

"Aye, my lady."

Nola played with Mary until the child became cranky, and then they sat in the rocking chair until the little one fell asleep. Nola rocked a while longer and looked upon the angelic face. Despite her longing for travel and adventure, something about the feel of a child in her arms let her know that she would enjoy being a mother some day.

Nola laid the sleeping toddler in her bed and pulled a soft blanket over the swaddled form. Then Nola went into the solar where Suisan kept her harp. The rosewood gleamed in a beam of sunlight that shone through the narrow window of the west wall.

Suisan sat behind the harp and ran her fingers across the strings, adjusting them as needed to ensure all were in tune. When she was satisfied, she played a slow, haunting melody. Nola loved to listen to the older woman play. Lady Suisan's face transformed as the music settled over them, as if it soothed her weariness.

When she finished, she rose and indicated that Nola should take her place.

Nola did so, settling her skirts. "I don't think I will ever coax such beautiful music from this instrument, my lady."

"You may, in time."

But Nola doubted it, almost hoped that she would never play music that spoke so eloquently of loss and longing. She wondered what made the lady so sad and dared to probe. "Mother says you were to marry my da, but you changed your mind."

"Aye. And though I regret the callow girl I was who deserted Adam when he needed me, still, I have found love with William and I am content."

"Have you ever left the glen?"

"Never."

"Did you ever want to?"

Suisan pondered for a moment. "Perhaps long ago. But as I said, I am content with my life as it is."

Nola thought of her own longing to see what the outside world had to offer. She doubted she could be content like Suisan if her dream never came true. Nola was more determined than ever to travel before she settled down to marriage and babies. Not that there was anything wrong with marriage and children, she just wanted something grand to look back on.

Nola played the harp, choosing lively music that spoke of nuances and texture and excitement. For that is how she planned to spend her own life.

IN THE DAYS AFTER KEIFER ARRIVED at Homelea, he had little time to miss Nola, despite the reminder of her "favor" on his wrist. Though he doubted that Uncle Angus still harbored ill will toward him, Morrigan had insisted that Keifer use his mother's family name of MacTaggert. So that is how he introduced himself to the only other boy who was to train with Keifer. Donel was a tall, sullen young man with dull blond hair who kept to himself unless he was playing a practical joke.

For the next two years Keifer's days began before sunrise with feeding and grooming his horse. After chapel and breaking his fast, he learned how to ride a war horse. Seamus could not have taught him this because there were no such large animals at Moy. The beasts required quantities of grain and hay that were not readily available in the highlands.

Sir Bryan was certainly a wealthy man, for he had three such horses. Two were used for schooling the squires. The third was the knight's personal war horse, trained to allow only Bryan to mount it. The beast was magnificent—the son of the horse Bryan had ridden when he conquered Homelea and married its mistress.

Keifer had mixed feelings about the beasts. He'd long heard the story of his father's death from a fall from his horse. And though his grandfather had worked with him at Inverlochy, Keifer still feared the animals' power and strength. But Sir Bryan taught him to harness his fear, to respect the strength, and to direct the power in appropriate response to specific cues.

"You must understand how a horse's mind works, what their natural instincts are. Then you can use those natural tendencies to your advantage," the knight explained.

Sir Bryan demonstrated what he wanted the boys to learn by riding his horse in a fenced ring. As he showed them the horse's movement, he told them how to apply leg pressure and shift their weight in the saddle. Then Keifer and Donel would attempt the same manuevers, to varying degrees of success.

"Even if you never own a destrier such as these, you can train whatever horse you ride to respond to you without hesitation. Your horse's willingness and abilty to do so can mean the difference between success and failure in a fight with other mounted men."

Bryan related the story of their own King Robert who, while mounted on a small, well trained garron, had bested an English knight on a much larger destrier. The knight had couched his lance and raced toward the king and his smaller horse. Bruce's mount had remained steady until given the command to swerve. At just the right moment, Bruce stood in the stirrups and brought his ax down on the man's head, ending the encounter and the knight's life.

Horsemanship was not Keifer's strong point, but hearing stories such as this let him know he must master his fears, and so he applied himself. In time he came to enjoy working with the horses, and it showed. Indeed, Keifer became so proficient that Sir Bryan surprised him one day.

"Keifer, give your mount to Donel and come here."

Keifer handed the reins to the other squire and walked to where Sir Bryan and his great destrier stood. The horse shook its head at Keifer's approach, jingling the bit and looking as if it disagreed with whatever the man had in mind.

Sir Bryan said, "You've mastered the lesser horses, let's see what you can do with Shadow."

Keifer drew back. "But he will let only you mount him. He'll throw me."

"Aye, he would if you approached him without me near. But if I hold his head and give him permission, he will allow you to get on and will obey you."

Keifer eyed the big horse and his stomach clenched. He fought his apprehension.

"Go on, you'll be fine."

With that assurance, Keifer determined to trust Sir Bryan's confidence in him. He fixed the stirrup leathers to the proper length, took the reins, and climbed aboard. The war saddle cradled him with its high front and rear, designed to hold a man in the seat during battle.

"Are your stirrups all right?"

He flexed his legs, standing in the stirrups to ensure they were even. "Aye, sir."

"Then take him for a walk around the arena." Sir Bryan let go of the bridle.

Anticipating an explosion of action, Keifer clung to the pommel of the saddle. The great stallion stood deceptively docile, shifting its weight, obviously waiting for Keifer to let go of his death grip and signal it to move out.

"Go ahead," Sir Bryan said. "Take him around the ring and make him respond to some simple commands."

Keifer urged the horse into a walk, gaining confidence as the bit made contact with the horse's mouth and the beast obeyed the cues. When he nudged the stallion into a trot, Keifer soon realized how much horse he had under him. Within minutes his shoulders ached from the powerful animal's pull on the snaffle bit.

At the canter, Keifer forced himself to relax and flow with the rocking motion, convinced he had harnessed the very wind—powerful and unpredictable. The horse tested him constantly, pushing his nose forward in an effort to take the bit, shying from the corners. But using his legs in the manner Sir Bryan had taught him, Keifer kept the horse steady and collected.

As Sir Bryan called out the manuevers Keifer had practiced on the other horses, Keifer gave the cue and the stallion responded. When he finally brought the horse to a halt in front of its master, Sir Bryan caught hold of the bridle and said, "Well done, both of you." He stroked the horse's face and looked up at Keifer. "You handled him very well. You may begin to train the horse you brought with you in these manuevers."

Keifer patted the stallion's neck. "This one is a challenge, but worth the effort, sir. Thank you for allowing me to ride him."

"You're welcome. Once you master these commands, you'll be ready to train on the quintain for the joust. Now, let's see if Donel can do as well as you did."

Donel couldn't keep the stallion from taking the bit and shoving its head down. He ended up in the dirt when the horse put its head to its knees and bucked his hind legs toward the sky.

Donel picked himself up out of the dirt and walked toward Sir Bryan and Keifer, frowning. "I may need a few more lessons, my laird."

Sir Bryan chuckled. "Aye, a few. Get back on and try again."

Donel landed in the dirt several more times before he learned how to keep the horse's head in the proper position. After a successful canter, Sir Bryan called him over, and Donel brought the horse to a halt and dismounted.

"Practice every day and soon you can learn to ride with a lance. Keifer, in light of your horsemanship, I'm naming you senior squire. You will come to me each morning for the day's orders."

With that, he dismissed them. Keifer and Donel cooled the horse and set about their other chores. As he worked, Keifer realized that although Sir Bryan was every bit as tough a taskmaster as Sir Adam had been, somehow Keifer didn't resent Sir Bryan's heavy hand the way he'd resented Adam's.

Perhaps it hadn't been Sir Adam's fault. Maybe Keifer's anger and resentment had been unfounded—a result of Keifer's determination to become a knight. Or perhaps it was the title of foster father that had irked Keifer. He had no father of his own and resented another man taking on the position.

Aye, there was truth to that. Some of the anger would be better directed toward the man who had died when Keifer was only two. His father had not been there to encourage Keifer's dreams. Keifer didn't know who he was supposed to become because he didn't know who he came from.

Adam Mackintosh hadn't been trying to douse Keifer's enthusiasm. Keifer could see now, with distance and time between them, that Adam had done nothing different than Sir Bryan. Keifer could see the results of both men's training, could see that he was well ahead in every area of instruction.

Maybe, just maybe, he owed Sir Adam an apology.

WILL MACPHERSON was quite handsome and knew it. Nola thought him tall and well made. She could admire his pleasant features and rich brown hair and dark brown eyes and even admit he was charming on occasion. But try as she might, Nola couldn't care for him the way she cared for Keifer. Will never passed up a chance to remind her he would one day inherit the lands and castle at Inversie, as well as leadership of his branch of Clan Macpherson.

If he told her once more how joining their holdings in marriage would create a wealthy alliance for their families, she thought she might run screaming all the way to Edinburgh.

Nola spent as much of her time at Inversie avoiding Will's company as she did helping his mother with little Mary. He tried to steal a kiss and Nola let him, hoping he'd stop once she gave in. His lips were hard and demanding. Keifer's had been gentle. Did hard kisses mean a man cared more? She hoped not, because she didn't like Will's kiss at all.

The day after her harp lesson, Will cornered her in the narrow walkway leading to the kitchen. Putting a hand on the wall to either side of her head, he grinned. "Come, Nola. Give me a kiss."

"No. I told you the last time not to try this again."

"It's just a kiss. I want us to be betrothed," he said. "Why do you object?"

"Will, I can't accept a betrothal to you," she said, growing cross with him.

He stood with his hands on his hips, his expression angry. "But I thought that's why you were sent here to foster. So that we might know each other and perhaps come to an agreement."

"I'm sure our parents hope for such a thing, Will. But I came to help your mother. Nothing more." And have a change of scenery in hopes of curing her adventurous spirit. But if anything, her longing to get away had grown stronger than ever. She knew that her next opportunity to travel would not come for another two years—for Keifer's knighting ceremony. And she didn't think she could remain at Inversie that long. She would have to speak to her mother the next time she went home to visit.

How could she make Will understand? "Tell me, Will. Do you ever long to see Edinburgh or Paris, or even Ireland?"

"No, not really. Should I?"

His answer didn't surprise her. "So you would be happy to spend your entire life here in the glen."

"Of course. What's wrong with that?"

She sidled away from him. "Not a thing if it satisfies you. But I want more."

He leaned against the wall again, trapping her, and she feared he would try to take another kiss. She ducked under his arm and moved a safe distance away.

He scowled. "Nola, traveling to far off places to see strange things and stranger people is a waste of time and coin. You just need to settle down with a husband and children of your own to keep you busy. You'll see. We can make a home together."

Nola dared not retort; the words on her lips were hurtful, and though she didn't love Will, she didn't want to hurt him either. But at this moment, Will's narrow vision for his future spoke volumes about why she could never marry him. Why she hoped and dreamed that Keifer would wait for her.

Keifer. Her heart fluttered whenever she thought of him. How tall and strong he must be by now. And what would he think when he saw that she had become womanly in form? She kept her eyes from straying to her bodice, not wanting to draw Will's attention there. Not that she needed to—he stared at her far more often than she was comfortable.

"You are thinking of Keifer again, aren't you? Why can't you just forget him, Nola? If he cared at all about you, he would make an effort to come see you. Or at least write. You can be certain he has forgotten about you."

But Will did not know of the two precious letters she had received from Keifer, telling her of his training. Two letters in two years, and none for almost ten months. Still, she could not believe that Keifer didn't care. Despite Keifer's avowal to remain a bachelor, Nola believed she could change his mind if she only had the chance.

The prospect of spending the next two years away from Keifer and in Will's presence stretched before her endlessly. She prayed that she would soon be allowed to go home before Will spoke to her father and asked for her hand. Da wouldn't force her to marry against her will, but her only excuse not to marry Will was Keifer. A weak hope at best. But before Nola had a chance to speak with her parents, Suisan Macpherson announced that she was expecting a baby. As her health was delicate, she was thankful to have Nola's help. Nola could not desert the woman at such a time and so resigned herself to spending another year at Inversie.

But if Will tried to kiss her again, she would slap him until his eyes crossed. Immediately after that thought, Nola went to the chapel to pray for forgiveness. And while she confessed her shortcomings, she prayed for patience and for Lady Suisan's good health as well.

EIGHT

Homelea, 1324

ONE MORNING THREE YEARS AFTER HIS ARRIVAL at Homelea, Keifer awoke to the sound of the nearby abbey's bells ringing. That in itself wasn't so unusual, as the bells were often used to signal news. But this was a jubilant cacophany beyond the norm. Keifer hurried through his morning ablutions and hurried to the hall to find out why the bells still rang after more than a quarter of an hour.

A messenger raced into the hall just behind Keifer and hurried to where Sir Bryan sat at the high table. The man gave his news, and Sir Bryan's face broke out in jubilation. All eyes were on him, and everyone, even the servants, became quiet.

"Our queen has been delivered of twin sons!"

A son! A long-awaited heir to the throne. And a second boy in case one of them didn't live past infancy. Surely God had blessed the king and his line with these children. Keifer prayed for the infants' good health and long lives. Until now, Sir Bryan had been the king's only son, but he'd not been born of either of Bruce's marriages and thus could not assume the throne without a great deal of dissent among Bruce's nobles.

The birth of a legitimate heir strengthened Bruce's hold on the monarchy and gave promise that Scotland's throne would not sit empty. It would also give the greedy English one less cause to come north again. As if Edward of England needed an excuse. The peace between the two countries was an uneasy one, with raids over the border a common thing.

Indeed, Keifer had heard there was fear that Edward, whose hold on his kingdom lessened with the passing of each year, would come north again with an army in an effort to prove that he was still in control. But in truth, Edward's traitorous queen and her lover, Mortimer, were winning the loyalty of Edward's nobles and eroding his power.

Keifer's thoughts came back to the present. The infant princes could well mean the beginning of peace for his country. But if Edward marched north, Keifer would be ready for battle.

A WEEK LATER Sir Bryan sent for Keifer. He was cleaning his weapons, but he laid his sword aside and went to the man's solar as instructed.

Sir Bryan indicated that Keifer should have a seat. When Keifer was settled, he said, "I have received word that your uncle Angus has petitioned Bruce to get his lands back."

Keifer wasn't surprised. "My sister warned that he would try that. Was he successful?"

"No, the king denied him. Apparently Bruce doesn't trust Angus to keep his word to be content with what he has. The king has ordered your cousin to be held in surety for your uncle's good behavior."

Keifer hated the thought that his cousin, a young man his same age, might be sent to prison for his father's misdeeds. "Where will he be held?"

"Actually, he's coming here. Tomorrow."

"Here? To train as a knight?"

"Bruce didn't want to send the boy to prison. The boy isn't much of a threat now, and who knows how prison might change him.

Sending him to me gives the boy some freedom while still controlling the father. I can keep a watch on him and limit his activities."

"I see." Keifer hadn't seen Owyn since they both were children. Wouldn't recognize him in a crowd.

"The king hopes that you and Owyn might mend any differences and end the division of loyalties in your clan."

"I guess that will depend on whether or not Owyn wants to be laird of clan Macnab." A new thought struck him. "Does Owyn know I am here?"

"No. Your family has been very quiet as to your whereabouts. Using your mother's family name has kept your identity a secret."

"Still, I'll watch my back until Owyn gives some proof of his intentions. Perhaps he and I can find a peaceable solution as to who should be laird."

"Good idea."

Sir Bryan then gave Keifer the day's assignments and Keifer left for the stable.

Owyn Macnab arrived the next morning riding a small Scottish garron and wearing a bright smile. It was obvious the boy hadn't been sent here to train as a knight. While Keifer's physique showed promise of the strapping man he would one day become, Owyn was thin shouldered and wiry. And a good head shorter than Keifer. A swordsman's physique, but not one to stand up to the heavy demands of mounted warfare.

While Donel showed Owyn where to put his things, Keifer kept his distance. Then Donel brought Owyn to be introduced.

Donel said, "Keifer MacTaggert is the head squire. You and I answer to him. Keifer MacTaggert, this is Owyn Macnab."

Owyn lifted an eyebrow and Keifer wondered if the man had recognized the unusual first name. They had both changed in appearance in the years since they'd seen each other at Keifer's father's funeral. "Good to meet you, Owyn. Your training begins on the morrow."

Keifer was prepared to dislike his cousin. As he readied his pallet that night, he recalled the day Uncle Angus had tried to kidnap him. He had been terrified, especially after his mother explained that Angus might very well have killed Keifer.

Owyn and Donel joined him in the hall. When Owyn rolled out his pallet, he jumped back and yelled, "What the . . . who put the frog in my bedding?"

Donel bent over laughing. It wasn't hard to know the culprit. Keifer laughed. "If you were a girl, Owyn, I'd say Donel likes you."

Owyn advanced on Donel. He might be small, but Owyn didn't back away from confrontation. "I'll show ye—"

"Cease, Owyn. You are in no danger from Donel. He visits a lady friend in the village every chance he gets."

Owyn lowered his fists and the frog croaked. Then Owyn grinned good-naturedly. "Donel, would ye be so kind as to escort my little friend here back to wherever ye found him?"

Smirking, Donel picked up the poor creature and left the hall, returning a few minutes later empty-handed. No one seemed tired, so they sat before the dying fire.

Over the course of the next several days, Keifer assessed his cousin's worth. One afternoon they sat in the stable and cleaned their tack. As he rubbed the leather saddle with a damp cloth, Keifer said, "You seem uncomfortable giving orders, Owyn. How will you command men in battle?"

"I don't expect I ever will, which is fine with me."

Donel looked up. "What do you want to do then?

Owyn shrugged. "I'd be happy as a squire but . . ."

"But what?" Keifer was curious to know why someone would be a squire rather than a full-fledged knight.

"Ye know how fathers are. Mine has plans for me, and he doesn't much care what I want."

Keifer's hands stilled and he forced his voice not to betray emotion. He didn't know if he could trust Owyn. The man had seemed to recognize Keifer's name but had not said as much. Innocence? Or treachery? "Actually, I don't know. My father died when I was two."

"Oh, well." He cleared his throat. "Sorry to hear that. Maybe not all fathers are like mine. He was laird but supported England. That's why I'm here, as surety for his behavior. He petitioned to get his lands back, the king denied him, and now Bruce wants to make sure that Da doesn't switch his allegiance again."

Sir Bryan had said that very thing, so Keifer knew that Owyn spoke the truth. Though he had reason not to trust the boy, Owyn seemed quite open and honest.

"So, you don't want to be laird?" Donel asked, plainly taken aback by the thought.

"By the saints, no. My cousin is welcome to it. What of ye?" he asked Keifer.

Trying to sound bored despite his anxiety at the turn of the conversation, Keifer said, "I am to be laird of my clan."

Owyn nodded and looked up from his chore. "Ye'll do well at it. Ye've the instincts of a leader."

Keifer didn't feel right not admitting to his identity. He would dance around the issue for just a while longer—give Owyn a chance to say or do something to reveal or condemn himself. Keifer changed the subject.

"You did well in the sword play today, Owyn. You could be very good at it if you would apply yourself."

"That I could. But as I said, I don't want to become a knight."

Donel rose to hang his bridle on its peg. "Will you hire yourself out, then?"

"Aye, I'll sell my sword arm, such as it is." He held his arm out in front of him, fist clenched, and tightened the muscles of his upper arm. Looking at the less-than-impressive mound of flesh, he grinned. "As if anyone would hire a squire the size of a small boy."

Keifer laughed. "It's not as bad as that."

"I appreciate the fighting moves ye showed us this morning. Perhaps I will be able to outwit an opponent and take advantage of my speed, as ye said."

"Aye, speed can be used to advantage. But all the skill in the world wouldn't get you into my army, did I have one. I value loyalty more."

"Well, ye have mine, Keifer, after saving me from Donel's frog."

They laughed, even Donel. Donel pushed his hair from his face. "You will be laird of your clan—why become a knight if you've something like that to look forward to?"

"King Robert has need of men trained for war. And I have need to protect my clan from . . . those who covet what isn't theirs."

"Ah, someone else thinks he should be laird." Donel nodded in apparent empathy.

"I was never meant to be laird, but my uncle chose to serve the English king. Bruce took away his lands and gave them to me when I was but a child. My sister and her husband hold them for me."

Owyn peered at him, his expression puzzled. "Ye don't sound enthused at the idea of leading yer clan."

"It's my duty, nothing more." Keifer fingered the braid on his wrist.

"That's an interesting piece of jewelry," Owyn said.

Keifer looked at the braid and then at Owyn. "My foster sister gave it to me before I left to come here."

"Foster sister or lady love?" Donel teased.

"Sister. I have pledged not to marry." Keifer thought of Nola with a touch of regret for what would never be. But she would always be his foster sister. That thought comforted him.

"Sounds like a fool's pledge to me," Donel said. "I caught a glimpse of the lass on her way out. Perhaps you'll introduce me to her should the occasion arise."

"Perhaps I will." But the thought of introducing Nola to a prospective suitor left Keifer decidedly unsettled.

MacPherson Castle

THE MONTHS PASSED IN ENDLESS PROCESSION. Mary was nearly three years old, and Nola enjoyed taking care of her. With Suisan expecting her child any day, Nola took on more and more responsibility for the little girl.

On a damp summer day Nola was helping Suisan sew the last of the new baby's buntings while Mary took an afternoon nap. Suisan stood often and paced about the solar.

"My lady, what is it? Are you not feeling well?"

Suisan put her hand in the small of her back. "I believe it would be wise to have Will go for the midwife."

Nola grabbed her cloak and went to the stable to find Will. But only William was there. "My laird, Lady Suisan needs Will to go for the midwife."

William set aside the shovel he'd been using to clean the barn. "Will's in the pasture with the sheep. I'll have to go."

He rushed toward the keep and Nola hurried after him. Nola remembered her own father's nervous energy at the birth of Nola's youngest brother. Nola entered the solar where Suisan still sat sewing, her husband now hovering over her.

Suisan smiled at him. "Go, William. I am fine. But I need mistress Grania to be here."

William cupped her cheek. "Do not have this babe while I'm gone."

"I will order the child to obey its father," she teased him.

William kissed her forehead and left.

"What shall I do?" Nola asked.

"If you could see to Mary, that would be most helpful," Suisan answered.

"Aye. But until your husband returns, Mary and I will stay with you."

Suisan walked about the castle, giving orders to the cook for the next day's meals. She found it increasingly necessary to sit down, and after an hour or so she retired to her chamber.

Mary awoke from her nap, and in an effort to keep the child busy, Nola and Mary fetched the birthing stool and took it to Suisan. She had stripped to her chemise and seemed distracted.

Nola stifled her anxiety. She hated to see her friend and mentor in pain. "Are you all right, my lady?"

"Aye. But the babe is coming faster than the last. I wish William would soon return."

So did Nola. She knew of Suisan's history of childbearing difficulties, and the knowledge made her nervous. Though she'd helped with lambing, and even with her mother's last confinement, Nola had always had someone more experienced to go to if there was a problem. Where were William and the midwife?

Nola kept Mary occupied by playing patty cake with her. But she glanced nervously at the child's mother from time to time.

Suisan gasped. "I think it would be best if you sent one of the other women to me, Nola. Take Mary elsewhere. And send the midwife as soon as she arrives."

Nola went to the kitchen and asked Cook to send one of the women to Lady Suisan.

Nola and Mary were playing in front of the fireplace in the hall when William returned with the midwife. The two hastened to the master's chamber.

It seemed like only a few minutes later that William strode into the hall and came to his child. He picked her up for a hug.

"Where's Momma?" Mary asked.

"She's asked a dozen times and doesn't seem to like my answer," Nola said.

William set the girl down. "Momma is going to give you a brother or sister today." He looked to Nola. "The midwife said it won't be much longer."

"How is Lady Suisan doing?"

He swallowed hard, looking at the child at his feet. "Well enough. Suisan asked for you to come to her. Go now, I'll watch Mary."

Nola hurried to the chamber, then hesitated outside the door. She said a quick prayer for Lady Suisan's safe delivery and prayed that she could be of some help. Nola blew out a breath and pushed open the door. She walked to where Suisan squatted in the birthing stool.

"Won't be long now, my lady," the midwife said. "Yer doin' fine." She dabbed a damp cloth on Suisan's red face. Though she spoke soothingly to Suisan, she cast a worried look toward Nola. Suisan groaned through a contraction. When it passed, she reached out her hand to Nola. Nola took the lady's hand and looked into Suisan's eyes, eyes filled with fear. Suisan opened her mouth to speak but was overcome with another pain. With a loud moan Suisan pushed the baby into the world.

"A boy, my lady! 'Tis a boy!" Nola said. But Suisan laid backward, limp, her eyes closed.

Nola soon realized why. A great deal of blood seeped onto the floor. The midwife cleaned the babe and had Nola cut the cord. They wrapped him in a blanket and laid him on Suisan's chest. She did not respond.

The midwife gently scraped the sweat-plastered hair from Suisan's face. She turned to Nola. "Fetch the laird, lass."

Nola gestured to the mess they had yet to clean up. "But—"

"No time! Go now!"

Nola ran from the room and found William and Mary where she'd left them.

"You have a son. The midwife bids you come. Quickly." She warned him with her eyes, of what she wasn't sure. But she feared for Suisan's life. Nola watched William's broad back disappear.

For what seemed like an eternity, she waited while Mary asked over and over where her mother was and could she see the new baby.

A short time later William walked into the hall, holding his new-born son. Tears tracked down his face as he showed the infant to a curious Mary.

Mary took a quick glance and said, "Want to see Momma."

"Momma is resting, little love. You may see her later." William exchanged an anguished look with Nola. "Nola. Would you help the midwife? I'll stay with the children."

Nola walked slowly to the chamber and discovered what she dreaded—the midwife was washing Suisan's lifeless body. Suisan looked peaceful, her travail over forever. Nola's tears would not be held at bay and she grieved for the woman who had befriended her. Although Nola had helped her mother with her last confinement and knew the trials and dangers, seeing Suisan suffer and die was too much.

She ran from the room, bumping into Will on her way to the chapel. "Oh, Will, I'm so sorry for your loss. So sorry. So sorry for all of us!" She laid a quick hand on his arm and then fled to the chapel, not wanting him to think anything more of her gesture than kindness. There she prayed for Suisan and the family that must go on without her.

Marriage and children were the accepted course for a woman's life. Providing a nurturing home for a family would challenge Nola to use all of the gifts God had given her. She would welcome the challenge one day. But she wasn't ready for children. And when she did have them, she was determined it would be with a man she loved, just as Suisan had done. A man Nola was willing to die for.

And that man was not Will Macpherson.

NINE

Homelea

A WEEK OR SO AFTER THEIR CONVERSATION, Keifer came across Donel in the stable, looking up into the rafters. A rope hung from one of the beams. Owyn was near the top, hanging onto the rope with Donel holding the end. Every time Owyn started to climb down, Donel raced about with the rope, causing Owyn to swing wildly. He clung fast, shouting at Donel to stop.

"Aye. Enough Donel. Let him climb down in peace." What was the man thinking? Owyn wasn't laughing; it was a prank gone too far already. Could Donel not see it himself?

Donel seemingly obeyed Kiefer's command, stopping immediately with a sly grin. So abrupt was the stop that it caused the swinging rope to whip backward, flinging Owyn fifteen feet to the stable floor.

Keifer ran to the fallen boy. "Are you all right?"

Owyn had the breath knocked out of him and didn't move. Keifer rolled him over as Donel bent down to see. Owyn's arm exploded upward and connected with Donel's nose.

Unfortunately, it was this blow that Sir Bryan witnessed. "What is the meaning of this?" the knight yelled.

No one said anything.

"Well?" he asked Keifer.

"A prank gone bad, my laird. Nothing more." Keifer defended his friends. No harm had come of this aside from minor injuries.

Sir Bryan surveyed the bloody nose. "Your loyalty to your mates is admirable, Keifer. Make sure it isn't misplaced."

"Aye, my laird."

"As for you two, keep in mind that I'll not abide a man who is so stupid as to harm the very men who will fight with him in battle. Do I make myself clear?"

"Aye, my laird," Owyn and Donel said in unison.

"Good. Now, since all of you seem to have too much time on your hands, see if you can work together to repair the axle on the hay wagon before you come into the hall for supper."

"Donel," Sir Bryan said. "I will take you to see Lady Kathryn. She will see to your nose before you join the others."

As Owyn climbed into the rafters and untied the rope, Keifer watched Donel walk away. Keifer wondered how long it would be until the young man's foolishness had more serious consequences than a bloody nose.

OCCASIONALLY SIR BRYAN left Homelea to attend to business with the king or, as today, to take his wife to Edinburgh to the market fair. The lady hoped to find new cloth for a dress, and Sir Bryan hoped to find a new milch cow. They would be gone for three days. Sir Bryan's steward would oversee day-to-day dealings. Keifer, as head squire, would see to the squires' activities.

Today, the first day of Sir Bryan's absence, was to be a day of rest for the boys and the horses. Owyn had volunteered to remain at Homelea and keep Keifer company. Donel did his chores before he went into the nearby village to spend time with the girl he was courting.

Keifer decided to use his free time to write to Nola. He'd only sent her two letters in all this time. Part of his excuse was lack of time. Part was the expense of buying writing materials. And partly he feared creating too strong a bond when he had no intention of courting her. It didn't take much to encourage Nola, and he didn't want to give her false hope.

Still, he missed the give and take of their friendship. Nola had sent six letters to Keifer, and only in the latest did she chastise him for not writing more often. But she mentioned Will Macpherson frequently. Keifer hadn't gotten much beyond the salutation of his letter when Owyn burst through the hall doorway and raced to where Keifer sat before the fire.

He skidded to a halt in front of Keifer and gulped air. "By all the saints above, come quick!"

Alarmed, Keifer stood and put a steadying hand on Owyn's shoulder. "What? Are we under attack?"

"No, not that!" He tugged on Keifer's tunic. "Donel has gone too far this time. Come before it's too late."

Owyn wasted no breath in explanations but sprinted toward the enclosures where the horses had been released for the day. Had Donel given too much grain and foundered one of the beasts? Quickly Keifer reviewed in his mind what little could be done for an animal stricken with severe indigestion. The malady often proved fatal, and Keifer hoped he was wrong about the cause of Owyn's agitation.

But when Owyn stopped and pointed into the pen, neither of the horses was down. Indeed, what Keifer saw almost made him wish it *was* founder. Sir Bryan's new mare, Skye, was in the pen with a stallion. And she appeared to be quite interested in the stallion's advances.

Disaster! The mare had been purchased to breed with Shadow, Sir Bryan's war horse, not the inferior animal who had his nose at her tail. Sir Bryan would be furious if the mare accepted this stallion. It would be another year before the man could breed her again. And what if she should be hurt in this encounter or in the birth of an unwanted foal?

"Donel put these two together?"

"Nay. He was in a hurry to leave, or so he said, and asked me to put the horses out for him. The mare must have been behind the hay rack—I didn't see her in there."

Or Donel put her in there himself and Owyn was covering for him.

Owyn wrung his hands, as aware of the seriousness of the situation as Keifer. "What are we to do?"

"Get one of them out of there. Somehow." Keifer had watched Sir Bryan with the mare when she arrived. She was well bred but high strung. And far too interested in the stallion—obviously she was in season. The two stood side by side, the stallion reaching to nip her withers.

She neighed an invitation but sidled away. Keifer's heart sank. Neither of the beasts was going to appreciate an interruption to their tryst. But it couldn't be helped. Donel was going to pay for this.

The halters hung on pegs beside the gate. Keifer grabbed the one for the stallion. "You take the mare's halter and try to catch her."

"Wait. I'll get some grain to distract them." Owyn hurried away and soon came back with two buckets of grain.

Within minutes it became obvious that the stallion wasn't hungry. Furthermore, he seemed to consider Keifer and Owyn as rivals for the mare's attention. Over and over he put himself between the men and the other horse. When they got too close, the stallion bared his teeth.

Their only success after a quarter of an hour was that they'd kept the animals from mating. With the stallion's attention on the men, the mare lost interest in him. This was a good sign that she wasn't truly ready and Keifer's first hope that this might turn out well after all.

"Maybe we should rope the stallion and tie him," Owyn suggested.

"And watch him throw himself to the ground in a frenzy to free himself?"

"What then?"

"I'm going to saddle my horse. I will cut the mare away from the stallion and herd her to the gate. You will open the gate for us to get out without letting the stallion out, too."

"Ye think it will work?"

"Do you have a better idea?"

"Ye mean besides killing Donel for this?"

Keifer smiled at the jest. "I think we'll let Donel take his chances with Sir Bryan."

Owyn gave a weak smile. "We will all answer to the laird for this, I fear."

With a grim nod Keifer walked off to saddle his horse. He rode the gelding into the pen with the other two. The stallion stood protectively between Keifer's horse and the mare. Slowly Keifer rode closer, praying the mare would come from behind the stallion out of curiosity. She did, but the stallion quickly chased her back with a nip of his teeth.

Owyn shook the grain bucket, and she trotted from behind her protector and toward the gate. Keifer couldn't believe his good luck. While Keifer and his gelding shielded him from the stallion, Owyn continued to shake the pail of grain until the mare put her head in the bucket. With practiced moves, Owyn got the halter on her. She followed him out of the gate, and Owyn closed it behind her.

"That went surprisingly well." Keifer urged his horse to a walk. The mare whinnied, unhappy at being separated. The stallion pawed the ground and snorted. Keifer needed to get out of the pen as fast as possible. But Owyn was busy tying up the mare. Keifer didn't want to agitate the disappointed stallion by running his own horse toward the gate, so he walked slowly until Owyn returned.

Keifer's horse was within five feet of the the opening when Keifer heard the sound of the stallion running. He kicked his horse into a trot and Owyn prepared to open the gate. The stallion cantered around the pen, getting closer and closer to Keifer and his horse. The stallion headed toward them from the right. When the gate opened, it would open into the horse's path and give Keifer a clear shot at the exit.

Three more steps and they'd be there. The stallion slid to a halt inches from Keifer's horse, bared his teeth, and lunged. Keifer gripped tightly, knowing his horse would shy from the bite. The gelding side-stepped successfully—the stallion's teeth missed his horse. But Keifer screamed in pain as the strong teeth and jaws clamped instead around his right arm. Distantly, he heard bones crunch.

The stallion released his grip just before Keifer would have been pulled from the saddle. Keifer and his horse shot through the gate and Owyn slammed it shut behind them.

Keifer crawled down from his horse, cradling his throbbing arm against his chest. He prayed the sound he'd heard had not been his bones, but instead the glove.

Owyn took the reins. "I'll see to the horse. Go stick yer arm in cool water. When I've put up yer horse, I'll fetch some cloth to make a sling."

As he walked to the hall, Keifer removed his gauntlet, allowing the glove to fall to the ground. He tried to wiggle his fingers and could not. The whole wrist and hand felt numb. When he reached the kitchen, he poured cool water into a basin before pulling back the sleeve of his tunic.

The large, semi-circle of teeth marks was clearly visible on both the upper and lower sides of his forearm. Redness was quickly giving way to blue, which would no doubt become purple in a few hours.

With relief he noted that the skin wasn't broken. Now if the same could be said about the bones . . . Keifer placed a wet cloth on the injury, wishing he had ice instead. Still, the cool water took some of the sting away.

Owyn came into the kitchen carrying Keifer's discarded glove. "Let me see."

Keifer removed the cloth.

Owyn whistled. "Ouch." He held up Keifer's riding glove, made of soft leather to allow greater flexibilty of the fingers. The sleeve of the glove was made stiff with whalebone and cuffed just above the wrist.

The cuff of Keifer's right glove showed teeth marks and hung limply, the whalebone useless. Keifer realized the bone that had snapped had indeed been in the glove, not his arm.

When the steward inquired how Keifer was injured, he said only that he'd been bitten. 'Twas the truth, and no more than the man needed to know. Time enough to deal with the episode when Sir Bryan and Lady Kathryn came home.

TWO DAYS AFTER THE HORSE BIT KEIFER, Donel returned to Homelea and Keifer sent for him. But before he had a chance to talk with the other squire, Keifer's benefactor and lady wife rode into the bailey. Half the surrounding countryside seemed to be there to welcome the lord and lady home. At least that's how it appeared to Keifer's disgruntled eyes.

He dreaded telling Sir Bryan the story—didn't want to get either

Owyn or Donel in trouble. But they would have to own up to their deeds. Keifer spied Donel in the crowd. He jerked his head and indicated Donel should follow him so they might talk privately. But Donel shrugged his shoulders as if he didn't understand.

Just then Sir Bryan saw Keifer and walked over to him, no doubt anxious for a report of the happenings during his absence. Bryan clasped Keifer's right hand, and he winced.

The knight pulled up Keifer's sleeve. "Well, what have we here? A horse bite, from the looks of it."

"Aye. The bay stallion caught me." Keifer hoped Donel would confess and free him from telling. It would go better for Donel if he did so. Keifer would not cover for him this time.

Donel and Owyn stood close by. Sir Bryan looked at Donel, who stood with his head averted, then at Owyn, who was shifting from foot to foot. "I would like to hear all about it. Wait here. All of you."

Donel paced back and forth, running his hand through his hair. "I need ye, man," he said to Keifer. "I cannot be dismissed. What will I do?"

Keifer glanced from his friend to his lord, then shook his head. "This is out of my hands. You made a bad decision. Now you'll need to own up and be accountable for your actions. I'm sorry, Donel."

The knight walked over to Lady Kathryn and spoke to her. She smiled at him and went into the hall. When Sir Bryan returned, he asked for an explanation.

Keifer answered, "The stallion was released into the wrong pen."

"Who put the stallion in there?"

Owyn said, "I did, my laird."

"Why?"

"The mare was hidden by the hay rack. I didn't know she was in there, and I thought it's where he belonged."

"Why did you think that?" the knight demanded.

Owyn bowed his head.

Sir Bryan looked at each boy in turn. "Tell me the truth, Owyn. Loyalty to friends is an admirable trait, but this prank could have had serious consequences to my livestock. And Keifer suffered a grievous wound."

Donel said nothing.

Keifer bent to Donel's ear. "Tell him, or I will."

Donel, red-faced and scowling, admitted what he'd done. "I told Owyn where to put the stallion. 'Twas meant to be a jest, a prank and nothing more."

Sir Bryan pointed to Keifer's injured arm. "Then you should have stayed for the fun. How did this happen, Keifer?"

Keifer told them in as few words as possible.

After hearing the tale, Sir Bryan scowled. "As head squire, you may mete out Owyn's punishment, Keifer. You will inform me of your decision in the morning. Donel, come with me and help me with my chain mail. Keifer, have my wife take a look at that."

Keifer feared the knight would dismiss both Owyn and Donel. When the other boys came to the stable a quarter hour later, Keifer had still not decided on Owyn's punishment. Donel was subdued. Owyn grabbed the other boy's tunic and pulled him close. Donel was a good six inches taller, but Owyn appeared to barely notice. "If ye ever harm Keifer again, ye'll answer to me."

"I didn't mean for him to get hurt," Donel said.

"Maybe not. But this time ye went too far. Next time I'll skewer ye on my sword."

Donel had the good sense not to make light of the threat, as Owyn's swordsmanship had become second to none. "There won't be a next time. I've been dismissed."

Donel gathered up his gear as Keifer exchanged glances with Owyn. "Dismissed?"

"Aye, no thanks to either of you."

Keifer shook his head at Owyn to warn him to stay out of this. "Frogs in our beds were harmless enough. I even stood up for you when you convinced Owyn to climb the rope and caused him to fall. You brought this on yourself."

Donel brought his horse out of its stall and threw the saddle on its back.

Keifer handed him his bridle. "Where will you go?"

"Can't go home. My father will not take me in again."

Owyn stood beside Keifer, looking unhappy. "Then what will ye do?"

Donel finished bridling his horse. He turned to fasten his saddle-bags to the back of the saddle. "Well, I certainly won't be able to marry Sarah now that I have no means to support her."

He gave the strings that secured the bags a savage tug and grabbed the reins from Keifer's hand. "Don't waste your time feeling sorry for me. I'll find someone in need of my services."

Glaring over his shoulder at Keifer, Donel said, "Some laird you'll make if you won't stand up for your men."

For a brief moment, Keifer allowed himself to feel guilty. But again he reminded himself that Donel had probably sealed his fate when he hadn't confessed without coercion. "I'm sorry you see it that way, Donel."

"I won't soon forget what you did this day. You are no friend to me, Keifer MacTaggert."

Keifer and Owyn watched as Donel mounted and rode out of Homelea's gate.

"Ye'd best watch yer back, Cousin."

Keifer turned from watching Donel's vanishing back to stare at Owyn.

Owyn shrugged. "I've heard my da speak of Eveleen MacTaggert often enough. And ye look like my da—it wasn't hard to make the connection."

"I've wondered if you didn't suspect it. Why didn't you say something sooner?"

"Didn't think it was important."

Keifer didn't know whether to believe him or not. "Until I met you, I thought you and your father still coveted my lands."

"I don't want them, and I mean it. I'm a simple man, Keifer. I am happy to serve others, to serve ye, if ye'll have me."

Keifer had no reason not to believe Owyn. Still, he hesitated.

Owyn held out his dirk, the blade glinting in the firelight. "Keifer, I need to do this. My father is wrong. He isn't interested in what's best for his son or the clan. Ye will make a far better laird than I ever would."

Owyn had shown himself to be a good friend and amiable companion. Could Keifer trust him? He thought so. "I almost envy you, Owyn."

"Ye don't want to be laird either?"

"Not really."

"Then why do it?"

Why indeed? "Duty. To honor my father's memory. To keep my family safe."

"I am determined to swear my loyalty to ye, to promise to protect ye."

"You would go against your own father?"

"Aye."

Was taking Owyn's pledge going to further that goal or hasten trouble? He looked his friend in the eye and could not believe he would do Keifer harm. God help him if he was wrong.

Keifer nodded. "All right. I accept your allegiance." He handed the dirk back to Owyn.

Owyn kissed the blade. "I swear my loyalty to ye, Keifer Macnab. May this very knife pierce my heart if I dishonor my oath."

"So be it. And I pray for your deliverance when your father finds out what you've done this day, Owyn Macnab."

TEN

Homelea 1326

At last the time came for Keifer to be knighted. Nola was delighted when her father agreed to take her to Homelea for the celebration. In fact, the whole family would make the trip. And Adam invited Will Macpherson to accompany them.

Will had been pressing her to let him ask her father for her hand, but while he had managed to needle his way into her heart, again she put him off. The promise she'd made to Keifer remained closer still. Was there any hope?

Nola was determined to enjoy the time away from the glen and to not obsess on Will's pressing ways or the worry over Keifer. The trip seemed to take much longer than her earlier one, not only because of Will's presence, but because Nola was anxious to see Keifer again. She was anxious for him to see that she was no longer a child.

She caught Will staring at her bosom—he had certainly noticed the changes. And if he mentioned his desire for a betrothal one more time, she would forbid him to speak with her!

Will had changed since his mother died. It seemed that without her hand to gentle him, his arrogance went unchecked. Will's father had all he could do to care for his land and tenants, and precious little time to deal with his son. Still, Nola had to admire Will's brash ways, his confidence. And he made her feel wanted and constantly admired.

Yet she worried that all the good things she saw in him would fade once he had her at his side for good. Will was a conqueror by habit, not a partner.

Nola no longer lived with the Macphersons at Inversie, but she went there once or twice a week to help with Mary. Nola loved the little girl and grieved for Suisan and the child that had died within weeks of its birth. This journey to Homelea came as a much-needed respite from caring for others. For once Nola planned to selfishly look to her own interests.

When they arrived at Homelea at last, the place bustled with guests. Sir Bryan came to meet them in the bailey and gave orders for their horses to be tended. As her father greeted Sir Bryan, Nola scanned the busy courtyard for Keifer. Her father drew her forward. "You remember my daughter, Nola."

Nola brought her attention back to her father and the handsome man she'd met on her earlier trip to Homelea.

"You've become a lovely young woman, just as I predicted," the earl said as he took her hand. She dipped a curtsy.

"And this is our neighbor, Will Macpherson. He and Nola and Keifer grew up together. Will's father and I thought it would be good for him to see some of the country."

Nola bit her tongue. She'd had to beg to get her father to bring her along. Yet he invited Will because it would be good for him to see some of the world.

"So, where is our knight to be?" Adam asked.

"He is in the village, helping with the preparations. Come, Adam, Will. We'll go fetch him."

Disappointed that she hadn't been included in Sir Bryan's invitation, Nola joined her mother as Lady Kathryn ushered them, along with her younger brothers, into the hall. Nola and her family would remain here as guests. Most of the other guests would have to stay in tents in the village. Nola waited anxiously for her father and Will to return, knowing Keifer might be with them.

THERE WAS MUCH WORK TO BE DONE in preparation for the ceremony that would take place tomorrow at the abbey. Keifer was assigned to set up tents on the outskirts of the village of Homelea. That's where Sir Bryan and his guests found Keifer near the end of the day.

As Sir Bryan and Adam Mackintosh walked toward him, Keifer noted Will Macpherson was with them but Nola was not. Keifer was disappointed—perhaps she hadn't come with them from Moy. Adam clapped his hand on Keifer's shoulder. "It's good to see you, Son. You remember Will."

"Aye, I do."

"Nola and I welcomed the opportunity to see you, old friend," Will said, reaching out his hand. Keifer didn't much care for the proprietary tone of Will Macpherson's voice when he said Nola's name. Nor his assumption of friendship. But he took the man's hand and looked him over, as a knight sizing up his competition. Competition? What was this roiling through him?

"Aye. My daughter is back with the women, Keifer." Adam smiled.

Keifer couldn't wait to see her but kept it to himself. And something in Adam's voice didn't ring true either. What was going on here? "If you will wait a few more minutes, I'll be finished and can accompany you back to Homelea."

Sir Bryan said, "Take your time. I'll show our guests the lay of the grounds."

They tied their horses under some shade trees, and Keifer continued to set up the tent he'd been working on. He had completed his work and was sitting under the shade with the horses when the others returned. As the sun began to set, the four men rode to the castle.

Sir Bryan and Adam rode side by side, as did Keifer and Will behind them. The two men in front engaged in conversation. Hoping Will would speak of Nola, Keifer asked, "How was the journey?"

"Uneventful." Then quietly Will added, "You will learn soon enough that I have been courting Nola."

That Will would court her didn't surprise Keifer. What would surprise him is if she encouraged him. "How goes your suit?" Keifer asked. He just couldn't picture Nola with Will, yet she could very well have changed in four years. Changes Keifer wouldn't know of from her letters.

"I hope to seal our betrothal when we return home."

Keifer's heart pounded. Nola and Will were as good as betrothed. Could he have misheard?

Keifer calmed himself and did not speak further. Much could happen in four years—perhaps she truly cared for Will. Hadn't he thought as much?

Still, she'd promised not to give her heart before seeing Keifer again. He expected her to hold true to that vow, if for no other reason than out of the depth of their friendship.

When he saw Nola, he would not act in an unseemly manner, hovering about another man's betrothed. By the time they reached Homelea, he had his emotions firmly under control. He hadn't spent the past four years training for battle for nothing. But he would find out the truth of the matter.

OWYN WOULD NOT BE KNIGHTED—he had decided to remain a squire—Keifer's squire. The position suited him. And unlike Keifer,

Owyn had no sponsor, no one to provide his weapons and horses.

Owyn walked to the church yard where he had agreed to meet his father. As a young boy, Owyn had spent three lonely years waiting for his father to be released from Bruce's prison. His mother had died, and Owyn longed for the company of his remaining parent. When Angus had come home, Owyn tried to listen to him, to understand him. But the old man had left prison near desperate for Eveleen Macnab to forgive him, and for the life of him, Owyn couldn't figure out why his father couldn't move on.

Apparently Angus had come to Homelea for the festivities. He had sent a message to Owyn, asking to meet with him. Today was the first chance Owyn had to get away. He walked through the yard to the cemetery behind the church.

The older man stood by a grave marker looking hale and hearty, belying his years. "Father. Ye are looking fit."

"Aye. Never better despite some disturbing news."

More disturbing than having his lands and title taken from him? Owyn's inheritance. An inheritance Owyn didn't want. "What is it, then?"

"Eveleen has married another."

"What?" Owyn wanted to feel sorry for his father, but he just couldn't. It seemed no sooner had Owyn's mother died but Angus had set his sights on marrying his brother's widow. Owyn feared Angus might not listen to reason. Nearly twenty years had passed, and still he obsessed over the woman.

"Six weeks ago. One of the neighboring lairds. He has an heir, no need of a young wife. But he has allied himself with Keifer and Morrigan."

"So that even if Keifer should die, Morrigan will have a strong ally to defend her lands and hold them for her own son."

"Aye."

"And Keifer has Black Bryan Mackintosh as an ally as well."

"Doesn't matter—I want Keifer dead."

Owyn had never heard his father sound so determined and it frightened him. "Da, ye don't mean that. He's Eveleen's son, yer brother's son."

Angus waved the words away. "Between the two of us we need to see it done, once and for all."

"I'm not killing him."

Angus slapped him, so quick Owyn had no time to react. His father's hand split Owyn's lip, and blood dripped onto his tunic. Owyn wiped his mouth on his sleeve.

Then in a perfectly calm voice, as if he discussed the weather and not murder, Angus said, "No, I don't suppose ye have the stomach for it. It'll be up to me."

With sudden clarity, Owyn knew he mustn't admit to his allegiance to Keifer. If Angus knew that, he would walk away and neither Owyn nor Keifer would be safe. In fact, the cold expression on Angus's face gave Owyn reason to believe his father would see Owyn himself killed rather than serve Keifer Macnab.

Owyn grabbed his father's arm. "Ye need to start thinking clearly. Keifer's death won't make any difference. I don't want the land."

"Not for the land. I have other lands that suit me well and a growing band of men who are loyal to me."

Other men? Men like his father who had ulterior motives for everything they did? Owyn didn't like this and tried again to reason with his father. "Keifer has powerful allies. Ye can't kill him and expect the king to hand over the land to me."

"I said it's not about the land."

"Then what is it about? Help me understand."

"She won't have me, never would have me. Now she will suffer as I have suffered for love."

He held his father's arm. "Don't do this, Da. Let it go. Go home and tend the sheep; lead yer men for Bruce. But forget about murdering yer brother's son."

Angus pushed past him without a word. Owyn watched his father walk away, distressed at the man's obsession and powerless to halt him. Their conversation haunted him.

He must warn Keifer of Angus's intent. Owyn was no saint, but he didn't want the blood of an innocent man on his conscience. He would confront his cousin when he returned to Homelea.

ANGUS STALKED OFF INTO THE VILLAGE and found the tavern. He went in and ordered a tankard of ale. The ale slaked his thirst for refreshment but not his thirst for revenge.

He would bide his time, enlist Owyn's help. The boy would change his mind. After all, the killing would benefit Owyn most of all. He had been wrongfully denied his birthright, no matter that Robert the Bruce himself had taken it.

Aye, and given it to Eveleen and Ian's son. Keifer. Ian had taken the woman Angus loved, and though Angus had married another, he'd never stopped caring for her. His woman, his land, his title. All taken from him.

He'd lied to Owyn. It wasn't just about Eveleen. The time had come to take things back. If she'd shown even the slightest appreciation for his honesty that day he'd confessed, he would have settled back and accepted her son as his laird.

But she'd scorned him. And now she had married someone else. Angus had received no forgiveness nor honor, and he would give none.

Keifer Macnab was a marked man.

That would teach her.

AFTER THE MEN LEFT to find Keifer, Lady Kathryn took Gwenyth and Nola into the hall. Da had made it clear that Nola was to stay with the women. She tried not to let her resentment show at being left behind. Lady Kathryn provided refreshments and introduced her children. Then she showed them to their guest chamber.

Nola's mother was nearly as anxious as she to see Keifer again, and both waited in anticipation for the men to return to the castle. After what seemed like hours, a knock came on the door of their chamber.

Nola opened the door to Lady Kathryn. "Do you have news?"

"Aye, the men have returned."

Nola raced to the winnock and looked down to the bailey where her father and the others were dismounting. She raced for the door-way and then remembered to walk. Until she reached the stairs. She ran down them, nearly tripping over her skirt, managing to resume a decorous walk when she reached the landing.

She walked out to the bailey. The first person she saw was Will, a deep frown on his face. Her father and Sir Bryan stood between Will and a tall, broad-shouldered youth. His short hair, darkened with per-spiration, was curled about his face and neck like a babe's.

Was that Keifer? The hair seemed too dark, but the curls were familiar. With all the discipline she possessed, Nola willed herself to walk like a young woman and not a child as she approached them.

This couldn't be Keifer. This man carried himself like a warrior, proud and erect. He seemed at ease with both Sir Bryan and her father.

Sir Bryan pointed to Keifer and said something to Nola's father. Adam beamed in that way he had when he was especially pleased with Nola or her siblings. It must be Keifer. She would know for sure when she looked into his mischievous eyes. Her heart stuttered, and she wiped her hands discreetly on her skirt.

What would he think of her? Would he find her pretty? Had he remembered their promise?

When she was but a few steps away, Will turned to her. She thought he called her name, but Nola kept her gaze on the handsome young warrior talking to her father. She stopped, and her father held out his hand to her. Taking it, Nola curtsied.

She straightened, and her father handed her to Sir Bryan.

Her father's friend kissed her fingers. He said something, but Nola's attention was on the man she thought was her childhood friend. She glanced at his wrist and saw the braided twine. She grinned.

"You remember Keifer, don't you?" Sir Bryan said.

"Keifer," she breathed, forgetting to curtsy, forgetting she was no longer a child, knowing only that her heart's desire stood before her.

But the boy she'd known was gone. There was no mischief in this man's eyes. Instead she saw wariness, an aloofness that had never been between them. Hurriedly she curtsied. He took her hand and kissed it. "My lady." No warmth in his voice, yet his gaze searched her. Where had her friend and companion gone? And why did his eyes reveal hurt?

She dared not act the child, would not give in to the impulse to leap into his arms. She drew her shawl closer, warding off the chill of the day and of his eyes.

Will's scowl faded, his expression triumphant.

Nola wanted to lash out at him. Just in time she remembered that if she spoke like a child, she would be treated like one. Curbing her tongue, she looked at her father. From his expression, Nola could see he was oblivious to the undercurrents swirling about her. And to the hostility raging between Will and Keifer.

Nola was not about to stand here and be humiliated by either of these posturing peacocks. Despite being devastated that this long-awaited moment had been ruined somehow, Nola managed to say that she was needed in the castle. Head high and heart dragging, she left them both.

Good riddance!

KEIFER WATCHED AS BEAUTIFUL NOLA hurried away from him. Nola, his Nola, was all but betrothed to the gloating frog of a boy standing next to him. It was all Keifer could do to politely disengage from the group with the excuse that his horse needed attention. But in truth, his horse was in better condition than Keifer.

He had not wanted to give a little girl false hope. But the little girl had become a woman. And that woman had chosen another over him. And yet why wouldn't she? No matter that he didn't want to marry. Seeing Nola was enough to make him question his resolve. He fingered the worn braid on his wrist. Had she noticed it?

Keifer led his horse to the stable. He offered the animal water, washed him down, and then turned him into a pen with some hay. He went to his quarters to wash off the day's dust.

Why had Nola run off like that? He threw his helm onto the bed. He'd been a fool to think a child would keep a promise. And what difference did it make? Recalling how she had looked standing there a few moments ago gave him his answer. Glory but she was every bit as beautiful as he'd foreseen. Had it been hurt he'd seen in her eyes just before she lowered her gaze?

One thing he knew for certain; Will had gloated at her hasty retreat and Keifer's evident acceptance of the impending betrothal.

Keifer slammed his hand on the table. No! He did not accept it. Would not until he heard it from her himself. All he wanted was a chance to know her again, to be friends as they once were. But the friendship he had once treasured would never be the same if she married someone else.

He would find her and talk to her before sundown, when he must return to the abbey. There he would be secluded with the other candidates to prepare for tomorrow's ceremony.

His stomach rumbled, reminding him of the fast he'd begun mid-morning. He drank some water, knowing it would do nothing to assuage his hunger.

The hours until his seclusion ticked away as his mother and her new husband arrived and took up his time. Dougal of Brodie seemed like a good man and obviously cared for Eveleen. Keifer was glad to see his mother so happy. Morrigan and Fergus were with them, but he had little chance to speak with them. He would remedy that tomorrow after the ceremony.

Nola didn't make it easy for him to speak with her—she seemed to disappear, giving Keifer no opportunity to come across her by chance. He was afraid to ask after her too often because if she truly was betrothed, his attentions would not be seemly.

Guests continued to arrive, and Keifer kept busy greeting them and seeing to their horses. After caring for the latest group of horses, one of the pages found him and told him to report to Sir Bryan's solar. When Keifer arrived, both the Earl of Homelea and his friend the Earl of Moray were there. They indicated that Keifer should sit down, and he did so gratefully.

It seemed a bit odd to Keifer that someone like Sir Thomas Randolph would come to this knighting ceremony. Keifer couldn't recall that any of the other fellows had ties to the man.

He fought the urge to squirm, knowing he didn't have much time until he must saddle up and ride to the abbey. He and the other postulants would spend this night in prayer. Keifer had much to pray about and wondered if this meeting would add to his burdens or lighten them.

"The king sends his congratulations, Keifer," Randolph said.

"I thank you for coming to deliver his greeting. Please tell the king that I am at his service."

"I am glad to hear that, because I come also to tell you the king wishes for you to accompany me to Paris for the treaty negotiations."

"Paris?" Keifer recovered from his surprise. "I shall be delighted."

"You will act as a guard for the delegation of the king's advisors."

Paris! An important assignment as well as a chance to travel. He could barely conceal his excitement at the prospect. "When do we leave?"

"I'm afraid the ship sails from Edinburgh in two days' time." Randolph gave him details as to when and where to meet the ship and directions to his house in Edinburgh, where he could spend the night before departure. "There will be no time to go to Innishewan."

Keifer was thrilled to be part of the venture, but now he simply must speak with Nola, wish her well with her marriage plans, before he left.

"I wasn't planning to go to Innishewan for some time. My holdings are not rich, and I am in need of cash. I had thought to compete in tournaments for a year or so to increase my wealth."

"I see. A wealthy wife could solve that problem for you. Shall I look to arrange one for you?"

Keifer tread carefully, not wanting to anger such a powerful man. "You would do that?"

"Aye. Robert needs you to defend your holdings, not tour Europe for funds."

"In truth, Sir, I do not plan to marry. I will formally name my nephew as my heir tomorrow."

The earl seemed taken aback. "I see. You appear to be serious about this."

Keifer had been serious until he saw Nola. Now he wasn't sure of anything. Still he repeated, "I do not wish to marry."

"Think on it," Sir Thomas urged again. "A wife is a great comfort to a man, even a knight."

"I will."

Keifer headed for the stables. He found a rope and caught his horse. When the beast was securely tied, he went looking for a brush to clean him up before saddling. He had much to think about and not much time.

But all he was sure of at the moment was that he must talk to Nola and set things to rights between them. As he cleaned the horse's coat, his mind wandered through conflicting images and emotions.

Tomorrow he would become a man, and once more he would pass a milestone without his father there as witness. Despite his success, despite the pride he felt, Keifer longed for something that eluded him. His father's words of congratulations, perhaps.

Marriage was another of the milestones of a man's life, and Keifer just couldn't see himself in the role. More to the point, he couldn't see himself as a father. To have a son of his own seemed like too great a responsibility.

He stopped brushing and sat on a bench. A son. Perhaps a son of his own would fill this empty space inside. He'd never thought of that. He shook his head. Seeing Nola again had him more confused than he realized if he was considering siring a child.

He stood to finish saddling up and became aware of someone behind him. Slowly he moved his hand to the dirk at his waist and turned around.

"Will." Keifer took his hand from the knife hilt and faced his boyhood acquaintance.

"Keifer." He jutted his chin toward the horse. "You are leaving?"

"Aye. I'm to spend the night in preparation for the ceremony."

"Ah."

Was that triumph in the other man's voice? Relief? Keifer turned back to the horse and began brushing it. Though he would like to settle this here and now, he dared not be late. "I'm sorry I can't stay and talk. I must be at the abbey within the hour."

Will took a lead rope off its hook and absently flicked the end of it. "Have you spoken to Nola?"

Keeping his voice neutral, Keifer said, "No, I haven't had time."

Will nodded. "You heard what I said? About us marrying?"

"I heard you say so, yes. I've yet to hear what Nola or her father have to say on the matter."

Will slapped the rope against the boards, making the horse spook. "She's mine, Macnab. Stay away from her. You saw how she ran from you today. Leave her be."

Keifer calmed the horse before saying, "Leave her to you, you mean. Is the betrothal set, then?"

"I haven't asked her father yet."

Keifer's betrayed heart lightened at the news. If Will hadn't approached Adam, it must mean that Nola hadn't said yes to him yet. All the more reason to hear what Nola had to say. "I won't time to speak with her tonight, but I will seek her out after the ceremony."

"You want to marry her?"

"I want to talk to her. You're the one who's bent on marriage."

"I am."

"I'll chat with Nola, and if she's willing—if she's *willing*—you can take her back north and marry her."

Keifer finished saddling the horse. Brushing past Will, he led the animal out of the barn, mounted up, and rode away. He needed to prepare his heart for the vows he would say tomorrow. But all he could think of was Will's confidence that Nola intended to marry him.

Why did the thought leave Keifer bereft?

ELEVEN

Owyn caught up with keifer on the road to the abbey. He reined his horse to a halt in front of Keifer's, and Keifer had to pull hard on the reins to prevent a collision.

"We must talk!" Owyn shouted.

Annoyed at yet another disruption of his day, Keifer said, "Talk then, but keep the horses moving. I'm late. Are you concerned about your part in tomorrow's ceremony?"

Owyn didn't move his horse. "Nay. I met with my father this afternoon."

Keifer attempted to rein his horse around Owyn's. "Your father is no concern of mine. Can't this wait?"

Owyn grabbed Keifer's bridle. "Nay. It cannot. My father intends to kill ye."

A chill of premonition went down Keifer's spine. Had he been wrong to trust his cousin? "He wants you to kill me? Why?"

Owyn explained. "My father is angry with yer mother for re-marrying. He will punish her with yer death."

Angus is angry at Mother? Keifer had thought all this settled in the years since Angus got out of prison. "Is my mother in danger?"

"I don't believe so."

"Does your father want the land and title back?"

"He says not, but I'm not sure I believe him. But he is determined to take revenge on Aunt Eveleen for choosing yer da, for rebuffing him when he got out of prison, and for daring to choose another man again."

Keifer tried to understand. "But most of that was years ago."

They sat on their horses in the middle of the road. Keifer checked the sun and knew he didn't have much time. He gathered his reins.

"Wait!" Owyn's expression looked pained. "Ye would turn yer back on impending danger?"

"Danger? Forgive me, friend, but your da is a powerless, foolish old man."

Owyn shook his head. "'Tis clear ye don't know how yer da died. Ye are in real danger."

Impatient, Keifer said, "My da fell from a horse."

"No. That's what *my* da told everyone. But the truth . . . our cousin Duncan says our fathers argued. My da knocked yers to the ground, and Ian broke his neck in the fall."

Keifer stared at his cousin as understanding set in. "Your father killed my da?"

Owyn nodded. "It was an accident, according to Duncan."

Keifer shook his head, hearing Owyn's words and not wanting to believe them. "Then why . . . then why the lie?"

"I don't know. But when my da confessed to yer mother after his release from prison, she refused to have anything more to do with him. It hurt him . . . worse than when she first chose Ian over him. It changed him, somehow. He wants revenge, and he's determined to hurt her through ye."

Keifer could not thank Owyn for the timing of this news. "All this time . . . How long have you known about my father's death?"

Owyn stared back at him. "I've known since just before I came to Homelea. But ye must believe me—until this moment, I thought ye knew the truth of it."

Keifer could feel anger rising, anger and frustration. "Your da murdered my own? And still you swore loyalty to me?"

Now Owyn grabbed Keifer's sleeve and looked directly into his eyes. "Aye. And I meant it. I still mean it." He let go of the sleeve. "I tell ye, I thought ye knew the truth of it. Ye must believe me."

Again Keifer looked to the west, not sure what to believe anymore, only knowing he had no choice but to trust Owyn. "I must go, Owyn. As you love me, find my mother and warn her that your da is nearby and he intends evil. I will see you tomorrow at the ceremony."

Owyn's expression was grim with what Keifer hoped was determination to serve him. "Aye, my laird. God go with ye."

Keifer spurred his horse to the abbey, toward a night meant for prayer and meditation. How could he open his heart to God when all he could think of was avenging his father's death? Aye, he would kill the man who had robbed him of his father!

NOLA SAT AT DINNER THAT SAME EVENING with her parents on one side and Will on the other. Will, solicitous to a fault, cut the meat on their shared trencher and presented her with the best morsels. His attention was that of a man intent on wooing his companion.

But Nola remembered Keifer in the bailey this afternoon. She remembered, too, the childish promise she had made. *I can't promise my heart, nor will I ask you to. But could we at least promise not to marry anyone else until we've spoken to each other again?*

The boy she'd made that promise to was gone, and his lack of warmth this afternoon still stung. Why had he behaved that way? Should she just accept Will's suit and forget her childish vow?

She reached for the wine goblet but Will got to it first. He lifted it to her lips but she pulled it from his hand, sloshing the wine onto the table covering in her haste.

"What's the matter with you tonight, Nola? You've acted peevish all through the meal."

They were friends and had often shared confidences over the years. But this . . . this distance from Keifer she could not share with anyone. Certainly not with Will. Why couldn't he just give her the time she had asked for to make her decision?

But despite her pique at his persistence, she just couldn't be mean. For once she wished she could. "I'm sorry, Will. Too much excitement."

"I know. I'm excited about our betrothal, too."

Nola took a deep breath and prayed for patience. "No, Will, you mistake me. 'Tis the excitement of our travel that has me on edge."

Lips pursed, Will asked, "Have you forgotten your father's request?"

How could she forget that Adam had asked her to give Will an answer by the time they returned home from this trip? "I have not." She remembered it well. And she truly did care for Will, despite his faults. She herself was far from perfect . . . Marriage to him would be good except for one thing. He wasn't Keifer. Yet after her encounter with Keifer today, she wasn't sure how she felt about either man. Certainly she was in no mind to make such an important decision.

"I don't mean to press you, love. But I would like to be able to announce our betrothal."

Nola rubbed her temples. "And what if I say no, Will? What then?"

"You will disappoint both our families."

"And you? Will I disappoint you?"

"What a foolish question, Nola. You know I care for you."

Aye, she did know that. And she also knew how much Will coveted the land she would bring to their marriage. No, that thought was unfair. Will cared for her and he would make a fine husband. But . . . "Give me more time, Will. You promised not to press me. I wish you would keep that vow."

His expression revealed his impatience, but all he said was, "As you wish."

She made her excuses to Will and her parents and left the hall. As she walked to her chamber, she tried to think of some way she could persuade her parents to let her stay here when they returned to Moy. Then perhaps she would have time to know Keifer again.

And if their childhood friendship could not bloom into something more, she would accept it and marry Will. Somehow she knew that despite repeated prayers, she would receive no clear vision of God's will in this matter. She simply needed to trust that His will would be re-vealed in time. Perhaps she wasn't meant to marry at all, like Keifer.

But if she and Keifer didn't marry each other, how would she ever recover from the loss of her best friend?

KEIFER AND THE FIVE OTHER YOUNG MEN who would be knighted along with him spent the evening at the abbey. One by one they were called to speak privately with the priest and confess their sins.

If Keifer told everything, he'd still be in there at dawn. Especially after what Owyn had told him. *Vengeance is mine, saith the Lord.* But the need to avenge his father's death burned in Keifer's heart.

And if that wasn't enough on his mind, there were his confusing feelings about Nola and his vow not to marry. Suddenly Keifer wasn't sure about anything in his life.

After confession Keifer went into the bathing chamber to prepare for the ritual bath. He disrobed and set his clothes aside for Owyn to gather later. Now the only thing he wore was the frayed braid upon his wrist that he had worn ever since the day Nola tied it fast. *Nola.*

She had turned her back on him this afternoon, had broken their vow. Sadly he cut the bracelet and laid it aside, just as he would lay aside his former life tomorrow.

Keifer entered the water and cleansed himself, refreshing his body if not his spirit. Then he donned a white robe and went into the nave of the church to pray before the altar.

He bowed his head. He should be praying for the strength and honor to be a good and faithful knight, but all through his vigil, those prayers were interspersed with ones about Nola. And fervent requests to help him deal with his growing hatred of Angus Macnab. It just didn't seem right to ask God to help him kill his uncle.

Dear Father in Heaven, I don't know if you mean for me to marry. If that is your will, help me to know, and to know if Nola is the woman you would choose for me. I have no idea how to conquer my hatred of Uncle Angus without your help. Guide me in this; show me your will, I beg of you.

By morning he was no closer to knowing God's will, nor did he feel entirely confident that God would guide him. He considered refusing to take his knightly vows, but how would he explain himself? That his heart wasn't free of entanglements? Whose heart was?

In the end he prayed that God would not desert him. He stood with the others when Sir Bryan came to fetch them for the ceremony. Keifer's knees hurt from kneeling and his stomach rumbled from hunger. But those discomforts paled beside the angry knot in his gut—a knot of hatred that the hours of prayer had not softened.

God forgive me.

ST. MARY'S ABBEY stood in the forested hills east of the village of Homelea, which took its name from the nearby castle. Eveleen glanced about the nave of the church as she and the other guests, mostly families of the six young men being honored today, waited for the ceremony to begin.

Light filtered in through fourteen round, stained-glass windows, each depicting a scene from the Crucifixion. On this day when her son would be recognized for his efforts, Eveleen was drawn to the window with Jesus and his mother. Like Mary, Eveleen knew the sorrow of losing a child. And a husband, for Joseph wasn't mentioned as being with Mary when their son died.

Eveleen shook off those sad thoughts and watched as Keifer and five other white-robed young men entered the abbey. Standing tall and proud, Keifer led them up the aisle to stand before the altar. If only Ian could have lived to see their son this day.

And in the same thought came Angus. The two brothers who had both courted her those many years ago. Short-tempered Angus, ambitious enough for both men. And Ian, content with his lot in life and trusting that God would provide. Eveleen feared her son took more after his uncle than his father. Which might be good for the clan, but at what price to Keifer?

She'd never regretted her choice of Ian for her husband. Except for one thing. That choice, and Angus's anger over her rejection, had eventually cost Ian his life. Owyn's warning yesterday evening had surprised her. She hadn't wanted to trust him. His words caused her to lie awake most of last night, not in fear for herself but for her son. Angus would strike back at her through Ian's son, of that she was sure. Eveleen feared that Angus's reprisal, when it came, would be silent and unobservable, something no army could detect.

Keifer's training as a knight was meant to give him the means to protect himself and his loved ones. As a knight sponsored by the king, Keifer would enjoy the loyalty and protection of the crown and the men loyal to it. Men Keifer could call upon if need arose.

One of those men stood beside her, Dougal of Brodie. Though his clan and holdings were small, he had pledged his honor and his men to Keifer's defense. Eveleen had not looked for love or marriage, but had found both in Dougal. She glanced up at him to find him staring at her. She smiled despite her anxiety, and he returned the smile before they both looked to the altar and the young men there.

AT SIR BRYAN'S NOD, Keifer and the other celebrants kneeled, their backs to the watching crowd. Somehow Keifer pushed thoughts of his uncle to the back of his mind and concentrated on the man before him.

Sir Bryan stepped in front of each man in turn, going through the ritual. When he stopped in front of Keifer, he asked, "Do you pledge to maintain and defend the faith of our fathers?"

In a strong voice Keifer replied, "I so pledge."

"Will you govern your lands with a firm but compassionate hand?"

Again Keifer said, "I so pledge."

"And will you uphold and defend your earthly lord?"

"I so pledge."

Sir Bryan turned to Keifer's squire. Owyn handed the earl a pair of golden spurs. Sir Bryan faced Keifer again and held them in his hands. "Wear these spurs as an outward sign of your commitment to serve God."

Keifer took the spurs. God would not be served with revenge, and Keifer bowed his head and vowed that so long as Angus left Keifer and his family alone, Keifer would not seek a confrontation. But given cause, Keifer would seek his revenge. 'Twas the best Keifer could promise, and it eased his heart. Then Keifer watched as the earl took Ian Macnab's sword from Owyn and tapped Keifer's shoulder three times, then placed the weapon into Keifer's outstretched hands. Keifer kissed the blade of his father's sword, vowing silently to honor his memory.

"Rise, Sir Keifer of Innishewan and laird of Clan Macnab."

To Keifer's surprise, Owyn handed the Macnab laird's ring to Sir Bryan, who in turn gave it to Keifer. Nola had not forgotten the request in his last letter, that she send the ring with her father. Or had she brought it herself? As he pushed the ring onto his finger, Keifer vowed to thank her for accomplishing the task.

Keifer stood, and Sir Bryan performed the same ritual with the rest of the candidates. When he was finished, the earl solemnly led the new knights down the center of the church, and the audience filed out behind them.

In the church yard, friends and families of the newly knighted men gathered around them to offer congratulations. As he accepted the well wishes, Keifer scanned the crowd for his mother. He needed to be sure Owyn had given her the warning. He would encourage her and Sir Dougal to return quickly to the safety of Innishewan.

He still needed to find Nola and set things right with her. He had little time before he must leave with Sir Thomas. Remembering his brief encounter with Nola yesterday, Keifer wondered if he was making too much of a childhood vow. But he couldn't stop himself. He had known Nola the child, and now he wanted time to get to know the woman she had become. He'd just found Nola in the crowd when his mother, his stepfather, and his sister and her husband walked toward him.

His mother stood beside him and looked in the direction of his gaze. "She is a beautiful young woman."

Wondering if he was allowing his emotions to show, he slowly turned away from watching Nola. "Who do you mean?"

"The Mackintosh girl. A mother notices these things."

He smiled. "You see what isn't there. Nola and I were best of friends as children. And I haven't had a chance to speak with her since she arrived."

"Do ye love her?"

"Of course not. You know my feelings about marriage. I've written to you of it oft enough."

The others drew close now and Keifer nodded to them while his mother spoke. "Aye, but feelings can change, Keifer. I never thought to remarry." She smiled at her husband.

"Nor did I," said Dougal. "Give it time."

Keifer didn't want to have this conversation. There were more pressing concerns. "Mother, did Owyn speak with you?"

"Aye, he did. I was a bit surprised that ye've taken him as yer squire."

"As was I," Morrigan said. "Do ye trust him?"

Keifer hadn't seen the man since the ceremony ended, and he had a moment of unease. He shook it off. "I trust him with my life or he wouldn't be my squire. He has sworn his loyalty to me and risked the wrath of his father in doing so."

Morrigan's eyes widened. "Angus knows?"

"He does now. Today his oath became public. That is why I urge all of you to return to Innishewan."

His mother looked confused. "We plan to leave with ye."

"That won't be possible." Keifer explained about his duty to accompany Randolph to Paris. "So I will feel better knowing you are safely home."

Fergus nodded. "I agree with yer son, Lady Eveleen." He said to Keifer, "Is Angus nearby Homelea?"

Grimly he nodded. "He was yesterday."

"But what of yer safety, Keifer? I agree with Owyn that his father will seek to hurt me through ye. Angus knows me too well. I would prefer my own death to yers."

Sir Dougal cleared his throat. "While I can applaud your motherly emotions, Eveleen, I would like to see you both alive and well for years to come."

Keifer saw Thomas Randolph in the crowd, reminding him of his imminent departure. Keifer wanted to find Nola, but duty and family must come first. He reached into his sporan and pulled out a sealed parchment. He extended his hand to Morrigan, and as she took the parchment, he explained. "I had this drawn up naming your son as my heir, as we agreed. I urge all of you to return to Innishewan with haste. I will come there upon my return from Paris."

Morrigan nodded and handed the paper to Fergus. "There is one other thing, Keifer. It's time ye knew how our father died."

"Owyn has told me."

"Did he also tell ye that Angus and yer father both courted me?" Eveleen told him the story.

Keifer was stunned by his mother's tale of the two brothers who had fought over a woman. His own mother. Angus and Ian had both wanted her. Had fought over Eveleen not once but twice. And the second time brother had killed brother. Could Keifer truly trust Owyn with such deep currents running between their families?

And what of this triangle with Will and Nola that Keifer found himself wrapped up in?

When she had finished, Eveleen said, "Promise ye will not seek revenge. What's done is done. I seek only peace."

"I want to promise it. But if Uncle Angus seeks me out and challenges me, I will not hold back."

"Very well. Find yer young lady and bid her farewell." His mother hugged him.

He kissed her forehead. "I will be fine, don't worry."

She patted his back and walked away with her husband. Keifer was thankful that she had a protector. His mother and sister had given him much to think about.

As he said good-bye to Morrigan and Fergus, Keifer wondered if perhaps he should just let Will have Nola and avoid repeating his father's mistake.

THAT THOUGHT DIDN'T HOLD FOR LONG. Keifer was ready to throttle Will Macpherson. Twice Keifer managed to find Nola, only to have Will barge through the crowd and join them. Will said Nola's parents were looking for her the second time. She promised to return to Keifer in a few minutes, and Keifer wandered about aimlessly.

Determined to get her alone so their talk could be private, Keifer walked up to her as she was speaking with her father and Sir Bryan. Will was nowhere in sight.

Keifer greeted, then turned to Nola's father. "Sir, I wonder if you would excuse Nola so I may speak privately with her?"

Sir Adam nodded. "Of course."

"Would you accompany me, my lady?" He smiled, hoping to soften whatever he had hardened in her heart in the bailey yesterday.

She stared at him a moment, and her hesitation pierced him, as did the wary look of her eyes. Where had the spontaneous girl he'd known gone? Had he chased her away, or had Nola changed so much? She looked at his bare wrist and he heard her breath hitch. But she said nothing, just laid her hand on his offered arm and allowed him to lead her into the abbey.

Just as they reached the doorway, Will walked quickly up to them, following them just as he had been doing all afternoon. "Ah, a quiet moment away from the crowd. What a delightful idea. I'll join—"

Keifer said, "You will not join us, Will. I wish to have a private word with Nola."

Will put his hand on her arm. "As your betrothed, I must object."

She pointedly removed his hand. "You are not my betrothed, Will. And even if you were, Keifer is my friend and I will speak to him. Privately."

Keifer's emotions went from anxious to anger to a stifled chuckle in the course of this exchange. Perhaps she hadn't changed so much after all—although she was more diplomatic than she'd been as a child.

"As you wish, my lady." Will's scowl was anything but conciliatory, but Keifer didn't care. Will was turning away and Nola was here, and they would talk at last.

Twelve

Nola had been glad when Keifer found her in the courtyard and asked for a private word. The way Will had hovered nearby all day wore thin, and she was especially relieved when Keifer made it clear that Will wasn't welcome.

Now she would have a chance to find out why Keifer had acted so odd, whether he had changed over these past four years into a stranger. But no matter what he said or did, she would not mention that he no longer wore her favor. A grown man should not be taken to task for putting aside the childish gesture.

Keifer allowed her to enter the empty church first and closed the door behind them. Again she noticed the graceful way he moved, as if perfectly at ease in his body. His shoulders were broad and she'd felt strength in his arm when she placed her hand on it. He wore dark trews and a white sark. A surcoat emblazoned with Sir Bryan's coat of arms proclaimed Keifer as Sir Bryan's man.

She knew she was staring, but Keifer did the same. Someone had to start the conversation. "Do you plan to remain in Sir Bryan's retinue?"

"Aye. Although I'll go home to Innishewan eventually, I will be assigned to him if we muster for a battle."

There was little warmth in his eyes and he seemed restrained. What had happened to the camaraderie they'd always shared? "You have changed," she blurted.

His gaze flicked up and down her person. "And so have you, wild one." His voice softened, and a hint of a smile graced his face.

She blushed. "Four years makes a difference. In both of us."

He didn't say anything.

"Why did you bring me in here?"

He seemed taken aback. "I wanted to thank you for bringing the ring. I thought we . . . perhaps it was a foolish idea. Yesterday . . ." he huffed out a breath.

"Yesterday what?" Why were they having so much trouble talking to each other?

Keifer's expression darkened. "Are you betrothed to Will Macpherson or not?"

"No!"

He paced away and back. "He seems to think the announcement will be made any day."

She tipped her head to one side and grinned. "Are you jealous, Keifer Macnab?"

He stopped in front of her and straightened to his full height. "Of course not. I'm simply . . . I simply want to keep my promise, *the one we made to each other.* Or did you forget?"

He was angry. Just as he'd been angry yesterday! "I thought *you* had forgotten. I haven't given my heart away, Keifer."

Was that relief on his face?

"Then you don't love Will?"

"No, I don't. I care for him, but I have not decided to marry him or anyone else."

Keifer's expression softened, but this was not the same rebellious boy who'd left Moy. "No wonder he didn't want to let you out of his sight."

She smiled and walked to the window to look out. She heard him move behind her and turned to see that he'd pulled out a bench for them to sit on. Nola took the seat he offered, though she felt much too restless to remain seated for long.

She waited for Keifer to speak, afraid that if she spoke first, she would blurt out her feelings for him and send him fleeing. But she couldn't wait for him. "I am so glad to see you again. I was afraid yesterday—"

"So was I. I thought our friendship hadn't survived the separation." He sat down next to her, careful to maintain a proper distance. "Just look at you, Nola. You've grown up. I'm surprised someone other than Will hasn't swept you away from Moy."

"I've been waiting for you."

His face clouded.

"What? Don't tell me you have given your heart elsewhere."

"No, of course not. I don't intend to marry. You know that."

With a dramatic sigh she said, "I thought you might have changed your mind."

"Looking at you is enough to make me consider it."

She grinned. She would not give up hope. "Perhaps if we were to spend time together, I could change it for you." A lady should not be so bold, but too much was at stake to be timid.

But her resolve was nearly shattered with his next words.

"I should like to spend time with you, Nola. But I am leaving in two days to accompany the Earl of Moray to Paris for the treaty negotiations."

"Leaving? For Paris!"

"Aye. I will be gone several months. And after that I must spend a year or more competing in tournaments to earn some coin. Innishewan isn't a rich holding."

He would leave and she would not see him for a year or longer! Will and her father would never agree to delaying a marriage that long. Something must be done. "Take me with you to Paris."

He stared at her as if she'd grown an extra nose. "Take you with me?" He shook his head. "Nola, how will it look if I ask to take a woman who isn't my wife?"

"Ask my da for permission. If he says yes, then no one can object to you escorting your foster sister." When he remained silent, she furthered her argument. "You know I've always wanted to see Paris. And you promised me an adventure."

His expression softened. Did he remember how many times Nola had told him of her dream of seeing the world before she settled down? He remained adamant, though he gentled his voice. "I'm not going on some great adventure, Nola. I'm going to Paris on the king's business. There won't be a lot of time for pleasure."

"Aye, you get your dream and I'll not get mine. I just want to see the sights my mother has told me about."

Patiently he explained again. "I'll have duties to perform, Nola. This is a not pleasure trip. I won't be able to spend my time defending the honor of a beautiful young woman."

She grinned. "You think I'm pretty."

"Don't change the subject. You know I do."

"Please take me with you, Keifer."

"Why aren't you pestering Will to take you there?"

"I did ask him once. He sees no reason to do such a thing. And for all the saints, why would you want me to go to such a romantic . . . Why are you being so difficult, Keifer Macnab?" Nola asked.

Keifer crossed his arms. "'Tis you who is being difficult. You can't go with me. Your father will never allow it."

"This may be the only chance I ever have to see Paris. And you promised to give me an adventure."

"So I did. But such an adventure would be more proper if we were married."

Nola bit her lip to keep from saying the obvious. Let him suggest it.

Keifer gave her a rueful stare. "You have changed. I fully expected you to suggest we marry before the day was up."

She laughed. "I almost did. But we should have my father's permission first, don't you think?"

"You can't come with me to Paris, but I will ask my mother to invite you to Innishewan when I return. We will have our time to become reacquainted, I promise. Just promise me you won't marry Will while I'm gone."

"I must make promises and keep them, but you don't?"

"We will have our time together, Nola. Then, if we decide to marry—should I decide to reconsider my decision not to marry—I will take you to Paris."

"If we marry I'll get to go to Paris? Call a priest, I'm ready today!"

He laughed, as she had meant him to. "Nola. Be reasonable."

If they were still children, she would push and wheedle until she got her way. However, this was not a boy but a man with responsibilities. Nola sensed that he spoke from conviction, and certainly not because he didn't want to take her. He truly believed he could not do so. She sighed, admitting a temporary defeat of her plans. At least he was speaking of marriage and her in the same sentence. That was progress. "I'm going to hold you to your promises, Keifer Macnab."

"That's *Sir* Keifer," he teased.

She gave a wan smile. "When do you leave?"

"Day after tomorrow." He blushed and looked away, clearly embarrassed by something.

"What? Why do you turn from me?"

His shoulders rose and sank with a deep breath, and when he looked at her again, she drew her own breath sharply. She was not a child anymore, and she recognized a man's desire in his eyes. He wanted her. Whether he knew the truth of it or not, she did.

She smiled, remembering the kiss they'd shared when they had parted at Homelea years past. She wanted his kiss. Wanted to see if there was any hope of marrying her best friend. "Perhaps you should kiss me."

"Aye. Perhaps I should." He hesitated, then accepted her dare. He held her arms, pulled her to him.

The kiss was every bit as sweet and as moving as the one they had shared four years ago. And his kiss told her that what she'd seen in his eyes a moment ago was real, told her what she needed to know about the feelings he tried to hide. He might fool himself that he didn't love her, but she wasn't fooled in the least.

As their lips parted and his hands fell away from her arms, she made up her mind.

She was going to Paris, whether he liked it or not!

KEIFER AND OWYN traveled with Sir Thomas Randolph to Edinburgh, where they assisted the earl in preparation for the voyage to Paris.

Just after midnight on the third day after his departure from Homelea and Nola, Keifer stood at the rail on the ship's stern and watched as the dark outline of Scotland's coast disappeared into the inky night. High thin clouds hid all but the brightest stars, and a half moon glowed through the hazy veil.

Salt air ruffled his clothing and soughed through the sails overhead as lanyards clanked against the mast. *He was sailing to Paris!* He had never dreamed his duties might take him away from Scotland.

His stomach knotted as it always did with farewells and new places. How many times had he left familiar surroundings and loved ones in his short life? But the gentle rise and fall of the deck soothed him. All that was missing was Nola.

Disappointment speared through him. It might be months before he saw her again. It shouldn't matter. But after their kiss, he knew that seeing her again mattered a great deal.

KEIFER SLEPT SOUNDLY despite the strangeness of his surroundings. He awoke refreshed in the morning, refreshed and hungry. The smell of food wafted under the door of the tiny stateroom he shared with Owyn.

Keifer stood and yanked the covers off Owyn. "Let's find the source of that delicious aroma."

Owyn grumbled at the rude awakening. "Couldn't ye warn a man before ye . . ." He lifted his head and sniffed, then grabbed his clothes. "One of the mates showed me the dining area last night."

They donned their clothes quickly and Keifer followed his squire to the small area that served as a dining room. It was empty except for a red-haired woman. For a moment, Keifer thought she looked like Nola. He shook his head. His thoughts last night had led to dreams of her, and now he saw Nola where she couldn't be.

It was going to be a very long voyage and sojourn in Paris if he couldn't get her off his mind any better than this. But when the red-haired woman turned to greet them, Keifer felt as if he'd been hit in the chest with a caber pole.

"Nola?" Shock turned to anger as he realized what his impetuous foster sister had done.

Stowaway!

"By the saints, Nola! What have you done now?"

She stared at him as if *he* were the one who had lost his mind.

"Your father will have my head!"

"Why would my father be angry?"

165

Keifer groaned. "Surely you didn't confide your plan to stow away aboard this ship?"

"Stow away?" She looked helplessly at Owyn, who shrugged. Realization came over her features. "Did Sir Thomas not tell you?"

"Tell me what?"

Nola peered behind him.

Keifer turned and saw the earl and his wife. Now it would all come down on him for sure. This prank of Nola's would have consequences as serious as her near drowning years ago.

"Good morrow, Lady Randolph," Nola said.

The lady looked at Keifer and Owyn, then at Nola. "Good morrow, Nola, gentlemen."

When had Nola met the earl and his wife? And why wasn't Lady Randolph surprised to see Nola this morning? "You two have met," he said, feeling decidedly half-witted.

Now Sir Thomas smiled, as did his wife. "We have indeed. While you and Owyn were at the docks yesterday, Nola and her father paid us a visit. I believe that in the hurry to finish preparations, I may not have mentioned that Lady Nola has agreed to be my wife's companion during our stay in Paris."

Nola laid her hand on Keifer's arm. "You are surprised. I'm sorry. I thought you knew." She chuckled. "You thought I was a stowaway."

Everyone had a good laugh at Keifer's expense. Though it was churlish of him, he wasn't quite amused. "Your father agreed to this?"

"Aye. It's perfect, Keifer. I will get the adventure I've always wanted." But her expression showed less enthusiasm than her words were meant to portray.

"And in return your father gets . . . what?"

Nola glanced at the others who were standing there, clearly entranced with this conversation.

"Excuse us, please." Without waiting for a reply, Keifer took

Nola's elbow and guided her to the other end of the small room.

"What have you promised your father?"

With a bright but obviously false smile, Nola replied, "I have promised to marry when I return."

"Will?" he choked out, louder than he meant to.

She only shrugged. "Da did not specify to whom."

A quick glance over his shoulder at the others convinced him to lower his voice. "But Will is waiting for your return."

She stared at the low ceiling, evidently finding the knotholes in the wood quite interesting.

"Nola, tell me all of it. I am relieved your father gave you permission to go to Paris. But I want to know how you convinced Will to let you out of his sight. Particularly aboard a ship I'm on."

Now she stared at her hands, and he knew he wasn't going to like whatever she had to say.

"Will thinks I am staying in Edinburgh with Lady Randolph."

She said it so quietly he almost didn't hear her. "You lied to him?"

Now she looked at him and carefully said, "He made an *assumption* and I didn't *correct* him."

Keifer shook his head. "Will and I are not the best of friends, but I would not see any man treated so."

She stuck her hands on her hips. "Will is *not* my betrothed. He has no say over me. I am here with Da's permission, nay, his blessing, Keifer Macnab. And you and Will are not going to ruin this opportunity for me." With that she shoved past him and sat down to finish her meal.

She'd certainly put Keifer in his place. Hunger and anger warred in him, and hunger won out. He took a seat by Owyn—as far from Nola as possible—and broke his fast.

Owyn raised his eyebrows in question.

Keifer shook his head, unsure whether to laugh at her audacity or bellow in rage. Typical of his feelings ever since Nola had arrived for his knighting ceremony, ever since he had met her, really. And his confusion had only worsened since their kiss. Their *good-bye* kiss.

He stole a glance at Nola where she sat with the Randolphs. He would do his best to stay angry at her, keep his distance. After all, he was a soldier with duties to perform. He couldn't be distracted by—

Then he saw her laugh, head thrown back and eyes dancing, and his anger dissipated as quickly as it had come. It had always been so with her.

Hadn't he prayed to be shown God's will? Now by some miracle God had granted them time together. Somehow, despite the demands of his work, Keifer would renew his friendship with Nola, see if there was something more between them that might tempt him toward Randolph's suggestion of reconsidering marriage. Only a fool would waste springtime in Paris with a beautiful woman.

And Keifer was no fool.

THIRTEEN

AFTER BREAKING THEIR FAST, Nola and Lady Randolph retired to the cramped stateroom they would share for the voyage. Sir Thomas had graciously agreed to sleep with the other men when no other cabin had been available at the last minute for Nola.

Lady Randolph smoothed the covers on the bed and sat down.

Nola sat beside her. "Your husband was kind to give up your company and his bed, my lady."

"You may call me Isobel in private, Nola. And Thomas is glad that I will have an agreeable companion. My sister had planned to come with us, but she discovered she was with child. This will be their first, and she and her husband thought it best not to risk the journey."

"I'm sorry for her but . . . I hope I will make a good companion."

"I'm sure you will. You have already proved quite interesting." She smiled broadly. "So, who is Will?"

"A neighbor and friend who thinks we should marry."

"And what of you? Do you want to marry?"

What could she say? "Not really."

Isobel stood and went to one of the three trunks that held her clothing. "My husband says you grew up with Sir Keifer."

"Aye. He came to live with us when I was about six years old and he was ten."

"From the way you look at him, I would guess 'tis him you prefer to wed," she said quietly. She removed a gown from the trunk and shook out the wrinkles before hanging it on a peg on the wall.

"I don't know if he'll have me. He swore when we were young that he never wanted to marry. But I thought, maybe, just maybe, if we had some time together now that we are grown, he might change his mind."

Isobel straightened, another gown in hand. "I suspect he is half-way there, Nola."

Nola couldn't help but grin. She'd thought as much after what he had said, after their kiss, but was glad to hear it confirmed by the older woman. "You really think so?"

"Aye. Now, let's hang up your dresses and you can tell me all about your adventures with handsome young Keifer."

Never one to disappoint, Nola told Lady Randolph all about the mishap in the creek when she had tried to save a lamb that didn't need saving. Lady Randolph seemed not to tire of hearing about Nola's childhood, so Nola regaled her with other stories. At long last, Nola returned to her task of removing her other dress from the small bag and hanging it on a peg. She would be glad to change out of the dress she'd worn for traveling and lamented that she had no other clothes to wear.

Lady Randolph said, "Is that all you brought with you?"

"Aye. I wasn't planning on such a trip when I left home, and there wasn't time to shop in Edinburgh. I'm going to be woefully under-dressed to stay in a royal palace."

Lady Randolph gazed at the three trunks of clothing she had brought with her. "Yes, you are. We will have to find material to make new gowns for you once we reach Paris."

"Da gave me money—will you help me choose something flatter-ing?"

"I will be delighted to help you find the perfect gown to capture your knight's heart. I will even help you sew."

"I can't ask you to do that."

"You didn't ask. I offered."

They smiled at each other and Nola sensed a mutual admiration forming. "I can hardly wait to see Paris. I hope you are a quick seamstress!"

THE BOAT DOCKED IN CALAIS late in the afternoon. Nola heard Sir Thomas say he was anxious to cover the 130 or so miles to Paris as quickly as possible. Owyn went with the earl to rent a coach and horses, and Keifer was given the duty of escorting the women.

After more than a week of the ship's rocking motion, Nola felt unsteady when she tried to walk across the dock. She glanced back at Keifer, who gallantly escorted the older woman.

Nola walked to shore unassisted and just a little peeved at Keifer. He had barely spoken to her for most of the voyage. It was as if every time he looked at her, he couldn't decide whether to kiss her or throttle her, so instead he turned away. Yet Nola found it difficult to be angry. She was in France! And she was tired of worrying over Keifer.

While their belongings were unloaded from the boat, Keifer escorted Lady Randolph and Nola to an inn. As she ate her meal, Nola talked excitedly with Lady Randolph, glad to have someone to share this adventure. Someone other than Keifer, who stood nearby, scowling. Keifer couldn't seem to make up his mind whether to be glad or not that Nola was with them. Nola would give him time—she could hardly believe she was here herself.

"Keifer," Lady Randolph said. "Why don't you join us?"

"I have eaten, my lady."

She indicated the open seat next to Nola. "Then sit with us, won't you?"

THE PROMISE OF PEACE

"Nay. I have orders." He smiled.

Nola thought he was being stubborn and tried to have him change his mind. "But surely—"

"I am not here to entertain but to protect you, Nola."

Nola was about to retort when Lady Randolph said, "My husband says we have reason to be vigilant, Nola, so don't take Keifer to task for doing his duty."

Chagrined, Nola whispered, "He isn't going to be much fun, is he?"

"No doubt there will be moments when he can let down his guard. You must be patient." The lady's air of importance let Nola understand that Keifer's role was serious. They might be in some danger in this foreign land. Perhaps that helped explain Keifer's odd manner toward her—she was adding to his responsibilities, the first official responsibilities of his career.

When the meal was finished, they went into the tavern's court-yard and the ladies climbed aboard the carriage that would take them to Paris. Although Sir Thomas joined them in the carriage, Keifer, Owyn, and the others rode on horseback. They were armed for pro-tection from bandits.

Nola said to Sir Thomas, "You would make better time without us, wouldn't you?"

"Aye. I would have ridden through the night. But in deference to your company, we will stop each evening." He smiled indulgently at his wife. "But 'tis well worth the inconvenience to have the company of such lovely ladies."

Lady Randolph smiled at her husband, and Nola wondered what it would be like to be married. She would certainly find out when she returned home. She half expected her father to be waiting at the dock with a priest. The thought made her smile. But then she realized that Will would be standing next to the priest. She drew a deep breath. She'd made a bargain and she would honor it. She would indeed marry upon her return to Scotland. She just hoped the groom would be Keifer.

They stopped a few hours later for the evening meal and to take rooms for the night at an inn. Sir Thomas exited the coach first, and Nola heard him greet someone. He turned to hand down Lady Randolph and Nola. As Nola and the lady found their footing, they were joined by Keifer and Owyn, who had dismounted. Nola saw that their hands rested on the hilts of their swords.

Lady Randolph said, "Richard! How delightful! We hoped to see you at court—what brings you so far from your king?"

Nola stared at the tall courtier as he bent over Lady Randolph's hand. His close-cropped, dark hair and swarthy skin contrasted with the finely drawn features of his face. Even in the gathering dusk she thought him quite handsome.

He straightened, and though he answered the lady's question, he addressed Sir Thomas. "King Charles sent me with a contingent of men to safeguard you and your party."

Sir Thomas raised an eyebrow. "I brought sufficient guards with me. Are we in need of the king's protection as well?"

"A few more men to protect such lovely ladies would not be remiss, *n'est-ce pas?*" The man named Richard bent closer. "We believe Edward of England has spies in France. He doesn't want to see the treaty succeed."

The man cocked his head to one side in a charming gesture that had Nola smiling.

He turned and asked Sir Thomas, "And who, pray tell, is this lovely lady?"

Lord Randolph said, "Lady Nola Mackintosh, may I present Richard de Fleury."

Nola felt herself blush as the man took her hand and kissed her fingers.

"It will be my pleasure to escort you and Lady Randolph." The man grinned at her and she saw the glow of male interest in his dark, sparkling eyes. "Delighted, mademoiselle."

She lowered her eyelids, not wanting to appear too forward. But already her journey showed promise of the excitement she'd hoped for.

She looked to see where Keifer stood, his expression impassive until their gazes met. For a brief moment Keifer allowed his feelings to show, and Nola's heart beat with joy. Another woman might have used Richard to make Keifer jealous. But that was a hurtful emotion, the weapon of a child.

Nola had put her childhood aside when she made the bargain with her father. She was a woman in love with a man who still thought of her as a child, a man unconvinced he should marry. She only had a few weeks to make him see her differently—she would not waste the time on a useless emotion such as jealousy.

THE CLOSER THEY CAME TO PARIS, the more people and carts filled the road. The countryside stirred with the promise of spring, and the early wildflowers were in bloom. They stopped each midday for a meal and to change the horses. Late on the third day they entered the city.

The heart of Paris and the seat of the French government lay on the Ile de la Cité, a large island in the middle of the Seine River. As they crossed a stone bridge, Nola stared out of the carriage window at the majestic towers of Notre Dame Cathedral. She could hardly wait to worship there on Sunday morning.

When the carriage came to a halt in the cobbled courtyard, Nola and her companions were surrounded by squires and stable boys who took charge of the horses and handed the ladies from the coach. Nola accepted the small satchel that contained the few belongings she had brought with her.

Richard escorted them to the guest quarters. Nola was delighted to have a room of her own. She put away her clothes and dismissed the maid who had been assigned to her. Nola went to the window and opened the shutter. Her room overlooked the Sainte-Chapelle with its soaring pinnacles and gilded roof.

Nola's mother had told her of the chapel built as a reliquary for the precious Crown of Thorns, which the French king had bought from the Emperor of Byzantium for 130,000 livres. An incredible extravagance, as the chapel itself had only cost 40,000 livres to build!

Anxious to see the holy relic as well as the inside of the chapel, she crossed the room and opened the door. As her foot passed over the threshold, a hand grabbed her arm and she shrieked.

"Calm down, Nola. 'Tis only me," Keifer commanded as he let go of her arm.

"What are you doing, standing outside my door?"

"You must not go about unescorted." His smile softened the sternness of his voice.

She had been about to do just that. "Well then, come, you can escort me to the Sainte-Chapelle. It's just—"

"I know where it is, but I've been instructed to take you to Sir Thomas before you begin exploring. So come with me."

They walked down the ornately decorated hallway. The walls were marble inlaid with Irish oak. The wood, highly desired in royal palaces, repelled spiders and thus prevented spider webs from forming in the high, dark recesses.

Keifer knocked at a sturdy wooden door, and they were admitted to the Randolphs' chamber. Sir Thomas and his wife sat at a small table in a chamber twice the size of Nola's. This room was a sitting room with comfortable couches and chairs. An escritoire sat against one wall next to a door that must lead to the sleeping chamber.

Sir Thomas indicated that Nola and Keifer should sit down. When they were settled, he said, "Nola, although my wife will no doubt wish to see the city, she and I have official duties and obligations that will limit her availability. You are free to come and go so long as you promise me one thing."

"Aye, my laird?"

"You will not leave the palace grounds without Keifer or Richard to accompany you."

She looked at Keifer and nodded her acceptance.

"I will have your word, Nola."

"I promise, my laird."

"Good. I don't wish to alarm you, but there are those who would harm our cause."

"This treaty is important, isn't it?" she asked.

"Aye, it is. I'm glad you understand."

Lady Randolph said, "As we discussed, I have arranged for a seamstress to fit you for new gowns, Nola. I will expect you here in our room first thing tomorrow morning."

"As you wish."

Nola and Keifer left the chamber and started back to Nola's room. She looked down at the dress she'd worn since leaving Edinburgh and knew that much as she wanted to explore Paris, she didn't want to do so in soiled and wrinkled clothes.

She stopped at her door.

Keifer looked surprised. "I thought you were anxious to see the chapel."

"I will wait until I have some proper clothes," she said.

"I think that is wise, Nola. That dress looks, well, it doesn't do justice to the daughter of a Scottish earl." He grinned and she felt better. She was in Paris. With Keifer. All was well with her world.

Fourteen

Nola spent the next two days being fitted for gowns and helping to sew them. She saw little of Keifer or Richard and spent much of her time with Lady Randolph. They were sitting alone in the lady's sitting room, as Sir Thomas had left for his business with the king.

Nola pricked her finger with the needle and quickly stuck the offended digit in her mouth to keep from bleeding on the material. She looked up to find Lady Randolph watching her. "I'm trying to sew too fast," Nola said with a grin.

"That you are, but I can understand your desire to see the city. And to spend time with Keifer."

Nola was more anxious for that than she wanted to let on. She changed the subject. "When will you meet with the queen?" Nola asked.

"The queen is not ready to receive many visitors so soon after giving birth, so I will meet her in a week or so. You may be invited as well."

Nola nodded. "I will look forward to it. My mother will be quite excited to know I met with the queen, as she is a cousin of Jeanne of Evreux."

"Your mother is cousin to the queen of France? Then I shall insist that you come with me when the time comes. Are you nearly done with that dress?"

"Aye. Just a bit more on the hem."

"Good. As soon as you are finished, go and change and we will get out of these rooms this afternoon."

Nola smiled. The rooms were lovely, but so was the weather, and she hated staying indoors. With a sigh of relief she tied off her thread and stood up, holding the gown in front of her.

"That color will look splendid on you, child. Now hurry and get dressed. I'll send for our escorts."

In her room Nola changed into the new dress with the help of her lady's maid, a luxury she wasn't used to. At Moy, Nola often left her hair undressed or covered it with a simple scarf. But here at court she would have to wear a more elaborate head covering.

As the maid pinned the wimple fast, Nola tried not to dislike the lack of freedom imposed by the material that now closely framed her face. A quick stab of homesickness reminded her of her family, and she hoped they were well. By now Will must know the truth, and she hoped he understood why she had to go. If she and Keifer should come to an agreement, Nola felt obligated to tell Will the news in person.

Shrugging off the homesickness and reminder of Will, Nola admired the green linen dress. Draped across the bodice in flattened folds, the material was belted just under her breasts. From there it fell in soft folds straight to the floor. A removable cape of heavier material in a contrasting green was fastened at her shoulders.

Though the material lacked the variegated colors of her usual woolen plaid, this linen was well suited to the French fashion.

Keifer and Richard were to meet her at Lady Randolph's room, so with a final adjustment of her wimple—and a wish that she could leave it behind—Nola left her chamber and walked down the hall. A light draft caused her to be glad for the cape, and she pulled it close.

When she entered the chamber, Keifer and Richard were in conversation with Sir Thomas.

Lady Randolph greeted her. "As soon as our escorts are ready we can leave."

Nola hoped they would hurry. Since she didn't need an escort for the palace grounds, Nola had decided to forgo the Sainte-Chapelle in favor of sights outside the castle walls. She planned to visit the chapel sometime when the men were not available to escort her.

Keifer and Richard joined them. Nola was glad when Keifer strode to her side and offered her his arm "Where is Owyn today?" she asked as they walked out of the castle and into a beautiful spring day.

"Sir Thomas has need of him. He may join us another time."

"I hope he will. I enjoy his company."

"I'm sure the feeling is mutual."

Soon they were walking down a paved street wide enough to accommodate two carts or carriages. In the distance rose the towers of Notre Dame Cathedral. Though construction of the great church had begun one hundred and fifty years prior, porches and chapels were still being added.

They spent an hour browsing through nearly two dozen booksellers in their stalls near Notre Dame, then walked along the narrower secondary streets where the various tradesmen had their shops. Stopping at the stall of a soap maker, Nola purchased lavender-fragranced soap for her mother. Lady Randolph made similar purchases for her family.

Richard walked them to the west side of the Island and pointed to a smaller island where the springtime green of hayfields mixed with budding fruit trees. "That is the Ile de Juifs, where Jacques de Molay, the Grand Master of the Templar Knights, was burned at the stake some years back."

Nola shuddered. "How could something so awful happen on such a pastoral spot?"

Keifer laid his hand over hers where it lay on his arm. He stared at the island as if deep in thought. "'Tis said that he lifted his eyes to the steeples of Notre Dame and professed his faith even as the flames consumed him."

Nola turned to him. "Did you learn of that from Ceallach?"

He nodded.

"Who is this Ceallach?" Richard inquired.

Keifer carefully said, "An acquaintance that was here at the time."

Nola raised her eyebrows and Keifer shook his head. She said nothing, realizing that Keifer sought to protect the former Templar from those who might seek him out to claim the ransom on his head. They strolled on, stopping at an overlook where Nola gazed out at the city with its sharply indented skyline, created by roofs of differing heights. Elegant dormers of white stone with blue roofs were topped with gilded weathervanes on every peak.

"What a charming and lovely place," she said. "My mother was here as a child and tried to describe it, but I'm afraid she failed." Nola smiled at Richard. "Is Paris your home?"

"I was born here, *oui*, but home is now wherever my king sends me."

WHILE NOLA AND LADY RANDOLPH perused the various shops, Keifer kept watch, as did Richard. The older man was attentive to their charges but remained alert to their surroundings.

At first Keifer hadn't been sure there truly was a threat. He thought Richard made it up as a means of ensuring time with Nola. But the man's actions spoke of his attention to duty above pleasure, and Keifer was glad for his assistance.

He and Richard had changed partners at the soap trader's booth, and Lady Randolph seemed content to walk quietly beside him.

Keifer let his thoughts return to that moment overlooking the Ile de Juifs, and the reminder of Ceallach and home. Paris was a fine city. The food, though strange, was tasty. Yet Keifer longed for the lochs and glens of his homeland. But it was years away, after he earned a good sum in tournaments and through turns such as this for the king. Then he would have enough money . . . With surprise he realized he looked forward to returning to Innishewan and settling down to his role as laird.

Even more surprising, he found himself imagining Nola at Innishewan, overseeing the castle folk and . . . playing with his children? Keifer shook his head, then glanced to where Nola and Richard stood examining some Flemish cloth. Nola ran her hands under the material, holding it to the light to see the weave, and smiling at Richard's comment.

A wimple covered Nola's glorious and untamable hair and he thought it a pity. Nola looked up, and their gazes held briefly. She grinned, and Keifer's heart stuttered. Aye, the minx would make a wonderful wife and mother. 'Twas a shame Keifer didn't have room for either in his life. Or did he?

THE SCOTS HAD RECEIVED AN INVITATION to a state dinner given in their honor that evening in the Grand Palace. Richard and Keifer discussed security concerns as the women continued to shop.

"After the dinner there will be a performance by a troupe of mummers," Richard said.

"Mimes wearing masks. How will we know they are friend and not foe?"

"We won't." Richard scanned the crowd. Apparently satisfied the women were safe, he said, "There could be several score of them but they, like us, will not be allowed to take weapons into the chamber with the king."

"Will the costumes be checked for concealed swords?"

"Aye. They have performed for the king before and will want to continue to do so in the future. I don't think there will be a disruption, but we must be on our guard, nonetheless."

They continued to follow the ladies and eventually, finally, the women tired of shopping. Keifer and Richard escorted them back to their quarters.

Several hours later, dressed in his best plaid, Keifer knocked at Nola's door. He would be her escort tonight while Richard and Owyn guarded the earl and his wife. The door opened and Keifer could only stare. Despite the wimple that covered her hair, Nola was lovely in a dress that fully complemented her coloring.

"You are a sight, Nola Mackintosh."

"A good sight?" she teased.

"Aye. A beautiful Scottish lass. I'll be busy fending off your many suitors tonight, I can see already."

She laughed and closed the door. He offered his arm, and they walked to the great salon where the festivities were to be held. They entered the salon through a high-arched door that echoed the arching of the ceiling. The walls were lined with statues of the French kings, past and present.

Keifer and Nola walked to the west end of the hall, toward the huge black table made of nine slabs of Alsatian marble. Keifer led Nola up the three steps to the dais and they were seated next to Sir Randolph and Lady Isobel.

Keifer almost forgot to be watchful, he was so entranced by his surroundings and the woman beside him. After surveying the crowded room, he turned to Nola.

"Why are you so quiet?"

He saw her swallow. "I am almost afraid to breathe for fear this dream will end before I am ready."

"I know how you feel. The opulence is a bit overwhelming."

They made small talk with each other and the others nearby. When the meal was finished, servants cleared the table and then urged those seated there to stand and move their chairs back several feet.

Nola turned to Richard. "Why is this necessary?"

He only smiled and said, "You will see, mademoiselle."

Trumpets announced the arrival of the performers and Keifer heard Nola gasp when the troupe, nearly one hundred of them, rode into the salon on horses. They dismounted and bowed to King Charles, and as pages led the animals back out of the room, the mummers leaped onto the table!

Keifer reached for the sword he wasn't wearing before he realized this was part of the act, that they meant to use the table as their stage. He laughed nervously and looked at Richard, who simply nodded. Keifer relaxed and watched as the actors performed an elaborate sword fight with wooden swords.

There was singing and music to accompany the fight, and a man dressed as a woman swooned when the hero was killed. But the hero was miraculously brought back to life with a magic potion, and with great celebration the entire group paraded around the salon before bowing once more to the king and taking their leave.

Keifer had never seen anything like it. It was hard to remember his duties as the crowd applauded and cheered and the main characters came back for a second bow. He looked at Nola and her face glowed with delight. Suddenly he was glad she'd been daring enough to find a way to join him in France.

The musicians began tuning up for the dancing to follow, and Richard came to stand by Keifer. "We should take turns dancing, so one of us is near Sir Thomas at all times."

Keifer nodded in agreement.

Richard smiled shrewdly. "And which of us shall have the first dance with the lovely Nola?"

Keifer didn't back down. "I believe that honor will be mine, monsieur."

Throughout the rest of the evening Nola danced with the two of them, as well as a number of other men who gathered around her. But after each dance she had her partner return her to Keifer's side, honoring him as . . . as a wife would do. What was she up to now?

Too soon the evening was over and he accompanied her to her chamber. She stood with her back to the wooden door, peering up at him beneath her lashes in a way that invited him to take liberties he shouldn't be thinking of taking.

"Ah, Nola. You are doing your very best to wear down my objections to marriage, aren't you?"

Her smile no longer hinted of childhood pranks and gray kittens and orphaned lambs. Now it spoke of the way of a woman with the man she loved. Could it be possible? Did she love him? He feared the answer; and though it would brand him as fainthearted, he dared not kiss her again to find out.

He bid her a hasty goodnight.

And did not see her delighted grin as she watched him run away from the inevitable.

SEVERAL BUSY DAYS WENT BY, and Keifer saw little of Nola. He heard from Owyn that she and Lady Randolph had received a flurry of visits from the French nobility, both male and female. So when the summons came to escort the two women to the open-air market, he was only too glad to do so.

He and Richard allowed the women to walk in front of them. Keifer couldn't take his eyes off Nola's gracefully swaying form.

"You would do well to see to her safety and admire her later," Richard chastised.

Keifer straightened. "I wasn't . . . You are right. I should pay more attention to our surroundings."

They were jostled in the crowded marketplace, and it was only prudent to be watchful. He scanned the crowd as they stopped at various stalls.

Basket filled with fresh bread and vegetables, Nola turned to the men. "Lady Randolph and I are ready to return to the palace."

Richard pointed and said, "Head that way."

They broke out of the crowd and walked toward the carriage where Owyn kept guard. As they drew near, Owyn shouted but Keifer couldn't make out what he said. Then Owyn pointed in agitation, and both Richard and Keifer reached for their swords at the same time.

Before he could get his weapon unsheathed, Richard was knocked to the ground from behind. Owyn ran toward them as a masked assailant grabbed Lady Randolph. Keifer, sword now drawn, attacked the man and broke his hold on the countess. He pushed her toward Owyn. But while Keifer continued the sword fight, a third man moved in toward Nola.

"Nola! Behind you!"

She whirled and ducked, but the man grabbed her sleeve. And in a move Keifer remembered well, she jammed her foot sideways down his shin. The man howled in pain and let her go.

With Nola in the thick of it, the odds were in their favor. But he wanted both women safely in the carriage. With a burst of strength, Keifer knocked the sword out of his assailant's hand, and the man backed up out of Keifer's reach.

Just for a minute Keifer allowed himself the distraction of seeing where Nola had gone. She was walking toward Richard, who was sitting up and looking dazed. Lady Randolph stood next to Owyn. Two of the men had run off, but the third now grabbed Nola's cloak and began to drag her away. She screamed and swung her arms, landing a fist in the man's eye. He let go and ran after his friends.

Evidently Nola's scream caught the attention of the gendarmes because several soon went in pursuit of the attackers. While Owyn helped Richard to his feet, Keifer hurried the women into the carriage. When all were aboard, he ordered the driver to return them to the palace.

In the safety of the carriage, Keifer asked, "Are you all right, Lady Randolph?"

"I'm fine, but Richard is bleeding."

Indeed, a trickle of blood ran from his temple, and he looked ill. Nola used the hem of her cloak to dab the blood. Keifer could see that her hand shook. He feared if he held his hands out they would shake as well.

"It's a small cut, Richard. You will have only a tiny scar with which to impress the ladies, I'm afraid." Nola smiled, and Richard smiled back.

When had the child Keifer had known become a woman of such beguiling looks and words? As Keifer relived those moments when the would-be robber or kidnapper had held fast to Nola, he could feel more than his hands shaking.

He could have lost her!

For the first time, he found himself hoping the treaty negotiations would conclude quickly. He'd been enjoying this time with Nola in this beautiful and exotic city. But now he just wanted to take her home to Scotland. Home. To Innishewan.

They arrived safely at the palace, and in the midst of answering the earl's questions, Keifer lost sight of Nola. No doubt she was seeing Lady Randolph to her chamber.

When Keifer and Owyn had satisfied the earl's inquiry, Owyn left to care for their weapons and Keifer made his way to Nola's chamber. He needed to see for himself that she was all right.

NOLA ANSWERED the knock on her chamber door, and to her relief, Keifer stood there.

"Nola, I've come to tell you that the earl has decided that you and his wife must remain on the palace grounds until we leave Paris."

She nodded slowly. "I don't think I want another episode like that to ruin my time here."

"And I would like to ask a boon of you."

Her heart tripped faster. "And what would that boon be?"

"That you have an escort even here in the palace."

She smiled. "I will grant your boon if you will grant mine."

His expression became wary. "What favor would you ask of me?"

"Only that you be my guardian."

Now he smiled, that wonderful smile she loved, would never grow tired of. "As you wish, my lady."

"Are you free at the moment?"

"Aye."

"Then let me get my shawl and you can show me the royal orchard. I think a soothing walk would shake off my confounded trembling. Such excitement for the day!"

She went back into her room and grabbed up her favorite shawl, woven from the sheep at Moy. When Nola closed the door, Keifer offered his arm and she rested her hand on his muscled forearm.

They spoke of mundane things, but Nola's heart was too full to care. The orchard trees were in bloom and the fragrance filled the air like a blessing as they strolled down the grassy aisles. Bees buzzed as they flitted among the trees collecting pollen.

"It is hard to believe in this peaceful setting that we nearly, that those men . . ." She stopped and Keifer reached for her, pulling her into the safety of his strong arms.

He put his lips near her ear. "Those men didn't have a chance with my highland lassie fighting them."

She drew back, ready to dispute with him if he mocked her. But his eyes held no rebuke, only tenderness. The boy she'd known had become a warrior, a man who fought to protect those he loved.

"You were quite ferocious in your defense, Sir Keifer."

"Some things are worth fighting for." He bent down and kissed her, and she put her arms around his neck.

And there in the blossom-filled orchard, Nola was sure of her heart, sure that she was in love with Keifer, always had been. Always would be. Should she tell him so or wait? She was sure he loved her, too, if he would just admit it. Probably best to wait.

FIFTEEN

Keifer pulled away from Nola and watched her face. Her eyes were closed and a smile played on her lips. A loose tendril of her hair caught his eye and he wrapped the silken strand about his finger.

With his other hand he tugged on the wimple. "Take this thing off," he murmured.

"Hmm? Why?"

"So I can see your hair."

She unfastened the ends and unwrapped the cloth from her head.

Keifer took it from her and let it fall to the ground. Then he stared at her beautiful fiery hair. Corkscrews sprang from the braids and he ran his hands over them. She closed her eyes again, and bless her, reached up and pulled out the pins. The long, curly ropes fell free to her waist.

He grasped a handful just as she opened her eyes and, looking over his shoulder, gasped at what she saw. Keifer dropped his hands from her hair. He spun, shoving her behind him and reaching for his sword in one swift motion.

Sword drawn, he faced the last person he expected to see. Will Macpherson. And behind him, Nola's father. Keifer wasn't sure if it was safe to sheathe the sword. Both men looked very, very angry. And both were armed, though they hadn't drawn their weapons.

Will clenched and unclenched his fists but didn't speak. The expression on his face said everything. The man loved Nola.

But so did Keifer. "Sir Adam. Will. What brings the two of you to Paris?"

Adam laid a restraining hand on Will's shoulder and stepped beside him. He jutted his chin out at Keifer and said, "Will insisted on coming after Nola. I thought it best if I came along. Looks to me like his fears for her welfare were well founded."

Nola pushed against Keifer's back and he moved out of her way. She stood next to him and he saw her hands were shaking. Was she angry or afraid? The sun blazed off Nola's bright, unbraided hair. An unmarried woman did not let down her hair for a man unless promises had been made and returned.

"Da. Will. Please don't be angry with Keifer."

"Quiet, Nola." Adam stared at Keifer. "I allowed my daughter to come here, knowing she would be under the supervision of a lady and protected by a man I've long trusted. But now that man has dared to touch you in a most intimate fashion, and dares to hold me at sword point! I'll be as angry as I please."

Keifer sheathed the sword, hoping to placate his foster father. "I can explain—"

"You will step aside and return my daughter to me. I'm taking Nola back to Moy to give Will time to decide if he will still marry her despite . . . her unchaste behavior."

Keifer looked at Nola's father and Will, afraid he understood them only too well. Anger welled in him that Adam could think that Keifer had dishonored Nola, had done more than gaze at her hair and kiss her. Keifer glanced at Nola, and if she'd been afraid earlier, now he saw her temper rising in the deep red flush of her skin.

Her eyes sparked with rage and Will wisely took a step backward. Chin thrust forward like her father's, arms crossed, Nola said, "I will not marry a man who believes the worst of me without so much as a thought to listening to what I have to say."

"Nola, be reasonable," Will said.

"Be reasonable? You have never listened to me, never taken my thoughts or feelings into account. Why must *I* be the reasonable one?"

Adam grabbed Nola's arm. "You will come with me." He turned to Keifer. "This is all your fault. You are no longer welcome at Moy."

The ties that bound them ran deep, and Adam's lack of trust cut to the quick. Keifer straightened and stepped between father and daughter, breaking Adam's hold on Nola. "You could at least hear what Nola has to say before banning me, before thinking the worst of your own daughter."

Keifer held tight to his temper, knowing that Adam had reason to be angry. Keifer never should have asked Nola to remove the wimple. The veiled accusation that he and Nola were lovers was understandable. But the refusal to hear her out was not.

He looked at Nola. Her hair, a tangle of red curls on the best of days, fell unrestrained down her back. She was his best friend, and she was a woman worth fighting for. Keifer knew that he would not allow Adam, or Will, to take her from him.

Keifer could not bear the thought of never seeing her again. And close on that thought came the realization that he would not let another man have her to wife. Not Will, not anyone.

To Keifer's relief, Adam backed off. "All right. I'll listen. Say your piece before I take my daughter home."

NOLA HAD SEEN AND HEARD ENOUGH. She refused to be bullied by her own father, and she would not marry Will Macpherson, even if it meant a lifetime as a spinster. Seeing him again, seeing the proprietary look in his eyes, convinced her of it. She was not a milch cow to be traded to seal some union! She certainly would not return to Moy with her father if he made good on his threat against Keifer. The thought of being forbidden to see Keifer again could not be borne.

With her gaze fastened on Keifer's face, she took a deep breath and spoke to her father. "We are betrothed."

Will gaped at her.

Her father said, "Betrothed? Without my permission?"

Keifer's mouth had fallen open at her pronouncement. As her words sank in, she thought she saw the beginnings of a grin on his face. If she was wrong, if she'd made him angry, he might say something foolish. Like the truth.

In the moments before he spoke, Nola's heart nearly burst with anxiety. Would he deny her?

Keifer studied her, then appeared to make up his mind. "My laird. Would you excuse us for a moment?"

"I'll not let Nola out of my sight."

Keifer regarded her again. "I believe I feel the same way, my laird." Her hopes rose.

"Now just a minute," Will blustered.

Keifer ignored Will and searched her face, his smile rueful. "'Twas a fine adventure, was it not?"

Nola's heart sank to her feet. All she could do was nod.

"I would hate to see it come to a bad end, wouldn't you?"

Tear-filled eyes were the only answer she could give him.

Keifer took her hand and faced her father. "What Nola meant to say is that we would like your permission to marry. And I need a moment with her."

Without asking for Adam's leave, Keifer walked Nola a few paces away. Nola threw a glance at her father and Will, who seemed as surprised as she at Keifer's statement.

Once again she had acted without thinking, and her impetuous words were forcing Keifer to do something he didn't want to do.

She'd known only too well that he didn't want to marry. "I'm so sorry, Keifer. I should not have said—"

"Hush." He kissed her, and it was everything she remembered, everything she wanted for the rest of her life. But she had ruined it.

They parted, and Keifer looked into her eyes without speaking. She thought she saw forgiveness in his gaze. Was it possible? His silence—she had to say something, anything. "I'm sor—"

"If you keep apologizing, I will have to keep kissing you and we will never finish this conversation." He smiled. "I like the idea of kissing you some more, but your father and Will are waiting none too patiently."

She saw Keifer swallow, as if reluctant to say whatever else was on his mind. If she had ruined their friendship, she would never forgive herself.

"I am tired of pretending that I don't care for you. I do care, Nola."

He cares. She breathed a sigh of relief. "I know you care." *But does he love me?* And was she brave enough to ask? No, she was not. But she, too, was tired of hiding her feelings. However, too much was at stake and she couldn't look at him, couldn't bear to see his reaction. So she stared at his chest and whispered, "I think I have loved you forever."

He placed his finger beneath her chin and raised her face. "I have loved you since you kicked me in the shins." He smiled again, and the tenderness she saw was what she had hoped for but had not expected to see. "But I fell in love with you in Paris."

"You did?"

"I did."

"Where exactly?"

He chuckled. "Let me think on that answer."

Nola heard her father clear his throat, but she paid him no mind. Only Keifer mattered. "I think we should marry, don't you?"

"Aye, sweet Nola. That we should. Will you marry me?"

She threw herself into his arms. "Aye! I want kisses and so much more, Keifer. Let us marry yet today and send Da back to Moy."

Keifer threw back his head and laughed. "Ah, Nola. Don't ever change."

They walked back to Nola's father, whose expression had softened somewhat.

Keifer said, "Your daughter has agreed to marry me."

"I see it didn't take much persuasion."

Keifer glared at Adam, clearly disliking his disrespect.

Sir Adam put up his hand. "No need to defend her honor. I suspect you'll marry her with or without my permission, so I may as well give you my blessing. Will?"

Nola looked at Will. He appeared to be genuinely disappointed. "I'm sorry, Will. I should have broken off with you before I left. I let you and Da assume I meant to return and marry you, and that was wrong. I ask for your forgiveness."

But Will did not answer her. He simply turned on his heel and strode away.

THE BELLS OF THE SAINTE-CHAPELLE RANG VESPERS as Nola, her father, Keifer, and Lady Randolph walked toward the abbey. Keifer looked up at the sky and its threat of rain as they walked across the courtyard toward the chapel. Nervously he glanced at Nola. Although she clutched her father's arm, she gave an impish smile to Keifer.

It would be all right. In those moments of decision, when her father and Will had threatened to take her from him, Keifer's path had become clear. He wanted Nola in his life and in his heart. Friendship would no longer do.

Adam had located a priest and persuaded him to perform the ceremony yet that day. The small chapel was damp and cold. Lady Randolph stood next to Nola, and Adam stood with Keifer as they faced the altar.

And then it was just Nola and Keifer, kneeling before the priest as Keifer placed the Macnab laird's ring on Nola's cold finger and said the words that bound him to her forever. The ring slid from her finger. He put it back and closed her fingers around it, anxious to find her a proper wedding ring when they had more time.

When the priest finished the blessing, Keifer took his wife, his best friend, into his arms and kissed her soundly, properly, and with promises of what awaited.

After the ceremony, Nola said good-bye to her father. "When you catch up to Will, tell him . . ." Tell him what? She had already apologized. "Just tell him God's speed."

"I'll do that, Daughter. But I'm not heading for Moy. And I doubt Will is either. We had talked about going to Homelea to join Bryan, see what Bruce has planned in the way of disappointing young Edward of England."

"You will fight?"

"Aye, if it comes to that. I'm not in my dotage, you know." Adam turned to Keifer. "Enjoy this time with your bride."

"Thank you, sir. For everything, especially for your daughter."

"See you take care of her," he said gruffly. Her father hugged her and wished her well, then left for the ship that would return him to Scotland. Keifer moved his things into Nola's chamber. The restriction to the palace grounds did not infringe on their enjoyment of Paris or of each other. Nola felt no shyness with her bridegroom, only joy. They laughed and played and enjoyed each other in the way of newlyweds.

THE WEEKS PASSED QUICKLY and the Treaty of Corbeil was signed, strengthening a long-standing alliance between Scotland and France. All too soon it was time to return to Scotland. Keifer stood on the deck of the ship, watching as the shoreline grew smaller and finally disappeared.

Paris had been a perfect spot for a newly married couple to spend their first weeks together. Keifer smiled at the memory of his lovely wife in her night shift. Aye, he liked being married to Nola.

Sir Thomas joined him. They both stared out at the sea for a time, lost in thoughts of Paris. "I am anxious to be home," the earl remarked."

"So am I, my laird."

"Do you plan to take Nola to Moy or to your own holdings?"

"To Innishewan. I hope to spend some time with my family. Then I must find a way to obtain more funds."

"You will always find employment with me," he said. "Please, stay with us in Edinburgh until arrangements are made for the trip to Innishewan."

"But—"

Sir Thomas held up his hand. "No use arguing. My wife says it will be so." The man grinned.

Keifer smiled back. "Aye. I've already learned there are times when it's best not to argue with the wife."

"Good. Then it's settled. Enjoy the voyage."

The weather remained good and they arrived in Edinburgh a day earlier than expected. Keifer and Nola gathered their belongings and walked off the ship toward the waiting carriage. Owyn had left immediately, intending to look for his father and ascertain if he was still a threat. He was to meet them at Innishewan.

As they rode in a carriage to the Randolph's home, Keifer looked forward to extending their holiday. But those hopes were dashed in less than an hour of depositing their belongings in the earl's guest room. A messenger arrived, and as soon as the man left, Sir Thomas called his wife and houseguests into his solar.

"I'm afraid our plans must be changed. Edward is dead."

Keifer took a moment to absorb this news. England's king was a relatively young man in good health. "How did he die?"

The earl took a deep breath and blew it out. "Rumor has it he died at the hands of his own wife and her scheming paramour, Mortimer."

Lady Randolph said, "Oh my." Edward's wife was the sister of France's king. "Will this affect the treaty you have worked so hard to negotiate?"

"No. I don't think so. Of more concern is that Edward's fifteen-year-old son has been crowned Edward III, and he blames 'the Scottish rebels' for his father's death."

"'Tis just an excuse to amass an army and come north," Keifer said.

"I agree." The earl didn't look pleased.

Keifer knew that Randolph had played a principal role in the defeat of the English on their last foray north. No doubt he had hoped not to have to repeat that role a dozen years later.

"Do you think he will? Come north?" Nola asked.

The earl strode over to a winnock, seemingly lost in thought. "Aye, he's going to want to finish what his grandfather started and his weakling father never finished. A victory over Scotland would establish his reign and his superiority."

"Then I best get Nola home quickly and return to prepare."

"There won't be time. I'm afraid that will have to be delayed until we know how imminent is the English threat."

Keifer glanced at Nola. She nodded, more subdued than Keifer had ever seen her.

"Are you all right, Nola?" he asked.

"There will be war again, won't there?"

"'Tis likely, yes."

"And you will fight."

"That's what I've trained for. And if God smiles, I will return with additional lands and spoils. Who knows?" he said, trying a smile. "This might be a godsend. I'll fight, we'll return home the victors, and then I can remain there the rest of our lives."

Sir Thomas cleared his throat. "I will go to the king, learn his plans, and either return for you or send for you. No need to cut short this time with your new wife."

"Thank you, Sir."

Nola did not smile, did not look at Keifer. Miserable and afraid, she glanced over toward Lady Randolph.

The countess gave her a tender smile of courage and said, "And when he must leave, Nola, you will remain with me until 'tis safe to travel."

ON THE THIRD DAY after Sir Thomas's departure, Keifer answered a knock at the front door late in the afternoon to find Owyn standing there. Keifer clasped Owyn's arm. "Good to see you, man."

"Come, sit by the fire and tell us your news," Nola urged. A serving girl came to her, and after instructing the girl to bring refreshments, Nola sat next to Keifer. As had become her habit, she took Keifer's hand in hers. He liked that she felt comfortable doing so in front of others.

Owyn raised an eyebrow.

Keifer smiled at his friend's surprise. "We are enjoying married life."

Owyn grinned. "Well done, my laird."

Keifer gave Nola's hand a squeeze before returning his attention to his friend. "Did you see your father?"

"Aye. Didn't have to travel far, either. He's with Sir Bryan." Owyn straightened in his chair. "As I was taking my leave, Da shared that he no longer wanted to see ye dead."

Nola sucked in a breath. "Dead? Your uncle wanted you killed?"

"Aye. It's a long, complicated story which I will be happy to tell you later." Keifer wiggled his eyebrows in a suggestive way. "Much later."

She blushed becomingly, and for a moment he entertained the hope that Owyn would not stay long.

She recovered her composure. "You needn't try to distract me from the fact that someone wants you dead."

"Wanted, my lady," Owyn assured her.

Keifer pondered this news. "Why the change of heart? Do you suppose Angus was covering his tracks?"

"I hadn't thought of that. He seemed sincere, Keifer. And in good spirits. The best I've seen him in some time."

"Perhaps so. But I would like to know why he's had the change of heart before I trust him. I will need to guard my back until then."

"Leave yer back to me, my laird."

"Aye. That is your duty. You've heard about the English coming north?"

"Aye, heard it myself from Sir Bryan. And I brought these orders for ye," he said, pulling out a folded piece of paper from his pocket and handing it to Keifer.

Keifer scanned the brief words on the paper and glanced up at Nola, then to Owyn. "We need to be ready to ride in the morning."

"Thought that might be the way of it. I'll see to the packing and getting the horses ready."

Keifer looked out the winnock at the lowering sun. "Aye. And you'll sleep here tonight."

"Are ye sure? Don't want to impose on yer honeymoon."

"We're sure," Nola said. "I will feel better about Keifer's leaving knowing he has you to watch over him."

"That I will do, my lady. That I will do."

A HEAVY MIST shrouded the sun the next morning as Owyn and Keifer saddled their horses.

The time had come to leave Nola, and Keifer was having second thoughts about the wisdom of marrying. Not of marriage to Nola—there was no doubt that she was the only woman he would ever love. But doubts about the wisdom of marrying at all. The dreary weather didn't help his spirits. When he'd tightened the girth, Keifer turned to Owyn. "Will you finish here while I get our provisions from Nola?"

"Aye, my laird."

Keifer started toward the manse, shoulders drooping.

Owyn laid a hand on his arm as he passed. "Keifer."

He looked back at his friend.

Owyn squeezed his arm. "Take yer time."

Keifer nodded in acknowledgment and continued walking. There was not enough time in a whole lifetime to say good-bye to Nola. They had parted any number of times over the years, and each time had been painful. But never like this.

The sharing of their hearts, souls, and bodies these past weeks had deepened his love for Nola to a level he could never have imagined. No wonder that God ordained the marriage bed to be sacred.

He should never have married her. If he should die, she would be abandoned, just as he had been by his father and brother. As his mother had been when Ian Macnab died. A fresh burst of anger at his uncle surfaced, as it was wont to do now and then.

Keifer would not nurture that anger, for his own sake and for

Owyn's. But Angus would be riding with them against the English. Could he be trusted? Keifer reached the door and walked into the kitchen where Nola stood with her back to him, staring out the small window that faced south. She turned to him. She was not crying as he had feared, and he thanked God for that. He didn't think he could ride away from her knowing there were tears in her eyes.

She held out her hands and walked to him. Taking her offered hands, he drew Nola close, then crushed her to his chest.

"I do so hate good-byes," she murmured.

"As do I." He held her, kissed her, drank in her sweetness. "Are you sure you don't want to come as far as Homelea with me?"

She pulled back and looked at his face. "Much as I would treasure another day with you, I feel I should stay here. Lady Randolph will need company with her husband gone, too. 'Tis the least I can do to repay her for her kindness. And surely this will be the best place to hear news."

He nodded. "Think how many times that good lady has seen her husband ride into conflict and waited to hear of his fate."

"Most of their married life."

"Perhaps this time we will win a lasting peace so that you won't have to do the same."

"I will be waiting here for you, Keifer. Husband." Her voice caught. She blew out her breath. "I will not cry. Absolutely not." She stood on tiptoe and kissed him. "Now then." She reached for two identical sacks tied shut with string. "Here are oats enough for both you and Owyn, as well as some dried apples. Do you have your oilcloths packed?"

He smiled at his always practical wife. "Aye."

"And here." She held out the Macnab laird's ring. "You should wear this."

He took it from her. "But you have no wedding ring other than this."

201

"You will buy me one when you return."

"That is a promise." He put the ring on his finger but couldn't make himself turn for the door.

She sighed. "Let us not draw this out."

"One more kiss?" he pleaded.

She grinned. "Aye. And no long-drawn-out farewell in front of Owyn."

"I remember." As he kissed her, he also remembered that the last time she'd said such a thing she'd gone back on her word and flung herself into his arms.

They parted reluctantly and walked hand in hand into the small courtyard where Owyn and the horses waited. Keifer checked the girth once more and—satisfied that it was secure—gathered the reins and mounted.

"Thank Lady Randolph for all she has done, Nola." He wanted to say so much more, but the time for words was over. Though he had spent the last years of his life training for battle, he prayed this would be the first and last time he ever had to ride away to war.

True to her word, Nola kept her chin up and he detected no tears as he spurred his horse and trotted away from his wife. But he couldn't help wishing she'd embraced him one last time.

SIXTEEN

KEIFER AND OWYN met up with Randolph and the others at their camp just north of the English border late that afternoon. The very next day the Scots headed south through the Kielder Gap and down the valley of the north Tyne. They traveled light, each man carrying his provision of oats, which could be made into a paste and grilled directly on their plates. They carried no wine, not even water, relying instead on the rivers for their refreshment.

Keifer admired Randolph's methods—by killing local cattle, he kept his army in meat. That and the oatcakes made a satisfying meal. Though the food was monotonous, Keifer found it met his needs. And most importantly, without the added weight of wine or water casks, they could travel swiftly through the countryside. The lack of wagons gave them superior mobility. And from what Keifer knew of English tactics, they would need that advantage to be victorious.

They crossed the border into England and raced south, splitting into three columns, each led by a different commander. Keifer stayed with Sir Bryan's group. As Keifer and Owyn sat around the campfire on their third evening, Keifer knew they must be getting close to the English army. He asked Sir Bryan about the battle plan for the coming days.

Bryan picked up a stick and drew a crude map in the dirt. He pointed to the ground. "We are about here, well into English territory.

Our scouts tell us Edward and his troops are still south of us. It looks like they plan to enter Scotland by traveling up the eastern march. 'Tis what they've done in the past." Bryan drew the low country of the northeastern-most English counties. "They will expect to feed off the land and thus save their supplies for when they enter Scotland."

"But we won't let them get that far north," Keifer said.

"Aye. And just to be sure, tomorrow we will begin burning and looting the English countryside between here and the border. If they do make it past us, they won't have enough provisions left to come deep into Scotland."

"Would we burn our own lands to prevent them from coming north?" Owyn asked.

"Aye. Randolph and Bruce have done it in the past and would do so again."

"Speaking of Bruce, where is our king? Did he ride with one of the other troops?" Keifer asked.

Bryan said, "He is in Ulster, dealing with his wife's inheritance there."

Disappointed, Keifer said, "Ireland? What if we need him to fight this battle?"

Bryan shook his head. "We will not engage the English. They have far superior weapons and over two thousand heavy cavalry. 'Twould be suicide to meet them head on."

"So what will we do?"

"As we have done in the past. Lure them to us by day, using the terrain to our advantage. Then slip away at night and disappear."

"To what purpose?" another of the men asked.

"To get them to make a mistake we can take advantage of."

Keifer grinned with sudden insight. "You want to capture the king!"

Sir Bryan clapped him on the back. "Can you think of a better way to force England to sue for peace on our terms?"

"Then we may see battle yet?" Keifer asked, hoping he didn't sound overeager.

"On a very limited basis, perhaps. And only when conditions are in our favor."

Keifer looked at Owyn, and the other man shrugged. They had trained for war, were willing and ready to meet the English on a battlefield. Keifer stifled his disappointment that he might not even draw his sword on this campaign.

THE FOLLOWING DAY Sir Thomas Randolph, Earl of Moray, watched as the slow-moving English army, led by young Edward III, advanced on the Scottish position north of Durham. In the several miles between where Randolph stood on an overlook and Edward's army, the English countryside lay in devastation. While Randolph disliked putting common people—even though they were English—out of their homes and destroying their crops, he had to use these tactics against such a superior force.

The death of Edward II and the widowed Isobella's takeover had created a crisis within the English government. With luck, Randolph hoped to use the confusion and division amongst England's nobles to Scotland's advantage. While Randolph and his three columns of raiders ransacked the northern counties of England, the English marched north with a mighty army, the pride of which were 2,500 heavily armed Flemish knights.

Randolph's own troops, on the other hand, traveled light. Sir Thomas had no intention of engaging Edward's superior forces.

Instead, he would lead the young, inexperienced king farther and farther from his supply source, allowing hunger and frustration to take its toll. It was a good plan. He'd thought of everything. Today they would put the plan in motion.

Sir Thomas turned to Bryan Mackintosh. "We have succeeded in making them dependent on their baggage train. Now we must separate them from their supplies."

Sir Bryan nodded. "How do you plan to defend against the new weapon?"

The baggage train included a gunpowder cannon. Randolph had seen one demonstrated while he was in France. It wasn't terribly accurate, but the noise and fire were enough to immobilize an enemy with fear. "We must stay out of range of its projectiles and lead the English into terrain where the cannon cannot be taken."

"Aye." Bryan pulled out a map and spread it open. "I suggest that all three columns band together, move south, and wait for them to come to us."

Randolph stared at the map Bryan held. Bryan was an excellent tactician, much like his father. Sir Thomas carefully weighed what the younger man said. "Agreed. But what if we were to put out the word that we are headed for the Tyne at Haydon Bridge?"

"You think Edward will be fooled into thinking we are done raiding and headed home?"

"Aye. But we will move west of the burned area and wait to see if he takes the bait. If he heads for the Tyne, he'll have to abandon the wagons when they reach the boglands. His army should be on short rations by the time they reach the river."

Bryan smiled grimly. "And we won't be there or even close by."

Randolph nodded. "We'll let them wait there for awhile before we split into two groups and lure them after us. You and Douglas will lead the forward raids and I'll remain behind to cover the rear. Gather your men and move out."

Bryan left, and Randolph looked to the overcast sky. Rain threatened, and not for the first time he wished he were safe and warm in his home in Edinburgh.

EDWARD III, the fifteen-year-old king of England, paced back and forth as his tent was being set up at the end of another wet, dreary day. A mild drizzle still fell, chilling him despite layers of warm garments and a waterproof oilcloth. *Blast the weather.*

Though old enough to wear the crown and lead troops, Edward needed to prove himself as the rightful leader of England so that he could oust his mother and her paramour. A victory over Bruce would allow him to do so.

Acting on reliable intelligence information, Edward had taken his army north to the Tyne River at Haydon Bridge to await the retreating Scots. The certainty of victory had balanced out the need to leave their supply wagons behind. Or so he had thought.

Eight wet, miserable days later, days when the supplies they'd been able to carry with them had dwindled to nothing, there was still no sign of the Scots. Saddles rotted in the damp, fires could not be built with the water-logged wood, and the men were hungry and grumbling.

So he had offered a reward to any man who could bring back word of the location of the Scottish army. Two dozen squires had scattered in all directions, seeking the elusive enemy.

Yesterday one of the men returned—the earlier reports had been false, and Edward had been sitting here in the miserable weather for naught. The Scots were camped on the south bank of the River Wear, twenty miles to the south near Stanhope Park.

Edward hastened his hungry army south, finding the Scots camped with the raging river in front of them and a marsh to their backs. They were trapped, and Edward eagerly anticipated moving in for the kill.

His tent, always first to be pitched, was soon ready. He entered the tent and gladly shed several layers of garments as the peat fires in the braziers warmed the enclosure. Warm and fed, despite his army's hunger and cold, Edward looked forward to morning. Tomorrow would be his day of glory at last.

KEIFER AND OWYN stood beside Sir Bryan and watched the English set up camp on the other side of the river. Keifer wondered why they didn't attack now—he itched to take part in his first combat.

Sir Thomas joined them in the gathering dusk. "Our opportunity has arrived. You and your men will circle around to the south and cross the river. That will put Edward between you and me. Attack when their camp is quiet for the night. You will attempt to capture the English king."

Keifer looked at Owyn, whose grin must surely match his own. To capture the king! Quickly Keifer brought his attention back to Randolph and his instructions.

"Once you have him, make for the river, there. His men will not be able to cross the river on foot, which will delay their pursuit until they can saddle their horses. Send a few men to cut the horses loose so the English will have to round them up before they can follow you."

Keifer was puzzled. "But the marsh will prevent our retreat."

Randolph smiled. "I'm sure Edward thinks so, too. My men and I will make it possible to retreat through the marsh."

"How?"

"We have scoured the countryside for wooden planks which we can lay over the bogs, cross over, and then pick the planks up as we move forward. It will be slow, but until they find planks of their own, the English will not be able to follow."

Keifer was exhilarated to see action at last—to be one of the men chosen to raid the English camp in hopes of capturing the young king. The English nobles would have to pay a hefty ransom for their king—nothing short of a treaty of peace and recognition of Scotland as an independent country.

His enthusiasm did not dim in the nearly three hours it took to circle around the camp. The water was high at the river crossing from the recent rain, and the mud sucked at the horses' hooves. They traveled slowly and as quietly as possible, as their success depended on taking the English by surprise.

Keifer saw his uncle among those who would set the English horses free. The man's presence unnerved him, but he'd given no indication thus far of any animosity to Keifer. Still, he was glad to have Owyn at his side as they moved into position.

At the earl's signal, Keifer and Owyn followed Sir Bryan into the sleeping camp, slashing at tent ropes and trampling anyone in their path. The king's large tent had been easy to spot at a distance and in daylight. But in the confusion and cover of darkness, Keifer lost his bearings. He turned his horse this way and that, fending off half-dressed enemy soldiers until the alarm was sounded.

Keifer wondered if his uncle had been successful with the horses. When he'd disarmed yet another Englishman, Keifer looked up to see Sir Bryan just ahead.

Sir Bryan pointed. "There! Go!"

Keifer spurred his horse in the direction the knight pointed and found himself heading straight for the pavilion that housed the king of England. By now the royal household guards—Edward's most trusted and well-trained knights—were awake and armed, and the fighting became fierce.

All the practice in the lists had not prepared Keifer for real combat. The confusion and noise overwhelmed him. He followed behind Sir Bryan, slashing with his sword, jostled by friend and foe. Twice Keifer had to curb a blow to avoid harming a fellow Scot. Though the guards were on foot, they were suicidal in their ferocious protection of their king. As the camp awoke, more and more English came to the defense of the king's pavilion.

After the initial shock, Keifer stood his ground, engaging and defeating several men. Now the hours of practice made sense. Sweat poured off him and his arms grew weary. Despite their best efforts, the Scots were driven back and it soon became apparent that the king could not be taken without serious loss of life and limb. Sir Bryan blew his horn to signal their retreat to the river.

Disappointed that they failed in their mission, Keifer turned his horse around and fought his way free to ride after his comrades. He and Owyn were among the last to leave the camp. Sir Bryan sat on his horse at the side of the trail and waved them on. He would wait until he was sure all the Scots had cleared the field before following them.

In high fettle, Keifer and Owyn whooped and hollered. They hadn't captured the king, but they'd come close enough to give the boy a good scare.

The English by now had started to round up their horses. It would be some time before they caught and saddled their mounts to give chase. Keifer urged his horse faster. The muddy ground slowed them, and Keifer's horse stumbled and regained its balance. As he came in sight of the river, Keifer looked over his shoulder and pointed to Owyn—a rider was coming up behind them. Keifer spurred his horse and pulled ahead of Owyn by several yards.

The land sloped gradually toward the river with a final thirty yards of fairly steep embankment before the water. Thick forest lay on either side of the trail. The ground was churned up by the several hundred horses that had already passed over it, and Keifer's mount struggled to keep up its pace.

By now the other rider had caught up to them. Uncle Angus! And he still had his sword drawn! Too late Keifer reached for his sword, barely unsheathing it when Angus swung his sword. Keifer raised his sword and stood in his stirrups to withstand the blow against his blade.

He felt his saddle shift to the right. He stood on the left stirrup to right it and heard a sickening snap of leather. Before he had time to react, the saddle slipped further right, throwing the horse off balance. It slid on the wet, muddy incline.

Keifer reached for the horse's mane, grasping the hair in a futile attempt to stay aboard. But the high cantle and pommel anchored him in the saddle. Where it went, Keifer would go too.

Owyn forced his horse between Keifer and Angus as Keifer's horse reared up in an effort to shake the unbalanced load off its back. In horror Keifer felt the animal lose its footing and go down, taking him with it. As the animal went over, Keifer kicked his feet from the stirrups but was unable to get free of the saddle before the horse hit the ground, pinning Keifer under its weight briefly before it lurched back to its feet.

Keifer looked up and saw Owyn, saw him wave his sword, saw his mouth moving as the cantle dug deep into Keifer's back. A sharp jolt shot down into his hips and legs and up to his head. His brain exploded in pain.

One thought filled his head and heart before the world went dark. *Nola.*

OWYN WATCHED IN HORROR as Keifer's horse went down. He barely checked his own mount in time to keep from running over Keifer where he lay, much too still. Owyn faced his father, kept his mount between Angus and Keifer.

But Angus ignored him and halted his horse a few feet away. "Well," his father bellowed. "Will ye finish him off or should I?"

Owyn just stared at his father. "Keifer Macnab is my laird. Ye'll have to kill me first." Owyn shook his head in disbelief as Angus charged toward him, sword drawn. The blow glanced off the chain mail on his left arm, stinging and bruising but not breaking through the protective barrier.

Angus came at him again. This time Owyn was ready, slashing and pushing his father back and away from Keifer. Their swords clashed and the hilts tangled, locked together as each man fought to disengage. With a mighty shove, Owyn freed his weapon and immediately attacked, catching Angus in the side. Angus leaned sideways to escape the worst of the blow.

Owyn pressed his advantage, slashing at Angus's sword arm. The other man's saddle did not have a deep seat for fighting. This made it easier for him to move out of range but it also made it easier to un-horse him. Owyn slashed repeatedly at his father's sword arm until the man dropped his weapon. Then, while Angus was off balance, Owyn shoved with his foot and sent him to the ground.

Angus picked himself up and grabbed his sword from the mud, ignoring Owyn, stalking instead toward Keifer. He stood over Keifer's still body, but instead of raising his sword to strike, he bent down and yanked the laird's ring from Keifer's finger.

Enraged, Owyn leaped from his horse, landing on top of his father. The ring flew from his hands into the mud. Angus grunted in pain and Owyn moved quickly away from him. From the corner of his eye, Owyn saw another rider approaching. Desperately he searched until he found the ring. Angus rose to his knees, stilling as the rider slid his mount to a halt. Sir Bryan dismounted and strode toward them. "What is the meaning of this?"

But Owyn returned his attention to Angus, who glanced to where his sword lay in the mud and inched toward it, still on his knees.

Fearing that any distraction would be disastrous to Keifer, Owyn ignored the knight and stood on the tip of his father's blade. "Do ye yield?"

Angus jerked his head toward Keifer. "Is he dead?"

Owyn didn't know for sure, but he wouldn't give Angus the satisfaction. "Nay, he's alive, ye miserable blackguard."

"Let me stand."

"Do ye yield?"

Angus eyed both men and let go of his sword. "Aye."

Sir Bryan walked over and knelt next to Keifer, his back to Owyn and Angus.

Owyn indicated that his father should stand and lifted his foot to retrieve Angus's blade.

In one fluid motion Angus came to his feet and pulled a dirk from his boot, lunging toward Keifer.

"Sir Bryan! Watch out!"

The knight spun toward them and reached for his sword hilt, rising to his feet to withdraw it fully. Angus was nearly upon him and, seeing the danger, Bryan didn't hesitate. He plunged his sword in Angus's gut and withdrew it with an upward flourish.

Surprise, shock, and anger crossed the wounded man's face as he slowly sank back to his knees. "Ye've killed me," he said in obvious disbelief. He fell sideways to the ground as blood stained his tunic.

Sir Bryan stared down at Angus and then at Owyn, his expression confused. "This is your father."

"Aye. He tried to kill Keifer."

"I'm sorry, Owyn. I should have tried for a maiming blow, not a lethal one."

Owyn's knees were shaking with anger at his father for forcing Sir Bryan to kill him. "Sir, I believe if ye hadn't killed him, I would have."

Sir Bryan stared at him.

"He attacked my sworn liege."

Sir Bryan gazed at Keifer's still form. "Is he dead?"

Owyn touched Keifer's neck and found the blood pulse. "He's alive." He looked about and found Keifer's horse standing quietly, as it had been taught to do after losing its rider.

"Aye. Alive but not conscious."

Owyn looked in the direction of the English camp. They didn't have much time. Surely the enemy was mounted and on the move by now.

"Let's move him off the path," Sir Bryan said.

They carried Keifer into the woods, then quickly fetched the horses and Keifer's saddle. Owyn heard hoof beats as he dashed back into the cover of the trees. The English rode past, about a half dozen of them, intent on their quarry. They paid no attention to Angus's body, no doubt seeing his plaid and taking him for a dead enemy.

Grief overcame Owyn but he shoved it aside. His father had made his choice, had forced Sir Bryan and Owyn to do what they'd done.

When the English were gone, Owyn said, "They will come back."

"Aye. But if they meant to engage us, they would have sent more. These are probably just scouts, sent to let Edward know our whereabouts. They won't want to be seen any more than we do." Sir Bryan gazed at Owyn. "We don't have time to bury your father."

"I know." Owyn went to stand beside his father's body. He said a prayer, then honored his da in the only way he could under the circumstances—he searched the ground for Angus's sword. Owyn unbelted the scabbard from his father's waist, sheathed the weapon, and fastened it to his saddle.

When he had finished, Sir Bryan nodded.

They must move on before they were discovered.

SEVENTEEN

Owyn heard keifer moan and went to him. His face was pale and his breath came fast and shallow. Owyn despaired of getting him to Homelea alive. While cool water might help as it had with Keifer's horse bite, they could not take the time for it now. They were deep in English territory and needed to head north with as much haste as possible.

"I don't see how we can take him on horseback, my laird."

"I agree. We need to fashion a litter of some kind to float him across the river. Then we can drag it on poles behind his horse."

They created a litter from two stout young trees and Owyn's large oilcloth. They debated whether or not to strap Keifer fast, and in the end decided that if they lost hold of him in the current, he was better off floating downstream tied on the cot than falling off into the water and drowning.

Since the girth on Keifer's saddle had given way, Owyn would have to tie the saddle fast to the horse using a length of rope. But first Owyn took his bag of oatmeal and dumped its contents into Keifer's. With a knife he slit the empty bag and placed it between the rope and the animal's hide, providing some cushioning for the horse from the abrasion of the rope. Then he looped the rope over the saddle seat and under the horse's belly, tying a sturdy knot to hold it. The stirrup leathers would hold the poles once they reached the other side of the river.

In the hour it took to prepare the litter, Keifer lay silent except for an occasional moan. If he didn't regain his senses soon, Owyn feared for his friend's life.

The sky was getting light when they entered the water. The litter floated surprisingly well, and the two men were able to steady it between their horses. Halfway through the crossing, Keifer's horse stumbled and water splashed in Keifer's face; he yelped in surprise.

"Steady, lad. We'll have you back on dry land in a few minutes," Sir Bryan said.

Keifer seemed to pass in and out of lucidity. Owyn wished he had some whiskey to give his friend for the pain, but they didn't even have wine.

They wasted little time. Sir Bryan inspected the litter's fastening to the stirrups, and they started off. Keifer grunted in pain each time the poles hit a rock until mercifully he passed out.

It took two hours to reach the marsh, and all the way there Owyn feared the English scouts would return. He wasn't too worried that their comrades would leave them behind since they wouldn't abandon Sir Bryan.

When they reached the edge of the marsh, half a dozen Scots awaited them. "What happened to the English who passed us by?" Owyn asked.

One of the men said, "We hid in the marsh, and when the English came, they split up. We must hurry. They could return at any time. We mustn't allow them to follow us into the swamp."

Owyn urged his horse to follow Sir Bryan's onto the planks set across the boggy area, and Keifer's horse followed behind. The six men pulled the planks up and then ran ahead to lay them down again where needed.

Exhausted, hungry, and worried about Keifer, Owyn was glad when they reached the other side of the marsh. He insisted that they rest, give Keifer time without the constant jostling. Sir Bryan found a secluded campsite near a small creek when the sun was well overhead.

Owyn sent two of the men to gather pine boughs to lay on the ground. When they returned with them, Owyn and Sir Bryan laid Keifer's litter atop the branches, hoping to give him some cushioning from the hardness of the ground. Again Owyn despaired at having nothing to relieve Keifer's pain.

Seeing that Keifer's eyes were open, Owyn brought him water.

"Get away from me, traitor."

Owyn stared at his friend, not believing he'd heard such hurtful words. He chose to pretend he didn't hear them. "Here." Owyn cradled Keifer's head and offered the water.

Keifer refused to drink. "Why don't you finish . . ."

"Finish what?"

Keifer seemed to gather the strength to talk. "What you and your father started?"

Owyn just stared at Keifer, settling him back down into the makeshift bed.

Sir Bryan approached and looked from one man to the other before addressing Owyn. "What is amiss?"

"He seems to think I tried to kill him."

Sir Bryan put his arm across Owyn's shoulders and led him out of Keifer's hearing. "Do not listen to him. He is in pain. Probably can't clearly remember what happened—he'll see things differently once he mends."

Owyn hoped it was true.

"Is there anything I can do?"

If Keifer hated Owyn now, he would hate him more before this next task was done. "Heat some water. I need to . . . wash him."

Sir Bryan bit his lip and hung his head—evidence of his aware-ness that Keifer had lost control of his functions. He nodded and walked away.

Owyn walked back to Keifer's side.

To see a warrior, a friend, reduced to this—not dead but not alive either—was enough to make the strongest man weep. Owyn fought his own tears and prayed silently for God's will to be done. *Heal him here or take him home, Lord.*

"Leave me," Keifer whispered so low Owyn wasn't sure he heard him right.

"I will not. I didn't do this to ye."

"Doesn't matter." Again Keifer hesitated.

"Ye want water?"

Keifer shook his head. "Leave me here. Go on without me."

Owyn was not shocked by Keifer's request. He thought he under-stood exactly why Keifer asked it of him and wondered if he might not ask the same thing in Keifer's position. But Owyn suspected it was far easier to ask the favor than to actually abandon a loved one.

Could he do it? Ride away and let nature take its course? But what if Keifer wasn't mortally wounded? Then Owyn would be no better than a murderer.

"I will not leave ye. Ye are my laird."

Keifer turned away.

Sir Bryan came back with the hot water and a bit of rough cloth. "Do you want help?"

"Nay. He's not going to like this. He . . . he asked us to leave him and go on without him."

The knight, a seasoned warrior, took a deep breath. "How do you feel about that?"

"I'm taking him home. To heal or to be buried, but I will not desert him."

"Good." Bryan smiled weakly. "I wouldn't leave him either."

When Sir Bryan had left, Owyn went about the task of washing Keifer's soiled body. He ignored Keifer's pleas, his humiliation, and did what needed doing. Then he covered Keifer with a warm plaid and tried desperately to ignore the tears on the man's face.

Sir Bryan came to him with a cup of broth and an oatcake. But Keifer refused to eat even when Sir Bryan—and not Owyn—offered the food. Owyn didn't have the heart to force the issue.

He rested, as did the others. Late in the day they awoke and prepared to depart the camp. Keifer drank some water but again refused food.

Owyn fastened the litter to the stirrups and then stood at Keifer's side. "I will not leave ye behind. Ye may curse me for the rest of the trip, for the rest of yer life. But I cannot do it."

"Then give me a knife."

Owyn closed his eyes and prayed for strength. "There is proof ye are not in yer right mind. We should make Homelea by nightfall. Lady Kathryn will know how to make ye more comfortable."

"Will she know how to make me walk again?"

Owyn swallowed. "That's in God's hands, Keifer."

"Well, it appears you are not the only one who has abandoned me."

Owyn had never been the most faithful of believers, but he'd been praying ever since Keifer fell. He vowed to continue until Keifer was released, one way or another, from this living hell.

They arrived at Homelea after dark. Lady Kathryn met them in the hall, and with one look at Keifer's pale face, she took charge. Owyn and Sir Bryan carried Keifer to the bed in the first floor chamber where Lady Kathryn led them. Briefly they explained his injury. He passed out when they moved him from the litter to the bed, placing him face down.

Within a few minutes a fire burned brightly in the fireplace as the lady examined Keifer's back. He still breathed, but his face was deadly pale.

"Owyn, I'll have the others tend to your horses. You stay with Keifer," Sir Bryan said, giving Owyn a meaningful look. Evidently the man wanted to protect Keifer's sensibilities from Lady Kathryn's nursing.

She finished her examination and Owyn stared at the swollen skin across Keifer's spine. A deep purple bruise, nearly black in some places, extended down into his buttocks.

A servant arrived with the poultice Lady Kathryn had ordered. "There's not much else can be done, Owyn. His back is very badly bruised, and I have no way to know what has been damaged inside."

Owyn just nodded, weary to the bone and beyond worried for his friend.

"I'll clean him and check on him through the night—you best get some sleep."

"No, my lady. I'll . . . Keifer did not appreciate my ministrations. He will be even more humiliated if ye . . ."

Maybe she sensed his need to be of service. Or maybe his eyes were bright with the unmanly tears that seemed too close to the surface. At any rate, she laid a hand on his arm, patted it like she might a child's.

"Of course, Owyn. You will want to care for him until Nola arrives. I've already sent a messenger to her."

"Thank ye, my lady."

"Now come, you need to rest."

"I'll just sleep here in case he needs me."

She studied him and must have seen his determination, for she did not argue. "I'll send you some hot water and cloths." She closed the door on her way out.

A servant brought the promised water, and again Owyn bathed

his friend, this time from head to toe. Keifer did not wake, or pretended to be asleep, Owyn wasn't sure which. When he was finished and Keifer was dry and dressed in a long linen shirt, Owyn rolled him to his back and covered him with soft blankets.

Though Keifer only took up half the large and very inviting bed, Owyn didn't want to lie down next to him for fear of jostling him. Instead he made a pallet on the floor with some extra bedding he found in a trunk.

But then, fearing he would sleep too soundly and miss hearing Keifer if he stirred, Owyn propped himself up against the wall. As he drifted off, Owyn dreaded facing Nola with the news that Keifer might well be mortally injured. And worse yet, that he hoped to die.

THE LIGHT DREW HIM and he followed the feeble glow, not at all sure where he was being led. As the light grew brighter, he became aware of the pain. He stopped following the light, sought the dark oblivion. At least there he couldn't feel the knife-sharp agony in his back.

But inevitably the light and the pain returned. When it did, Keifer opened his eyes. He was lying in a bed. Vaguely he remembered their arrival at Homelea and the agony of being moved from the litter. And the humiliation of soiling himself and of his friend washing him.

Friend? Or foe? All Keifer could remember was Owyn with his sword in his hand, looking down at him as he lay helpless.

A fire glowed on the hearth, and a candle sputtered on a lampstand near his head. Nothing looked familiar except for the man sleeping propped up against the wall.

"Owyn?" he whispered, unable to make his dry throat and mouth work properly.

Owyn roused nonetheless and stumbled to Keifer's side. "About time ye came back among the living."

The joking words belied the serious expression on Owyn's face.

"Water," Keifer said. He had no choice but to trust the man.

Owyn brought a metal dipper of cool water and held it for Keifer to drink. He took several sips, grateful for the soothing of his throat. Yet every movement, no matter how small, brought on a new wave of pain. The darkness closed over him again.

Keifer awoke again, not sure if it was minutes or hours later. Owyn was awake, seated at his side, his expression glum. Minutes, then.

Keifer tried to move but only his arms seemed to be working.

"Ye need to lie still, Keifer."

"Legs won't move." He could not even wiggle his toes, and panic and fear threatened him. Fear of what he would become now that he was . . . *Oh God, why have you deserted me?*

"Lady Kathryn says ye must be still, give the swelling time to go down."

"Why don't you just finish it?" The look of pain that crossed Owyn's face gave Keifer pause. Why was the man nursing him if he had tried to kill him? Was Keifer wrong to accuse him?

"Will I walk?"

Owyn didn't answer.

"Didn't think so."

"Nay, Keifer. Ye mustn't take my silence for an answer. The lady says there is no way of knowing how long yer legs will stay numb."

Keifer turned his head to face away from the pity in Owyn's expression. With bitterness he considered that his lifelong prayer, his request that he not ever be abandoned again, had been answered. Nor had he died and left his wife to grieve him. Instead he had been placed in this limbo—not dead but not fully alive. Aye, the prayer had been heard, but Keifer didn't like the answer one bit.

"Nola will be here on the morrow and—"

"No!" Keifer faced his friend once more. "I don't want Nola. Don't want her to see . . . this."

"Knowing Nola, I don't think ye're going to have much choice in the matter, Keifer."

"If you love me, keep her away. Promise!" He couldn't bear having her see him weak and crippled and utterly useless.

Owyn stood and went to the table where he picked up a cup and brought it back. "Lady Kathryn says to drink some of this; it will help with the pain."

"Promise!"

"I'll not make a promise we both know I won't be able to keep. Ye think yer wife will love ye less because ye are hurt? Ye don't regard her any more than ye do me if ye think that's true." He held out the cup. "Drink this."

Owyn steadied the cup so Keifer could sip the bitter drink.

He drank and sank back onto the bed and closed his eyes. *Take this cup from me, Lord. I can't do this, can't face a life as a cripple. Never to be a husband to Nola again. Take this cup.* A tear trickled from his eye. He didn't bother to wipe it away. *Let me die, Lord. Please! Let me die!*

225

EIGHTEEN

Keifer's color was better the next morning and his breathing seemed easier. However, Owyn remained discouraged by Keifer's refusal to eat or even to talk while he took care of the man's needs. Gratefully Owyn accepted Lady Kathryn's offer to stay with Keifer when she came to check on them.

Hoping that keeping his hands busy would help lift his gloomy mood, Owyn decided to mend Keifer's saddle. He set it astride a saddle stand to take a closer look at the girth. How could he have missed a spot so worn it would give way?

Maybe Keifer was right to accuse Owyn. Maybe Keifer's fall *was* his fault. He should have seen that the leather was worn and needed replacing. Guilt flooded Owyn as he thought of his friend lying so still, of his unwillingness to see his wife.

As if Nola would listen to such folly.

Owyn smiled, thinking of his friend's intrepid wife. He hoped he was in the room when she arrived so he could watch the sparks. And he hoped that Keifer would succumb to his wife's natural optimism and practical mind. If any woman could cope with Keifer's future, it was Nola Mackintosh.

Owyn brought his attention back to the saddle. He looked at the girth itself and saw nothing wrong with it. The end of the billet strap that had snapped was still buckled fast. Closer inspection made his heart skip a beat.

He shoved the thin leather skirt upward and found the billet straps on the right side of the saddle. The leather strap was cut clean until the final quarter inch, which showed a distinct tearing of the fibers not apparent on the rest of the strap. Holding the two ends together made it even more apparent.

Clearly the strap had been cut. There was no other explanation. The strap would have been covered by Keifer's leg and the saddle's skirt—no chance that a stray gash by a sword had done the damage. And it had to have been done after the horse was saddled, because Owyn was sure he would have noticed the cut if it had been there while he was tightening the girth.

Shaking with outrage, Owyn took the small piece of the billet with him while he searched for Sir Bryan. He found him at the corral, working with one of the horses. Owyn didn't wait for the man to acknowledge him before opening the gate and striding inside.

Sir Bryan halted his horse. "What is the meaning of this?"

Owyn just stood there, too upset to speak and holding the strap in the air. He shook it and finally said, "This was cut."

Sir Bryan tilted his head, his expression questioning. Then he jumped down from the horse and strode to Owyn, grabbing the leather and scrutinizing it. He cursed, something Owyn had never heard from the man before.

"This is from Keifer's saddle?"

"Aye, my laird."

"Dear Lord," he prayed. "Do you have any idea who might have done this?" They both knew that a bad fall from the high-cantled saddles often killed or maimed.

"My father must have done it—he wanted Keifer dead."

Sir Bryan stared at the leather. "What happened back there at the river, Owyn? Between you and Angus?"

Owyn told Sir Bryan of Angus's desire to kill Keifer, of the land and Aunt Eveleen. "He blamed Keifer for all his troubles."

"Is there anyone else who might benefit from Keifer's death?"

Owyn shifted from one foot to the other. "Me. It could have been me. I have the leadership of a clan to gain."

Sir Bryan shook his head. "No man who did for his comrade what you have done for Keifer these past days . . . no, I don't believe you wish him harm."

"Maybe I'm caring for him out of guilt." Owyn couldn't keep the bitterness from his voice.

"Others may think that, Owyn, but I do not. And I think Keifer and Nola will come to that same conclusion soon enough."

Sir Bryan glanced at the leather strap again. "There is no way to prove or disprove it, Owyn, but it does seem likely that your father was entirely responsible for cutting the saddle. But let us not speak of this to Keifer until he is better."

"He will get better, won't he, my laird?" Owyn asked.

Sir Bryan didn't answer, but Owyn saw him swallow. Hard. "We must pray without ceasing, Owyn. All things are possible with God." He handed the strap back. "Nola will arrive yet today. Will you tell her the extent of Keifer's injury, or shall I?"

Though he dreaded it, Owyn knew he must do this. He had failed to protect his laird; he would not fail him again. "'Tis my duty as his squire."

Sir Bryan laid his hand on Owyn's shoulder. "God give you strength." The knight began to unsaddle his horse.

Owyn started back to the keep to check on Keifer. As he rounded the corner of the stable, he saw three riders enter the bailey. Nola, her father, and Will Macpherson. Dread gnawed at Owyn. Dread and suspicion. *Who else might benefit from Keifer's death?*

Will Macpherson.

Nola saw Owyn and jumped from her horse before anyone could help her dismount. She rushed to him. "Owyn! You did not come to harm, thank goodness. How . . . where is Keifer?"

"I will take ye to him, my lady. But first tell me how it is that yer father and Will have brought ye here. They rode south with us."

Sir Adam dismounted and joined them in time to hear Owyn's query. "Aye, we did. Will's horse came up lame and there was no other for him to ride. By the time we found him a mount, the rest of you were long gone, so we went back to Edinburgh to wait. Now, how is my foster son?"

Owyn would check this story later. Not that he doubted Sir Adam's word. But a horse could easily be made to come up lame by pounding a rock into the soft tissue on the underside of the hoof. He didn't want to believe it of Will, and now was not the time to bring up his suspicions.

Owyn brought himself back to the earl's question. "Keifer is not good, my laird. He cannot move his legs and he is refusing to eat." Owyn turned to Nola. "Perhaps ye will have more success at feeding him."

Adam said, "Aye, Nola. Go to him. I'll visit with him later."

KEIFER LAY ON HIS BACK in the dimly lit room. Owyn had turned him earlier, and he'd cursed him in his pain. Lady Kathryn had assured him the pain was a good sign before she'd given him some tea to ease him, and now he was fairly comfortable.

He heard the door to his chamber open and quickly closed his eyes, but not before he saw Nola and Owyn enter the room. He gritted his jaw in frustration. Hadn't he told the man not to bring her here?

Nola, this wife who could never just leave things be, came to his side and took his hand in hers. "Has he awakened at all?" she asked Owyn the traitor.

"Aye, several times, but never for long."

Keifer heard the concern in Owyn's voice, in both their voices, and he felt a moment of guilt for deceiving them into thinking he was asleep. But he just wanted to be left alone until God came for him.

"And you have offered food which he declines?"

"Aye. He doesn't want to live, Nola, if ye'll pardon my saying so. And he accuses me of trying to kill him."

He heard her intake of breath. Owyn couldn't keep his mouth shut. Keifer had half a mind to end Owyn's service as his squire, if not his life, for trying to take his.

"You must tell me what happened later. But I say to you now—I do not believe you harmed Keifer."

"Thank ye, my lady."

He felt Nola's soft hand upon his forehead. "There is no fever. And no injury except to his back?"

"So far as we can see."

Keifer's heart beat quicker at his wife's touch. 'Twas very difficult to feel dead or even close to it under the circumstances. He might as well pretend to awaken.

He stirred and she took his hand again. "Keifer?"

He opened his eyes. From the disheveled appearance of her hair, Nola must have come to him as soon as she arrived.

"Can you talk?" she asked.

Reluctantly he said, "Aye." Yes, he could talk. But it was the only thing he could do unassisted. As soon as Nola understood how badly he was injured, she wouldn't want to stay with such a man. And if she didn't or wouldn't understand, he must make her see the futility of continuing this marriage to him. He would send her away, drive her away if he had to.

"Why are you not eating?"

"I'm not hungry."

"Nonsense. Owyn, go ask Lady Kathryn for some broth, please."

"Of course. Just the thing." Owyn was smiling, the turncoat.

Owyn left, and Nola said, "Keifer. Talk to me."

He turned away from her eager face. "What is there to say?"

She took her fingers and turned his face back to her. "Look at me."

He did and his heart nearly broke at the pain and the disappointment he had caused her, would continue to bring to her.

Owyn returned with a bowl of broth and some bread. He set it on the table by the bed and left again.

Nola added a pillow under Keifer's head, then picked up the bowl and spoon.

"I don't want that."

"Aye, but you'll have it anyway, to please me. If you won't eat it yourself, then I'll feed you." She put the spoon to Keifer's mouth, and when he didn't open, she pushed it against his lips. "I don't want—"

She pushed the spoon between his opened lips and he was forced to swallow.

"—to eat."

"You want to die, then? Is that what this is about? You face a hurdle and you quit, just like that?"

He could face this, he could! He just didn't want her to be there. For once in his life Keifer wanted someone to leave him, and Nola wouldn't. "I can't move my legs! I'll never get out of this bed and walk again!"

"So you've become God while I've been waiting for a mere man to return to me?"

Keifer was bitter. "No, I'm very aware of my mortality, Nola. All my life—"

"You don't appear dead to me, Keifer. And I'll be hanged if I'll stand by and watch you starve yourself to death!"

"Fine. I will eat. But I want you to leave Homelea, leave me."

"And why would I do something so wrong-headed as to desert my husband?"

How could he make her understand? "I've tried to live a good life, obey the commandments. And this is my reward. To end my days as a cripple."

"Don't be foolish. Your reward for serving God is eternal life and forgiveness for your many sins." She smiled and slipped the spoon into his mouth.

He swallowed the liquid. "Then what is this if not punishment?"

"A trial. We've faced others, Keifer. We've faced them together. Nothing has changed."

"Everything has changed and you know it."

"What I know is that you've been given a cross to bear. One that I will help you carry."

"I don't want to be a burden. I want my life back."

"You have life, Keifer. The question is, what will you do with it? Will you accept this and move on, or whine and complain for the rest of your life?"

"I'm tired, Nola. Leave me be."

"I'm not leaving. Not this room, not Homelea. Not without my husband."

"Husband? I can't be a husband now, Nola. How will you feel a year from now without a child, without the joys that we shared in our marriage bed?"

"How do you know that I am not already with child?"

He felt his face drain of color. "Are you? With child?"

"I don't know, but it is possible, Keifer. Will you abandon us both? I thought you didn't want to be like your father?"

Only Nola knew the points that would hurt the most. That she would say such a thing gave him an indication of just how desperate she was. He softened his voice, hoping that by being reasonable, she would listen better. "The man you loved doesn't exist anymore, Nola."

"You are still my husband and friend."

"Some husband. I can't provide for you, nor can I give you children."

"I still love you, Keifer. That will never change."

Why wouldn't she listen? "What do you want of me?" he shouted.

A tear escaped her eye and ran down her cheek. Another followed from the other eye. "I want it to be the way it was when you loved me."

He put his head in his hands, close to tears himself. "Don't you understand? That is over for us. I cannot be your husband."

She swiped at the tears on her cheek and raised her voice. "We don't know that, do we? Who can tell what might happen as you heal? And a marriage is more than a bed! It is a sacred bond between man and woman that connects our hearts, our minds."

She would not listen to reason. The time had come to send her away. "If I live, I want you to petition the church to dissolve our marriage, Nola. Go on with your life."

She stood so fast she tipped the bowl and spilled the broth. "I will not abandon you! God never promised that life would be easy. His promise is that he will help us bear our pain and welcome us home when he calls us to him."

"Who's to say he isn't calling me, Nola? At least we've had a chance to say good-bye—"

He sputtered as Nola shoved a hunk of bread in his mouth. "You will eat. You will get better. We will live to have gray hair together." Tears began to fall in earnest. "And you will pray, Keifer. Do you hear me? You will pray and stop this nonsense about dying and about me leaving you if you don't!"

She spun away, knocking over the stool she'd been sitting on, then whirled back to face him. "I believe if you were standing, I'd kick you in the shins again, Keifer Macnab!"

Sparks danced in her eyes, and he didn't remember ever seeing her so angry. But anger was better than pity any day. And if she was angry enough, she just might do as he wanted her to. He took the bread from his mouth. "Well, there's the crux of it, Nola. I'm not going to stand again now, am I?"

She fled the room and slammed the door so hard he thought it would bounce off its hinges.

Well, he'd succeeded—she was gone. Why didn't he feel relieved to have his way?

NOLA RAN, HEAD DOWN, right into Will. When his arms came up to catch her, she just stayed there, caught fast to his chest as the tears poured from her eyes. Will had been unusually kind to her as they rode here from Edinburgh, and she was grateful now for his willingness to comfort her.

He patted her back, and when she'd finished crying he handed her a small cloth to dry her eyes and nose. He took her to sit in a corner of the great hall, away from prying eyes. When they were seated, he said, "Is he so bad, then, Nola?"

She drew a breath and exhaled, fearing the tears would start again. "He wants to die, Will. And worse, if he lives, he expects me to desert him."

Will took her hands in his and she allowed it. "Is there no hope he'll walk again?"

"Lady Kathryn says it's possible, though none of us is truly hopeful."

Will dropped her hands into her lap and stood, walking a short distance away. He stood with his back to her for several minutes, and she began to fidget in her seat.

He must have heard her, because he was smiling gently when he turned back to face her. "You love him very much, don't you?"

She didn't know what to say except the truth. "Aye. I've loved him since we were children. I'm sorry, Will. I—"

"Stop. I know that, have always known it but chose to ignore it. I never took Keifer for a fool, but he is one if he won't accept your love." He came back to her and pulled her to her feet. "I'll speak with him, shall I? Maybe I can talk some sense into him."

Nola wasn't sure if Keifer would listen to Will. He certainly hadn't listened to anyone else. He needed to rest, to heal. Of course, no amount of rest would do any good if the stubborn fool wouldn't eat. "Aye, Will. Talk to him. It can't hurt."

"All right. Now, you go and find yourself something to eat—keep up your strength, Nola. He needs you."

She stared at Will. "You have changed."

He smiled, and it was genuine, not cynical as it might have been in the past. "Your father and I have spent a good deal of time together recently. He pointed out that I had two choices—I could stay mad and jealous the rest of my life, or I could grow up and find a woman to love me the way you love Keifer."

Relief filled her as if a weight had been lifted from her heart. She smiled at him, felt genuine affection despite—or perhaps because of—their past. "And have you? Found someone?"

"Not yet. But I'd like to think I've grown up a bit."

She stared at him. "I believe you have. Thank you, Will."

They stood, and Will put his finger under her chin, making it jut out in the way she knew she did when she was determined. "That's better," Will said. "I'll talk to him."

NINETEEN

Keifer heard the door to his room open. Now who had come to disturb him? Why couldn't they just let him go to his rest without all the fuss?

He sensed someone standing over the bed. It wasn't Nola—he could tell with his eyes closed that this person smelled of saddles and leather. Why didn't they say something? Minutes passed, and Keifer grew tired of pretending to sleep. He opened his eyes and was surprised to see Will Macpherson sitting in the chair by the bed.

"What do you want?" he growled.

"Hello, Keifer."

"Say your piece and leave me alone. You've got what you wanted."

Will looked surprised but said nothing.

Was the man that thick-headed that he didn't understand Keifer's meaning? "You'll soon have Nola." Keifer closed his eyes, hoping the man would go away.

"Really," Will said mildly. "That's going to present a problem since I no longer want her."

Keifer opened his eyes. "Of course you do."

"Why are you trying to push your wife off on me, Macnab?"

Will's behavior was confusing. He should be jumping at the opportunity to call Nola his. "I want to know that Nola will be taken care of when I'm gone."

"Where are you planning to go? You can't walk."

Keifer sat up, angry, and then in pain from the quick movement. He leaned on an elbow. "Come to rub it in, did you?"

"No, you fool. I came to tell you to stop feeling sorry for yourself. Don't count on me to take care of your wife. I don't want someone else's woman. I want one who loves me the way Nola loves you, you blind, pig-headed fool!" Will jumped to his feet, and Keifer could see the man was genuinely angry.

Then Will walked to the end of the bed and touched Keifer's big toe. "Can you move your toes, Keifer? Have you even tried?"

Keifer refused to try to move the digit. Hadn't he laid here in the dark and tried to do so in vain? It was better to simply give in to death than live as a cripple. "Go away, Will."

"Fine. I will. But Nola is your responsibility, not mine. Not her father's. Be a man, Keifer, and accept what you cannot change."

"And what would you know about acceptance of such things?" Keifer shouted.

Will came around the bed and stood close, so close Keifer felt himself shrink back into the bedding.

"I learned it well the day the woman I loved married another man." Will spun on his heel and strode out of the room, banging the door just as Nola had before him.

Keifer wept. Wept for the future that would no longer be his. Wept for the pain he would cause Nola. Wept for being a coward who would rather die than face whatever God had planned for him.

Exhausted from the tears and the emotions of the past few hours, Keifer fell into a troubled asleep.

IN A PIQUE OF TEMPER Nola stayed away from Keifer's room the rest of the day and all of the next. She would not go to him unless he sent for her. Furthermore, she considered returning home to Moy with her father.

She said as much to Owyn when she sat next to him to break her fast.

"Ye mustn't do that, my lady."

"Give me one good reason to stay."

Owyn stood up. "Stay right here and I will bring ye a reason."

Puzzled, she said, "All right."

In a few minutes Owyn returned carrying something in his hands. He put it in her hands and sat down beside her.

"Keifer's treasure box! Where has it been?"

"I left it here with Lady Kathryn for safekeeping." He handed her the key, still laced on the faded ribbon she had taken from her hair.

As she took the key, she stared at the box. "This is the reason I should not go to Moy?"

"Ye will find the reason inside, my lady." And with that he stood and walked away.

Curious, Nola placed the key in the lock. The mechanism stuck, and she had to use force to make the key turn. She undid the lock and opened the lid. There lay the Macnab laird's ring, encrusted with mud. Why wasn't Keifer wearing it? And what did it have to do with . . . ?

Her vision blurred as she gazed at the item laying beneath the ring. There next to the wooden horse lay the bracelet, Nola's favor. Keifer had kept it! Had worn it until it was faded and frayed.

It had been new once, just as their love was new. Just as their love would one day be old and frayed, so long as they didn't throw it away.

She clutched the braided twine in her hands, knowing what she must do. She made her way to the chapel. Once there, she dropped to her knees in prayer. She asked that Keifer would live, crippled or not. And asked for God's guidance in how to be the wife he needed in their changed circumstances.

As she left the chapel she felt stronger, more resolute, and ready to face her husband. Lady Kathryn informed Nola that Keifer was definitely getting stronger. But still he did not ask for her. Nola wandered Homelea's gardens and soon found herself among Lady Kathryn's roses.

The late summer blooms perfumed the air as she paced the walkway. Keifer would live. But he didn't want her to be part of his life. Even the beauty of the roses could not lift the weight from her heart.

She swiped away tears. Did Keifer think so little of her that he thought she wouldn't or couldn't love him now that he lay injured? What did he think would happen when his hair turned gray and fell out? Would he not love her if she proved to be barren?

She sank onto a stone bench, crying in earnest. How could she explain her feelings if he didn't want to see her?

Her father found her there, and Nola turned away when he sat down next to her. But she couldn't cry forever, and Da seemed patient enough to wait her out. She reached into the *ciorbholg* at her waist and found a shivereen of cloth, wiped her eyes and blew her nose.

Then Nola turned to face her father, and he folded her into his arms. The gesture of sympathy should have brought more tears, but his comfort soothed her spirit. She rested her head on his broad shoulder.

"Crying doesn't help, you know," Adam said.

"No, but I've prayed until I'm sure God is thinking, *Enough already.*" She smiled weakly and sat up.

"Keifer needs you to be strong."

"Ah, there is the problem, Da. Keifer says he doesn't need me at all. Doesn't want me or our marriage."

Adam studied her. "And how do you feel about that?"

"At first I was so angry, I went to my room and started gathering my things," she admitted.

"Angry or hurt?"

"Hurt. Then as I prayed, I saw clearly that his reaction is to be expected."

"How is that?"

"Keifer feels he has been abandoned over and over again."

"Since his father and brother died when he was so young, it's understandable."

"Aye. And he felt like his family deserted him when he came to Moy."

"He was troubled. I thought he'd gotten over it." He sighed. "So now he sends you away before you can do the same to him."

"So it would seem. And I almost did it. But I'm not going. I don't care what he says, I'm his wife and his friend . . ." The tears threatened again.

Adam held her close and patted her back. "Good for you, Nola."

When she composed herself, she drew away. "It occurs to me that he could learn some things from your experience with being wounded. Would you talk to him?"

"Keifer knows of my injury and my struggle to overcome it. But just now he's not going to believe me or anyone else. He will have to learn on his own. With his wife's help, as I did."

Nola smiled. "As mother helped you."

His smile was tender. "Aye. Just so."

"Do I go to him or wait?"

"Give him some time."

She hugged him. "I love you, Da."

"And I love you, Daughter."

"You must be anxious to go home. When will you leave?"

"I miss your mother and brothers." He paused. "But I believe I'll stay to see Keifer's reaction when he finds out you intend to stick like a cocklebur."

They laughed, and Nola knew that just as God had seen her father and mother through their difficulties, he would not abandon her or Keifer.

SIR BRYAN MACKINTOSH glanced about at the colorful autumn English countryside. A warm sun beat down as he rode beside Robert the Bruce, his father and his king. Twenty-one years had passed since that awful day in Carrick when Bruce had learned the fate of his family. Twenty-one years of near ceaseless warfare with England and the three kings named Edward who ruled there.

Though Bruce would not admit it, Bryan could see that age was catching up to the older warrior. It showed in the lines on his face and the gray in his hair. And in the bouts of the mysterious disease that laid the king low from time to time. Bryan said a quick prayer for Bruce's continued good health.

Today though, Bruce was in fine form, and well he should be. Both he and Bryan had their favorite hunting hawks on their arms, riding leisurely though northern England at will, uncontested by the English army.

Bryan chuckled.

Bruce turned in his saddle, a rare smile on his familiar face. "Will you share your amusement?"

"I was just mentally thumbing my nose at Edward III. And his father and grandfather."

"Ah, yes. 'Tis a beautiful day to hunt on another man's land, is it not?"

They both laughed.

"Do you think your bluff will work?" Bryan asked.

"When young Edward and his keepers hear that I am roaming his northern counties, exacting tribute from his people, and claiming the land for Scotland, he will have to act."

"You expect him to mount another war?"

Bruce's hawk ruffled its feathers, and he calmed the bird before answering. "I expect he will try. But this last pitiful expedition has taxed his treasury to the limit. I don't think his parliament will pay for another campaign."

Randolph and Bruce and their cat-and-mouse tactics had successfully exhausted and demoralized the English army. The expensive Flemish mercenaries with their great war horses had been decimated by the forced marches and insufficient food.

After a lifetime of struggle, Bruce was about to see the completion of his plan for a united and free Scotland. Peace was in the air, from here in the north of England all the way to Homelea, where Keifer lay struggling to overcome his wounds.

Bryan said another prayer, this time for the young man's healing and for the many who had lost homes, fortunes, loved ones, or their very lives in this conflict. They were so close to the promise; surely God would not turn his back now!

The words of the Declaration of Arbroath came back to him. *For it is not glory, it is not riches, neither is it honor, but it is freedom alone that we fight and contend for, which no honest man will lose but with his life.*

"God grant us freedom," Bryan said, his voice hoarse with emotion as he watched his hawk climb high in the sky.

"Aye, God grant us freedom," Bruce repeated.

Homelea

KEIFER GREW STRONGER EVERY DAY and soon realized that he would not die from his injury. Lady Kathryn said to be patient, to wait for the swelling to go down some more and the bruising to heal.

Only then could he know the full extent of the damage to his back and its impact on the use of his legs.

Just as surprising as the news that he was healing was the way Will had spoken to him. Keifer had expected the man to be anxious for Keifer's demise. But on reflection Keifer had to admit, to himself if no one else, that Will was thinking of Nola, putting her heart and dreams ahead of his own. Will must truly care about her to do that. Which in comparison, didn't speak too well of Keifer's recent behavior.

Still, it had to be easier to be noble when you weren't faced with being crippled, unable to care for yourself or your loved ones. What kind of husband would he be if he was unable to protect his wife? Unable to fulfill her dreams? But then, he'd given her Paris. Keifer smiled, remembering their time in France. And their precious few weeks as man and wife.

Keifer missed Nola and regretted chasing her off. He daydreamed constantly about her smile, her laugh, and her eagerness as a wife.

He hadn't believed her when she said she would stay with him, so he'd pushed her away. But he missed her. If he was going to live, and that seemed more and more likely, did he really want to live without her? His life would be difficult enough. Without Nola . . . it didn't bear thinking.

What if Nola was with child? The thought filled him with fear and exhilaration. All his life Keifer had vowed not to marry, not to abandon a wife and children as his father had done. But Ian had not left of his own accord. How could Keifer do such a thing?

He could not.

"I want it to be the way it was when you loved me." Her words haunted him. He still loved her—would always love her, no matter what. Why didn't she come to him, his stubborn, wonderful wife? He needed her. Didn't she realize that it was only his pride that had sent her away?

His pride had also kept him from seeking God's forgiveness. But he was done feeling sorry for himself. Done wishing for death, for release from this life.

Forgive me, Father. I will accept the cup, no matter how bitter, if you will but let me have Nola's love for the rest of my life. I don't deserve it, but you already know that.

Aye, he wanted her. If she would still have him.

KEIFER AWAKENED THE NEXT MORNING and felt even better. To his disappointment, once again Lady Kathryn came to tend to him, not Nola. He was anxious to heal the rift with Nola, but how long would it be until she came to him?

As Kathryn picked up Keifer's dishes, he asked, "Is Nola still at Homelea?"

"Aye, she is. She asks after you, you know."

His heart gladdened with hope. "But she doesn't come to see me."

"Why would she? You made your wishes perfectly clear."

And he had. Maybe too clear. Perhaps he must be the one to bend.

Lady Kathryn studied him. "I think it possible you will regain some use of your legs, Keifer."

"God willing, my lady."

She smiled. "Shall I send Nola to you?"

He made up his mind. It was time to get on with his life, accept things as they were, just as Will had said. With God's help and Nola's love, he would face the future. "I would like to wash and shave first."

She smiled. "May I send Owyn to tend to you?"

Another rift he needed to mend. "Aye. Send him."

"As you wish."

Owyn arrived a few minutes later. He did not close the door when he entered the room, as if leaving himself a quick retreat. "Lady Kathryn said ye wanted to see me." Owyn sounded almost fearful. But then his squire had taken the brunt of Keifer's anger and self-pity.

"I want to sit in the chair today, Owyn."

"Ye do?" He sounded hopeful, relieved. "Did Lady Kathryn say ye could?"

"She didn't say I couldn't. I want to bathe and shave and sit in a chair to see my wife."

Owyn closed the door and walked forward. "Do ye trust me to shave ye?" Owyn's expression remained neutral but his voice sounded anxious.

"I do, Owyn."

Their gazes met. Owyn must have seen Keifer's sincerity because his smile nearly split his face. "That's better, my laird. 'Tis a start, indeed."

When Keifer was clean and dry and safely shaved, he pulled a shirt over his head. With Owyn's help, he swung his legs over the side of the bed. They decided he should kilt a plaid about his hips instead of struggling to pull on breeches.

It took some maneuvering and more than a few twinges of pain in his back, but they finally managed it. Keifer was sweating by the time Owyn pulled the extra material up over his shoulder and attached it with a decorative pin.

Owyn held up his boots and Keifer shook his head. "There's a limit to my strength, Owyn. I'll have to settle for warm stockings."

"Of course." He found a pair in Keifer's trunk and helped pull them on.

Keifer looked down at his clothing with approval. He was ready to meet Nola. "You can't carry me to the chair, Owyn. I outweigh you by nearly two stone."

"Right. I'll get us some help."

Owyn returned in a few minutes with Will.

Keifer scowled, but Will had been the catalyst for Keifer's coming to grips with his situation. He owed the man.

Will stood with his hands on his hips. "So, you've decided to live."

Their gazes locked. "Aye. If you won't take care of Nola, what choice do I have?"

Will raised an eyebrow. "I'm sure it will be a burden."

They looked at each other, silently acknowledging a favor received and gratitude given in return.

"Well, let's get me in the chair."

"Wait," Owyn cried. He grabbed a pillow off the bed and placed it on the wooden chair.

"Good idea. Thank you."

Then Will and Owyn picked him up and carried him to the chair. In the scuffle of getting him settled, someone accidentally stepped on his stocking-covered toes.

"Ouch! Get off my foot!"

Will and Owyn both jumped back and started accusing each other of being clumsy.

Keifer watched them argue, and all he could do was grin.

Owyn and Will stopped mid-sentence. Owyn recovered first. "Ye felt it?"

Keifer nodded.

"You felt it!" Will shouted.

Keifer reached down and touched his foot, touched them both. The sensitivity had returned to the bottoms of his feet as well. He could not make his feet or toes move, but he had to believe this was a good sign.

"Don't tell Nola," Keifer said. He wanted to surprise her.

"Not a word." The two promised and went to find Nola.

Twenty

No matter what keifer said, Nola wasn't leaving. Whatever the future held, she was determined to face it at Keifer's side. Nothing he could say would change her mind.

Now to convince him.

He answered her tentative knock with a gruff "Enter."

Nola opened the door and stepped inside, peering at an empty bed. She raced around the foot of the bed, afraid she would find he'd fallen out and lay helpless on the floor.

But Keifer wasn't there, and panic surged through her. She spun about, searching the room until she saw him, seated in a chair, dressed and looking handsome and whole, if somewhat pale. This must be what Owyn and Will had been grinning about when they came to deliver Keifer's summons. And aye, what a wonderful sight!

Nola stared until he indicated she should sit in the chair across from him. She walked to him and sat down, folding her hands in her lap. This once she would be an obedient wife, her impulse to just shake good sense into him firmly under control. There were bigger battles to come.

"You look well, Keifer."

"As do you, Nola."

While Nola's hands remained in her lap, Keifer's fingers drummed on the arms of his chair. So, he was nervous, too. To see them thus, no one would believe they had been friends for half their lives.

Nola felt her control slipping and bit the inside of her cheek to keep her tongue silent. Finally she lost the battle. "Owyn gave me your treasure box."

He tilted his head, his expression puzzled. "He did? What for?"

"I think he knew that when I saw what was in the box, I wouldn't leave you."

He looked at her, clearly not knowing what she was talking about. She held out her hand, palm down. "Here."

Keifer reached out his hand, and Nola laid the bracelet in his palm. He stared at the braid, shook his head. "Owyn."

"What?"

"How could I have doubted him?" he whispered. He picked up the favor she had given to him years ago. "Owyn must have put this in the box after I cut it off my wrist before my knighting ceremony."

"You cut it off?" Maybe Keifer had never loved her after all!

"Aye. I thought you were going to marry Will, and I was angry. I cut it off and threw it atop my clothes. But Owyn . . . I owe him an apology for ever doubting his loyalty."

"And what of me, Keifer?"

Keifer stared at her, and she saw love and longing in his expression.

"I'm sorry—" she began.

"I shouldn't have—" he said at the same time.

They grinned at each other.

He lifted his hand to Nola, and she bent forward and took it between her own. But she needed to be closer, much closer, so she inched her chair forward until their knees were touching.

Keifer drew her hand to his lips and kissed her fingers, one by one. "I should not have sent you away."

"No. You should not have. But as you can see, it didn't do any good. I'm still here."

He laughed and held fast to her hand. "I love you, Nola. God knows I don't deserve you or your love after the way I've been acting. I don't know what God has in store, what the future holds. I only know that I don't want to face it without you."

"That was never in question. I'm not going to desert you, not ever."

"Good." He tugged on her hand and she leaned closer, bracing her hands on the arms of the chair. They kissed; a kiss of forgiveness that quickly warmed into one of promise.

Nola pulled away. "I promise to give you a new favor to wear, Husband."

"I promise to wear it until I die, Nola."

All was forgiven, forgotten, turned over to God. Together they would face tomorrow, man and wife as God had ordained from days gone by.

KEIFER AND NOLA remained at Homelea, postponing travel to Innishewan until such time as Keifer regained more of his strength. With each passing day, his back healed and feeling returned to his legs. Adam and Will left for Moy with the promise to bring Nola's mother and siblings to Innishewan in the spring.

A fortnight later they were sitting in Homelea's rose garden when they heard the commotion of horses' hooves in the bailey. With the crutches Owyn had fashioned for him and Nola's help, Keifer stood. He had improved to the point where he could swing both legs together and put his weight on them. He followed Nola slowly to the front of the castle. As they rounded the corner, the abbey bells began to peal in the distance.

Lady Kathryn and others came running into the bailey from the castle and the outbuildings as Bryan halted his horse and dismounted. He'd been with the king for nearly a week.

Nola clutched Keifer's arm. "What on earth has happened?" she asked, her voice echoing Keifer's fear.

Not war. Not again, Lord.

Sir Bryan strode toward them, grinning like a boy who'd just stolen his first kiss. "The English have sued for peace!" Bryan shouted as he embraced Kathryn and lifted her off her feet.

"Peace?" Lady Kathryn breathed and several others echoed.

Bryan set her back on the ground. "Aye. My brilliant sire has succeeded in bringing England to terms."

Everyone now crowded around Sir Bryan, anxious to hear more. The knight lifted his gaze to see Keifer, and he smiled broadly, pushing his way to stand in front of him. "Well, now. Seeing you upright is even better than my news."

Keifer waggled a crutch. "These are temporary, my laird. I plan to get rid of them in the coming days. But tell us more—what are the terms?"

Bryan spoke as his wife gently guided him into the hall and urged him to sit. Soon servants brought food and drink, and after a long pull from a tankard, Sir Bryan answered their many questions.

"The terms are non-negotiable. Our king is firm in his resolve to have the kingdom of Scotland free and clear to himself and his heirs forever, without any homage to anyone other than God."

"He has certainly earned that right!" Keifer declared.

Bryan agreed. "His son David will marry Edward's sister, Joan."

"They are but wee children!" Lady Kathryn exclaimed.

"Aye. Nevertheless, the marriage will take place next summer. Bruce wants this agreement sealed in a way that Edward must honor."

Keifer nodded. Too much blood had been shed on both sides to settle for less.

Bryan continued. "Robert insists that the English king should use his influence to persuade the pope to lift the interdict from Scotland and from Bruce himself."

"And Edward has agreed?" Nola asked, obviously incredulous.

"Aye."

"It is done, then," Keifer said in wonder.

"Done!" Nola cried, hugging him close.

Freedom at last.

TEN MONTHS LATER Adam Mackintosh stood with his wife Gwenyth as they awaited the bridal procession of the future queen of Scotland. Robert the Bruce's four-year-old son waited on the steps of the church for his seven-year-old bride, Joan Plantagenet, sister of Edward III of England.

For a moment, Adam remembered the day he had married the woman at his side. Actually, he remembered all three times he and Gwenyth had exchanged vows. He smiled. She had been hard to convince but well worth the effort.

He fingered the ring on his left hand, the one that matched his wife's. He and Gwenyth had once been enemies, just as David and Joan's families were. Peace and prosperity now reigned at Moy, and in a few short months, he and Gwenyth would become grandparents.

He glanced at Gwenyth and saw that her gaze was on the little prince. The boy hopped up and down and his half brother, Bryan Mackintosh, knelt down to speak quietly with the child.

Gwenyth took Adam's hand and drew him close. "Poor lad. His childhood is being snatched away from him."

"Aye. But this marriage is our only hope of holding the bride's brother to the treaty he signed. A betrothal is too easily broken."

"As are treaties, especially those with England." Gwenyth sighed. "We must pray that our countries and this marriage will be spared the turmoil of our generation."

Adam also hoped that these children would be spared, but before he could say as much, trumpets sounded, announcing the bride. Adam watched as a half dozen young girls followed the trumpeters, walking down the pathway and strewing flower petals from willow baskets.

Then came Joan herself, mounted on a prancing white pony and looking regal despite her tender years. Joan's mother, the dowager Queen Isobella, and Isobella's companion, Mortimer, rode just behind the princess.

Adam had attended the royal wedding of the ill-fated Marjorie Bruce some dozen or so years ago, and he watched as the familiar pageantry unfolded. The princess's pony was led to the steps of the church, where Bryan helped her to dismount.

Then the bride and groom, so young and full of promise, faced each other. Without prompting, David took the girl's hand as Bryan read the terms of the marriage contract. Joan's dowry was nothing less than the kingdom of Scotland, given over at last to her new father-in-law by way of her husband.

BRYAN FINISHED READING THE MARRIAGE CONTRACT and presented the parchment to the priest. The wedding party and family members then entered the church for the consecration of the vows. As David and Joan knelt before the altar, Bryan walked over to his wife, Kathryn, who was standing in the first row.

She smiled up at him, and her expression reminded him that, like

David and Joan, he and Kathryn had had little choice in their marriage. Bryan just prayed that the two who took vows this day would be as blessed as he and his wife had been.

When the priest pronounced the prince and princess as man and wife, Kathryn placed her hand on the enameled white rose she wore fastened to her shawl. Bryan had commissioned a silversmith to create the piece of jewelry for his wife to remember the peace offering he'd once given her from Homelea's garden. From that beginning they had forged a life together.

Now, after years of war, destruction, and death, Scotland stood on the brink of peace. Many men on both sides had given their lives or returned home wounded and maimed.

The priest's prayer broke into Bryan's dark thoughts. "Oh, Lord of Heaven, we ask that you would create from these two a single mind and purpose. And further, that you would form your faithful people in both England and Scotland into a single will. A will for peace. Make us love what you command and desire what you promise. Remind us that amid all the changes of this world, we should fix our hearts where true love and joy are found: in your Son, our Savior, Jesus Christ the Lord. Amen."

Bryan added a heartfelt "Amen" as the bridal couple faced the audience to accept felicitations.

Kathryn's daughter Isobel moved forward, and Bryan took Kathryn's elbow to follow. Isobel, the illegitimate daughter of Bryan's one-time enemy, had grown into a beauty. She had also become the daughter of Bryan's heart. Although he and Kathryn had three other children, Bryan and Isobel shared a special affinity because of the shared circumstances of their births.

Having congratulated the solemn couple, Bryan led his family to the church door. "You go ahead to the pavilion—I must accompany David and his bride."

Kathryn said, "'Tis a shame your father cannot be here to perform that duty."

"Aye. But Edward of England chose not to attend as well. 'Tis probably for the best, as I'm not sure they could have spoken civilly to each other."

Kathryn smiled. "King Robert could charm a smile from a stone, Bryan. Nevertheless, your point is well taken. Come, Isobel. We will wait for your father as he asked."

KEIFER MACNAB leaned on his cane beneath the shade of an old oak tree. Although he still limped and relied on the cane for balance, he was far from the hopeless cripple he had once imagined. He shuddered when he remembered how close he'd come to succumbing to the darkness.

But here he stood in the town of Berwick, gathered with his family and friends to celebrate the marriage of David Bruce and Joan Plantagenet. These two young children held the promise of peace for their respective countries. Keifer prayed for God's intervention in their lives—that genuine love might form between them as they grew up—much like it had between Keifer and Nola.

It seemed that all the nobility and half the peasant population of Scotland had been invited to the celebration. Robert the Bruce had spared no expense on the lavish wedding feast, even going so far as to purchase clothes for the guests to wear.

Children of various ages—including Keifer's nieces and nephews—darted among the guests as they played tag and blind man's bluff under the watchful eyes of their mothers. 'Twas a restful, pastoral scene, one Keifer savored in the sheer joy of being alive.

Sir Bryan joined him under the tree's sturdy branches. Keifer greeted Bryan and said, "'Tis too bad your father cannot be here today."

"Aye. He decided to remain in seclusion at Cardross. He just hasn't been the same since his wife died. I fear for his health. But this," he said, waving about him, "this is the culmination of all his dreams, everything for which we worked."

Freedom from an oppressor's rule. Men had given their lives—men like his father and brother and others before them. A pang of grief shot through Keifer, but along with it came assurance. Surely Da and Gordon looked down upon today's celebration and knew that their sacrifice hadn't been for naught.

On this beautiful summer day, as Englishmen and Scots celebrated an end to the seemingly endless issues that separated them, Keifer recalled the Bible verse the priest had quoted in today's wedding ceremony: *And God shall wipe away all tears from their eyes; and there shall be no more death, neither sorrow, nor crying, neither shall there be any more pain: for the former things are passed away.*

Keifer swallowed. The future was never a given, but it was always worth living for. He could see the future's promise in the scene before him. He saw it there under the trees where children of Scottish and English blood played together as if their fathers and grandfathers had never warred against each other. He saw it in his father-in-law, Adam, earnestly speaking of his prized new ram rather than of borders and battle plans. He saw it in the warrior, Ceallach, who once could barely care for a child but now reached out to hug his young daughter.

Keifer could see the future in his beloved Nola, her body swollen with his own child. Such hope! Such promise!

Keifer fingered the braided strand of silver on his wrist, Nola's favor, the one he had promised to wear until he died. He would keep his promise to her, just as God would keep his promise of peace for all those who believed in him.

He gazed again at the scene before him.

Keifer believed.